OFFERING OF SCANDALOUS LOVE

"I'm in love with you," Ben said. "I won't ask if you love me."

Pearl swallowed audibly.

"I will ask if you're still afraid of me."

How had he known she was afraid? How could he tell? "I . . . at first . . . not now."

"I'll not ask if you could ever love me."

"I—" She swallowed again.

"As things stand, the law won't permit marriage between us. I've been to an attorney, however, and there's no law that says you can't live at Rivard. Or that you can't be very close . . . and dear to me."

She bowed her head, overwhelmed by his warmth and sincerity.

"We've explored your situation," he said. "There's no work for you. But there is a place for you, where you're wanted. I offer myself, Pearl. For life. I offer you Rivard."

Carefully he drew her, rigid, into his arms . . .

CREOLE

SALIEE O'BRIEN

BANTAM BOOKS
TORONTO · NEW YORK · LONDON · SYDNEY

This is a novel. All characters are imaginary. Neither they nor the events depicted in the story have been taken from real people or real life with the exception of references to historic characters living at the time.

CREOLE

A Bantam Book / November 1983

ISBN 0-553-23712-8

Published simultaneously in the United States and Canada

Bantam Books are published by Bantam Books, Inc. Its trademark, consisting of the words "Bantam Books" and the portrayal of a rooster, is Registered in U.S. Patent and Trademark Office and in other countries. Marca Registrada. Bantam Books, Inc., 666 Fifth Avenue, New York, New York 10103.

PRINTED IN THE UNITED STATES OF AMERICA

O   0 9 8 7 6 5 4 3 2 1

Once again, for Thurlow Benjamin Weed

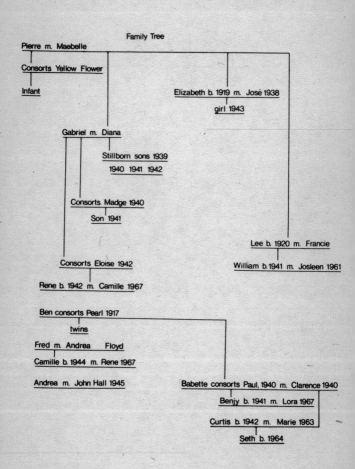

Family Tree

Pierre m. Maebelle

Consorts Yellow Flower

Infant

Elizabeth b. 1919 m. José 1938

girl 1943

Gabriel m. Diana

Stillborn sons 1939
1940 1941 1942

Consorts Madge 1940

Son 1941

Lee b. 1920 m. Francie

William b.1941 m. Josleen 1961

Consorts Eloise 1942

Rene b. 1942 m. Camille 1967

Ben consorts Pearl 1917

twins

Fred m. Andrea   Floyd

Camille b. 1944 m. Rene 1967

Andrea m. John Hall 1945

Babette consorts Paul, 1940 m. Clarence 1940

Benjy b. 1941 m. Lora 1967

Curtis b. 1942 m. Marie 1963

Seth b. 1964

PROLOGUE

1917

I

Pearl had never been so terrified in her life, not even of Pa. The little houseboat swayed, the rope which tied it to the pier creaked, and Pa stood spraddled, his black, wavy hair falling across his brow, his snarled, black moustache showing jagged, yellow teeth.

Pearl cowered in the bunk, listening to the two older boys shift in the bunk above. She knew how scared they were, even though they were old for their twelve and thirteen years.

She gazed fearfully into Pa's eyes, so black and piercing, so killing-mad. She couldn't swallow, yearned to cry out to her ma, Annie, standing helplessly in the doorway, one arm around each of her baby twin brothers so they wouldn't fall. But Pearl dared not cry, because Pa would turn on Ma and knock her into the middle of the other cabin.

He held the whip in his fist, its braided leather ends dangling. For now he didn't move, but kept his small black eyes piercing her. His cheeks were flushed with rage.

"Don't, Pa!" cried Pearl. "Please don't! I'll do what you say!"

He could kill her with that whip and would, if she couldn't talk her way out of it. Desperate, she cowered, pleading.

Her ma got out words. "No! Marcel . . . don't whip her! Don't make her go! She can work harder shrimping. She'll bring in more money—you'll see—and she'll marry and be gone, and it'll be just us and the boys!"

He gestured for silence, moving so violently that the

3

boat swayed on the predawn waters of Bayou Lafourche. His moustache quivered. "Not ready, eh?" he snarled at Pearl. "Let's see if the whip kin help you to move up!"

His arm jerked back, then forward, and the braided leather wrapped around Pearl's shoulders, cutting through her nightgown and into her skin. The whip made a sharp, vicious sound, and Annie cried out as if she were the one being lashed. Pearl was ashen, but she held back her cries. "Don't, Pa," she moaned. "Oh, please . . . no more! I'll get dressed fast!"

As if excited by each mighty blow, Marcel kept working the whip. Annie cried out at each stroke, holding the shrieking twins close. The older boys sobbed and pleaded for their pa to stop, but he ignored their pleas. Pa's chest was heaving, he was madder than he'd ever been before, his blunt Cajun features had turned hard and merciless as he plied the whip.

Pearl shrank against the wall of the bunk and endured. As each separate blow struck her, she felt the stinging impact of the leather, then the cutting in, and last, the wet trickle of blood. Holding her breath, she bent forward, wrapped her arms around her little body, and submitted to blow after blow.

She begged for him to stop. "Quit, Pa . . . please, Pa . . . I'll put on the dress and fix my hair. You won't be ashamed of me when we get there!"

But the strap rose and fell, rose and fell; the twins screamed; Annie pleaded; the boat swayed. Finally Pearl crept out of the bunk, trying to evade the strap. The strap is a living thing, she thought. It's glad and happy to hit me, to bite deep, to kill!

Blindly, she took her mended chemise, which the sobbing Annie thrust into her hands. "See, Pa!" Pearl cried out, "I'm getting dressed, just like you want!"

By some miracle, Pa's arm finally dropped. The whip hung from his fist, its ends still swinging. His face was

fiery and set in a mask of fury. He grabbed the chemise
away from Pearl.

"Where's your sense, woman?" he snarled at Annie.
"Get that gown off her and sop the blood. Stop the
bleedin'! She ain't to mess up her good dress with blood.
She's got to look decent, can't I get that through your
head?"

Annie passed the twins up to the older boys, then
flipped Pearl's gown over her head fast. Pearl's back and
shoulders were a welter of cuts and stripes; her buttocks
oozed blood. Her body looked like that of some wench
who had been put to the whip in the slave days.

She stood naked, bent forward to hide herself. The whip
caught her across the shoulders again. "Shameless slut,
letting your brothers see you bare-assed! Cover yourself!"

"Marcel," pleaded Ma, her long platinum hair dishev-
eled, "she's bleeding! She'll ruin her dress! You said so
yourself! Let me clean her first. She can't travel in a
bloody dress."

He grabbed a ragged towel. "Use this!" he roared. "And
do it fast!"

Pearl stood, her breath tearing through her, hurting. Ma
sopped the blood away and smeared on a thick layer of
yellow salve, which stung. Marcel watched and glowered,
whip ever ready. Muttering and cursing, he ordered Ma to
make it snappy, and when he would wait no longer, he
threw the chemise, soft from many washings and mendings,
into Pearl's face.

"Get your nakedness behind the curtain!" he ordered.
"Get into your duds fast, and do it proper!"

He swung on Annie. "Pin a towel in the back of her
dress so nothing'll show through!" When Ma didn't move
fast enough, he raised the whip, and she scurried to a
drawer, then gave Pearl pins and two thin towels. "Not my

Pearl in a sportin' house!" sobbed Ma. "Not my beautiful Pearl! She's so innocent, so pure—"

The whip laced across Ma's shoulders. "Quiet! She goes!"

Ma pleaded on, ignoring the whip. "A girl's own pa can't. . . . Marcel, you're a good man, you can't—"

"I ain't her pa, not me!" He gave Annie another lash, rocking her slim body. "I was a fool to marry American, a fool to fall for that blond hair. I shoulda married Cajun, good French Cajun! You took another man! Look at her, that hair like yours, no color to it! She ain't Cajun, not one drop of her! So she ain't mine! But now that I've fed her and dressed her and raised her, now that she's growed, she'll bring me some cash with her looks!"

"Marcel, she can't help the hair! She can't help being pretty! Give her time. She'll marry, and you'll be rid of her, and her life won't be ruint in a sportin' house!"

"Them girls has it good! Fine houses to live in, swell clothes, finest eats to be had, don't never turn their hands over! I'm doin' her a favor—she'll find out—and the day'll come when she'll know I'm right! Marcel Babin's no fool—she'll make me the richest man on Lafourche, richest man on the longest bayou in Louisiana!"

He whirled on Pearl, snatched away her chemise, and flung it aside. "Annie, get your chemise. It's better'n hers, won't come so near to tearin' and lettin' them cuts show while we're on the way."

Ma opened a drawer, took out a chemise, and handed it over. "It really won't tear easy, not if you're careful," she said.

Pearl took the chemise and the towels numbly, using them to shield her nakedness, afraid to move to the shelter of the curtain until Pa gave the word.

"Get behind that curtain!" he growled. "Get dressed and do it fast and proper!"

She dived gratefully behind the curtain and struggled into Ma's chemise, holding it away from her body as she pulled it up, so as not to rub away the salve. She felt the softness of the chemise and longed to lie face down until the pain eased.

She reached for her only slip and put it on cautiously. She had to take care, because if she did things wrong, if Pa saw one drop of blood, he'd strap her again. And this time he'd kill her, likely as not. Quickly but carefully, she pinned the other towel on the inside of her good dress, a worn white voile, then pulled it over her head, still sobbing in pain.

Pa yanked the curtain open as she fastened the buttons in the front of the dress. "Hurry it up!" he gritted. "I want to be on my way!"

She crossed the tiny cabin and went to the wash-shelf. As she peered into the mottled mirror, her silver-gray eyes filled with tears she dare not shed any longer. She poured water into the tin basin and washed her face, leaving her skin startlingly white and her lips pink and shapely despite their trembling.

With unsteady hands, she combed her hip-length platinum hair and pulled it back, tying it at the nape with an old, narrow ribbon. The hair tumbled down her back, waving softly, ending just short of where she could sit on it. Last, she tugged on her slippers, which were black and too short and hurt her toes. She was ready.

"C'mon," grunted Pa. "Let's go."

"Can't she take her other dress?" asked Ma. "And her clean chemise? What'll she do for a change?"

"That'll be tended to where she's headed for," Pa snapped. "These duds she's wearin' now, why they'll use them for rags! The madam, she wouldn't have no such junk in her house."

Ma's tears increased. "Won't you give it another thought,

Marcel?" she pleaded desperately. "Let's find her a husband here on the bayou and not send her away."

Pa's face turned uglier. "Nothin' doin'! If I'd of knew,
when she was fifteen and blossomin' out, I could have sold
her to this madam fer as much as eight hundred dollars!
Now the madam won't buy girls no more, never did buy
but the best, and I'm lucky I can farm her out there and
re'lize a damned good income from her!"

"C-can I come home to visit, Pa?" Pearl asked.

"You try to do that," Pa snorted, drawing the leather
thongs of the whip through his hand, "and you'll get
another taste of this! I'm tellin' folks you got a nursemaid
job in New Orleans, and you're not to show up here and
make a liar out of me! I got a good reputation on Lafourche,
and I aim to keep it."

"Can I go see her?" quavered Ma.

"Quiet, woman! Take a good look now, 'cause you ain't
never goin' to see this by-blow you foisted off on me again!
You got four good, legal boys to slobber over. From this
minute, it's like you never had a girl child! And I don't
want you talkin' to the other women about her. They'll
soon forget. They mention her, you just pass it off."

Ma moved for Pearl as Pearl reached out for her.

The whip streaked down between them before they
could kiss. It cut Ma's forehead, raising a welt instantly.
"You got your hands full, Annie," Pa said fiercely, "explainin'
how Pearl's a nursemaid and how you hurt your head. You
tell how you got that welt, any of you"—he glared at the
older boys—"and we'll have us a good old-fashioned whippin'
party, which you know, Annie, ain't my normal custom.
But when somebody crosses me, I take control. If I ain't
crossed, I'm a kind and lovin' man."

Pearl looked at her four brothers, huddled in the top
bunk. The twins were sucking their thumbs. The older

boys were no longer crying, but they looked sad and Pearl knew if Pa would let them, they'd hug her good-bye.

"March," Pa ordered Pearl. "Into the pirogue!"

With one last glance at her family, Pearl lifted her chin, went out onto the deck, and scrambled down into the pirogue. Pa thumped in behind her, untied the rope, then oared away from the houseboat.

Ma and the boys didn't come on deck. They didn't dare.

Pa oared swiftly along the bayou, gliding past the houseboats where Cajun shrimpers and their families still slept. The houseboats rocked gently on the water.

I hate him, Pearl thought. He's always been mean to me, even when I was a little girl. And now he's taking me to New Orleans, and I don't know what it is I'm to do there!

Through darkness they glided on and on. A sickle moon appeared now and then among the clouds. Then Pearl could see lush growth as they moved past—bushes and undergrowth and trees without end. She could even make out the giant cypress trees that knelt at the edge of the black water like women praying, their long moss hair touching the water. Pearl wished she were one of those tree-women, so calm, so reverent. So safe. She, too, felt rooted in the bayou that she loved, that she had never in her life wished to leave.

She listened to the song of the bayou. A bullfrog beat his notes on the black morning; a shrill, bell-toned frog answered. An alligator slid into the water. A night bird uttered its predawn cry.

Riddled by the burning pain of her body, by the fear that she would never see her ma or the boys again, by homesickness for her family and for this wondrous bayou, Pearl grieved silently, deeply.

And Pa oared on and on, carrying her to her fate.

II

"I really don't want to go, Pa," Pearl ventured at last. "Honest and true. I really don't want to go."

"You're goin'!" he snarled. "Hell, I made that clear to you last night! When Marcel Babin's mind's made up, it's made up. So shut your whinin' mouth, and keep it shut."

Fighting tears, she fell silent. She listened to the swamp sadly; she'd never hear its sounds again, not after Pa handed her over in New Orleans.

By the time they passed into Bayou La Vie, shrimpers were stirring about their boats. The flower smell thickened as blossoms opened to the warming sun, and Pearl breathed in the fragrance, clinging to it until the last possible moment.

Her back had begun to stiffen. The cuts pulled at the edges when she moved, and she knew the blood was clotting. It hurt, the ache was deep and sore beyond belief. Pa had strapped her before, but never like this; he'd never marked her up before.

"Turn your back to me," Pa commanded. Carefully, she did as he ordered, knowing he wanted to see if blood had seeped through the towels. He lifted her hair and grunted. She could almost feel his little black Cajun eyes poking into her back. The cuts throbbed anew, and she clenched her fists, willing that no blood showed, fearing what he might do to her.

He let her hair drop. "You are of good fortune," he said. "No blood has come through your dress."

Her spirit stirred. She was safe for the moment; she

10

could speak out. He'd not whip her now, not in sight of all the boats.

"If the blood had come into my dress, what would you do?" she asked, wondering if he would have taken her back home.

"I got a dollar or two in my pocket," he said. "I'd of bought you another dress, another towel to pin inside."

"On Sunday?"

"On Sunday. There's places. In New Orleans."

Again she fell silent. She knew she had to get away from him. If she'd bled, she could have run while he was bargaining for a dress. Now that chance was gone. She sat motionless, her mind seeking a way to escape.

Shrimpers and their women and children waved at Marcel and Pearl. Pa had waved back and now demanded that Pearl wave, too, which she did. The motion pulled at the wounds, and she hoped they'd bleed again so he'd have to buy another dress, giving her a chance to run.

"Where you go, Marcel, eh?" cried a brawny shrimper. "Not to fish, mon ami, not on Sunday. This is the day the Cajun does not fish, does not catch the shrimp, eh?"

"I take this girl to New Orleans, where she has the fine job!" Pa called back.

"What job is that, eh?" cried the shrimper's wife.

"A fine one—nursemaid! In a fine house. She is the girl of great luck to get such a job! Though I, her pa, had to find it for her and get the promise of work. And now we go today because I do not have to find the shrimp!"

After they had passed along the bayou, Pearl dared to ask, "What work will I do at this place, Pa? Ma . . . she said she'd not mind if I was to be nursemaid, anything but what I will be, she said."

She stiffened, braced lest he lash out at her.

"It's time you know about your job," he said harshly, "so you'll behave yourself and do what is expected. You'll live

in a fine, rich house, wear satin, eat the best, and get paid
for it. Paid high."

"And that's all? Why would anybody pay me for that?"

"There's a little more. You'll be nice to gentlemen . . .
customers. You'll eat with them, drink whiskey with them."

"But you've never let me drink! Ma says—"

"In this job, it is required. It is also required that you
do whatever else the gentlemen want."

"I can't sing for them or dance."

He gestured roughly. "You be nice, they'll be nice."

"Ma says—"

"Your ma don't know what she's talkin' about, her!"

"She says those girls in fine houses do bad things, have
bad diseases. They even have babies and no husband!"

"The smart ones don't have babies. It's up to the lady
that hires you to be smart. And up to you. One thing,
you'll earn lots of money—at least ten dollars from every
gentleman you please, twenty dollars if he thinks you're
special, and with that hair, there ain't no reason for you
not to be special. You'll pay board and room out of your
money, and I'll come to New Orleans regular and get the
rest of what you make. I'll even buy your ma a blue silk
dress."

"There's something wrong, I know it!" cried Pearl. "I
won't do it, whatever it is. I'd rather die!"

Real fast, Pa smacked her, rocking her head, numbing
her jaw. She went silent again, her mind numb, clumsily
trying to find a way out. If she could just get away from
him . . . run . . .

Where the bayou met the big road, while Pa tied up at a
tree she ran. Desperate, though her outgrown slippers
hurt her toes and her back was a searing flame, she ran.
Fear was like a rod in her throat. She heard Pa chasing
her. Panic stricken, she poured on speed, and then her

short slippers caught in a rut and she fell headlong on her face.

Pa forced her to her knees in the dust and shook her until her head flopped. Her dress, twisted around her legs at midcalf, felt like a rope. She felt the cuts open and tried to moan, but couldn't catch her breath.

Pa's face, when she glimpsed it once, twisted with anger. His dark eyes blazed red.

He hit her a couple of times more, rocking her head, and then he yanked her to her feet, clamped her arm with one fist, and marched her along the road so fast she had to trot. "Try that again," he warned, "and you'll find out what I've give you before is love taps. Faster! Walk faster! We got twenty miles yet to go."

"Pa," she quavered, "I can't walk twenty miles, not in these slippers. Let me take them off and carry them. I can put them back on when we get to this house."

"Keep 'em on. I ain't walkin' to New Orleans. I'll get us a ride, free or almost free. Just keep that mouth shut and walk."

She stumbled on, the dusty road and the fields becoming a blur. Once she saw a long driveway leading to a plantation house with white pillars across its front.

After what seemed hours, after many carriages had passed in both directions, Pa spied a wagonload of hay turning out of a drive and hailed the Negro driver. He clutched Pearl's arm as he talked. The Negro said his name was Sam and he was taking the hay to a stable on the edge of New Orleans, Sunday or no Sunday.

Pa offered ten cents to let himself and Pearl ride on the back end of the wagon, and Sam took the money and waited while they climbed up and sat on the prickly hay. It pierced through Pearl's dress and made her itch. Her back had smarted worse after Pa shook her, and the slow, rough jiggle of the wagon increased her pain.

She closed her eyes and rode. Occasionally, when she opened her eyes, she saw carriage traffic, the dusty, rutted road, the fields stretching away, and far off, another fine, tall plantation house. She noted that Pa looked sleepy, and saw that he and Sam nodded and dozed as they rode. Then Sam would wake up and shake the reins over the mule, and Pa'd open his eyes and glare at her before dozing off again.

But Pearl didn't doze; she was alert to every sight, every sound when she closed her eyes. She had only one thing in mind—escape. But not too soon, not until they were clear to New Orleans and before Pa and Sam perked up to settle on where Pa'd get out of the wagon.

After hours of riding and Pa and Sam dozing more and more, her chance came. She didn't know how far they were from New Orleans, but if she was going to run, it had to be now.

Sam's chin was on his chest; Pa was leaning against the side of the wagon, his own chin down. With utmost care, she slid along the hay, dangled her feet over the tailgate, and managed to drop to the ground without any noise. Instantly she was running, with one swift glance to see that Pa and Sam were still dozing. She veered, fleeing for the drive of a plantation they had just passed.

Suddenly she heard the pound of footsteps behind her. This time she didn't fall, but ran with every ounce of speed in her, faster and faster, to get to that plantation house, to safety. But a hand dug into her shoulder and jolted her to a staggering halt. Pa slammed her alongside the head again, dragged her back to the wagon, and she made the rest of the trip in a red haze, too weak to run even if she had another chance.

III

Before they reached the outskirts of the city, darkness had wrapped New Orleans except for streetlights and lights in houses and courtyards. At the waterfront, Marcel dragged Pearl out of the wagon, clamped her arm in one mighty hand and propelled her along the wharf. Ships of every sort rode at anchor, all showing a light, their naked spars reaching to the black sky, their sails furled. Boxes, kegs, and barrels set in rows, rank upon rank of them, lined the wharf, waiting to be loaded into the holds of the ships and carried off to faraway places.

Despite his cruel grip on her arm, Pa became expansive. "Them boxes and stuff, they hold sugar cane, molasses, shelled corn—ever'thing that's raised in Louisiana and crops from up the Mississippi, too. Some hold silks and ivory and high-class things from the East, waitin' to be put into warehouses. They won't be stole because there's watchmen—one over there, see?—so nothin'll be stole."

Pearl wondered what the watchman would do if she could get to him and tell him that she was Pa's captive. Could he save her? Would he? Now he was gone somewhere among the barrels and the darkness; her chance, if ever it had existed, was gone.

Pa was still talking. "The sugar cane," he said, "is likely goin' to Paris—that's in France—or to London—that's in England. You ain't got the wits to know it, girl, but this job I got for you is an education. You'll learn all kinds of things and be paid for doin' it. The day'll come when you'll re'lize I'm the best friend you ever had, done you the best turn."

15

She said nothing, and he began to name off New Orleans streets she'd eventually see—Carondelet, St. Charles, Bourbon, St. Louis, Royal. She'd see them all when the madam took her and the other girls for carriage rides.

Under a streetlight ahead, a group of soldiers in khaki stood talking. Pa spotted them and, as always, cursed the Kaiser. Half-listening, Pearl gazed at the tiny, unpainted wooden shacks which lined the far edge of the wharf. Each had a front door and a window with a lighted candle. Most of the doors were open, and in each, a scantily clad girl lolled, calling out softly to the loitering soldiers.

As one tall soldier broke away from the others and headed for a girl, Pa stopped. "Watch," he growled. "See for yourself how much better I done for you than this. See how these girls has to turn a trick, so after you get to Josie's place, you'll appreciate how lucky you are."

Her throat dry with fear, Pearl stared. The soldier went to the doorway where the girl stood with candlelight flickering on her white face, and they began to murmur. Pearl could just catch the sound, not the words.

"They're talkin' money," Pa said. "He'll want to pay fifteen cents—that's the goin' price—and she'll hold out for two bits. My guess is, he'll pay it. He's so bad off he can't hardly stand still."

Bad off? Pearl wondered, but wouldn't ask. She wanted to keep Pa's attention off her all she could.

"The hooker won!" Pa snorted. "See how spry he is goin' into the crib. He may try to get two for one."

Pearl saw the door of the shack go shut. She saw the girl that Pa had called a hooker blow out the candle, heard the window scrape shut.

The other soldiers went to other cribs. Pa pulled Pearl along. "Now you know," he said. "You'll be a ten-dollar whore, even a twenty-dollar whore if you're good at it. You reach twenty, and I'll let you keep some of the money."

Pearl shuddered. Pa gave her a shake, hurried her along the wharf and out onto a street. They walked along the banquette, so close to buildings she could have touched them. She forced her sore feet onward, forced her pained body to keep up with Pa. She wondered what the soldier and the girl were doing back there, closed into the crib.

Whatever it is, she thought, she'd have to do it at Josie's with gentlemen. She wondered if soldiers ever came to Josie's. She felt so frightened her scalp prickled.

On they walked, Pearl stumbling, Pa yanking. Now they passed along fine streets lined on both sides by great, important houses where soft lights shone behind draperies. She glimpsed hidden patios, rich and fragrant with trees and flowering bushes, and even finer courtyards. Carriages passed, muted laughter coming from them, the horses' hoofs clipping elegantly.

She studied one lovely house, made out delicate lace ironwork on windows and balconies and drew a shaking breath at such beauty. She wished forlornly that she might one day see inside the house, might even, wonder of wonders, live in it, though not with any gentleman Pa talked about, but she knew that was impossible.

"This," Pa said at last, "is Storyville, where we're headed."

"Storyville?" she repeated, surprised.

"That's what they call it. It was set up special for sportin' houses. Josie's is on Basin Street, top house of all. The madams pay the law, so they get along fine—all that money. The lawmakers, they come to the houses theirselves. The madams get rich, and the girls like you, they get rich. Some of them marry rich men, and their fortunes are made. You don't appreciate nothin', but there's a future in this job I got for you. See you make the most of it."

Still they walked. The houses had red lamps burning in the front rooms. The lamps were set right in the windows, like a signal. Carriages appeared on the street, too. Men would get out of the carriages and enter one of the many houses with red lamps.

"Storyville," Pa bragged, "is where the fancy houses are with the girls dressed in satin. They're bein' nice to gentlemen you see goin' in, and you know they get paid good, because I told you how much. You owe me for this, girl, owe me plenty."

Pearl was silent. Her whole insides seemed to shrivel up. She dreaded the moment when they'd reach Josie's house.

"You'll work in the finest house in Storyville," Pa said. "You can hold your head up."

Pearl was convinced now that the girls in the cribs and the ones in satin let the soldiers and the gentlemen do something shameful. Desperate with not knowing, she turned her face to Pa as she stumbled along.

"Exactly what will my work be?" she asked, trying to hide any quaver in her voice.

"Easy work, and don't you forget it," he said roughly. "You go to bed with a gentleman, and let him do what he wants—he'll show you. You'll learn. Lie on your back, smile at him, put your arms around his neck, spread your legs, he'll do the rest. It's up to you to give satisfaction. He's spendin' big money for your services, so do what he wants, no matter what, no argument. There's Josie's, the one with two red lamps in two front windows. The best house in Storyville—keep that in mind and be the best whore in the house. You can, because you got the looks and the hair. You'll be Josie's specialty. Why, you do right, you can get twenty-five dollars for all night with one gentleman."

They turned in at the short banquette leading to the

entrance. The four red lamps glowed with frightening beauty. Pearl's breath quivered. They climbed steps. Pa worked the brass knocker. It reflected the red light coming through the glass insets on each side of the heavy door.

The door swung open. A giant Negro in black velvet knee breeches with silver buckles stood there. His head was shaved and very black; the light from a great, candle-filled, red-crystal chandelier made pools of light on his black, shiny skin. He looked just past Pearl's and Pa's faces the way Negroes did with white people.

He spoke in a soft rumble. "Miss Josie expectin' you?"

"That she is," Pa said. "Tell her we're from Bayou Lafourche. She'll know."

Pearl got a swift, confused view of the entrance hall. The floor was covered in thick, blood-red carpet which also covered the steps of the curled stairway leading up to mysterious regions. The handrails were polished wood; the spindles between step and handrail were shining white. Off to the right was a vast double parlor, decorated with blood-red draperies, carpet, and upholstery. Even the glass in the chandeliers was blood-red. The mantel and woodwork were painted a gleaming white. She'd never seen anything like it. The walls were covered in heavy, embossed white, and white roses spread their beauty and their scent from blood-red vases. Fancily dressed girls, perfumed and bejeweled, smiled and murmured as they sat with finely dressed gentlemen.

The Negro butler disappeared into the parlor for a moment. He returned, preceded by a tall, voluptuous woman of perhaps forty. She was auburn-haired, white-skinned, and was wearing a blood-red velvet gown which enhanced every lush curve.

Her features were strong, but handsome, and the look on her face was kind. Her hazel eyes flew to Pearl, warming instantly.

"I'm Josie. In here, please," she said in a husky voice, and moved toward a door on the far side of the hall. It was then, awed by this woman, this madam, that Pearl became really aware of the soft music coming from somewhere inside.

"We'll talk in the music room," Josie said. "It's private. Other places, the men and girls hang around and ruin the music, but not there."

Pa nodded, grinned, mumbled. Pearl was surprised that he wasn't so know-it-all now that they'd arrived. Josie motioned him to a chair, motioned Pearl to a sofa where the blood-red cushions were so heavenly soft she could lean into them without pain. Pearl gazed at Josie.

"Look around, if you like," said the woman. "Call me Josie—all my girls do."

This room was small and red and white, except for the piano, which was glistening black. A very black, young Negro was at the keyboard, playing with his eyes half-closed, lost in his music. The comforting notes of the song seeped into Pearl so that she felt—well, welcome.

Josie looked her over openly. She had Pearl stand up and walked around her, looking. She lifted up the long spill of hair from Pearl's back, meaning to try it atop her head, when she spied dark spots of blood on the towel pinned inside the thin white dress.

She let Pearl's hair drop and looked at Pa. "The girl's beauty is classic," she said. "Amazing."

"I told you," Pa said. "Nobody can beat her for looks!"

Josie moved the back of Pearl's dress, peered down her back, saw the riddled flesh. "Did you have to beat her?" she asked. "I don't use girls who must be forced."

"She won't need no force, not when I'm gone."

"How do I know she won't run away?"

"She's got no place to go, her. And she's like her ma. Give her a taste of man, you can't drive her off. She'll stay. And like it."

Josie turned to Pearl. "Will you stay with me, dear? Or will you run?"

The tinkle of girls' laughter drifted in from the parlors. Those girls sound happy, Pearl thought. They aren't scared. Maybe she'd get used to things if she stayed. No telling what Pa'd do to her if he had to take her back.

Heart shivering, beyond tears, Pearl was too frightened to answer. She just stood and trembled.

"See?" Pa said. "She'll stay."

"You won't run, child?"

"I've got no place to run to, ma'am."

"I'll give it a try," Josie told Pa. "She'll have to stay out of sight in the attic room while she heals." She peered down the dress again. "I believe we can keep her from scarring. She'll get her keep, which will be deducted from her first earnings."

Pearl saw that Pa didn't like this, but he couldn't argue. "All right," he mumbled. "It's a deal. Three months. She'll be healed then, and she'll have money comin', which I'll collect for my fam'ly like I told you before."

Josie nodded. She didn't look pleased.

Pa left without another word. He didn't even grunt a good-bye to Pearl.

IV

"Let me take you upstairs," Josie said to Pearl. "I'll have one of the colored girls bathe those cuts and give you a cotton wrapper. And food."

"That's kind of you, ma'am," Pearl faltered, "but if I could just sit and listen to the music . . . just a while." The music was soothing, and sitting here would delay what was in store for her. She stood gazing earnestly into Josie's eyes, every line of her body asking, pleading to stay and listen to the music.

Pearl surprised herself that she had asked to be left alone in a room with the piano player. Ma had taught her to be afraid of Negroes, and this one was so big his very size made her uneasy. But somehow, the way he was drawing such beauty from the keys, stroking them, he didn't seem dangerous. Besides, Josie would never let a dangerous Negro into her fine house.

Josie relented. "You can sit here as long as you want, child," she said. "Just don't come into the parlors. Keep to that sofa, because it hides your back."

Pearl smiled wanly and sank gratefully down onto the sofa. Josie winked, smiled, and left.

Music enwrapped Pearl. She'd never heard anything so beautiful in her whole life. It cushioned her throbbing body, drifted out of the room and across the hallway where gentlemen continued to arrive. From where she sat, Pearl caught glimpses of beautiful girls, their hair stunningly dressed, wearing silk and satin and taffeta, sprigged materials fresh as the breath of spring. Twice she saw couples, the gentleman's fingers under the girl's arm, going up the stairs, smiling and chatting, and she marveled at the girls. They didn't look to be scared, not at all, and she wondered how they could be calm when she herself, untouched by any man, ever, was scared for them. She closed her eyes, leaned her head against the sofa cushion, breathed in the sweet, heavy scent of roses, and let her mind fill with music.

"You like music, miss?" asked the Negro, his voice like black velvet.

Startled, she looked at him, then nodded. And as he played on, eyes closed in that way he had, she stared at him closely.

He was coal-black. The wool on his head was closely cropped; his eyes, when they were open, were very dark. His features were heavily negroid, his lips thick. He was very large, at least six feet tall, and must weigh two hundred pounds. His hands, stroking the keys, were big and powerful and could probably break almost anything in half. She shivered. How dangerous!

He sang quietly, his voice the deepest velvet bass, and the piano quieted to a ripple, a sweet background to that voice which, if he let it go, would surely be as mighty as his hands.

Fascinated, she stared on at his color, at the power of him. She began to tremble, inwardly at first, then visibly. He opened his eyes and looked her way, and she knew he saw the trembling, but she couldn't stop.

"You don't want to work here, miss?" he asked, the words breathing out of the music.

She shook her head, swallowed. "I'll run away. Somehow."

"What can you do to earn money, miss?"

"I know how to shrimp."

"Folks here don't hire young ladies for that, miss."

"I can be a nursemaid. I've taken care of my baby brothers."

"Folks here hire colored girls for that, miss."

She sat and trembled. Why was she telling this fearsome Negro her troubles, admitting to him that she could do nothing to support herself? Fear of her plight made her stiffen. It was a fear of him, too. Yet despite these fears, she felt a warmth of understanding that he seemed to send her through his ceaseless music. Gradually, the music lessened her trembling; she even began to take courage. Somehow, she would escape.

The Negro played on and on. The sound of laughter and voices reached from the parlors. Pearl's back, her feet, her shoulders, ached.

"I'm Ben Rivard," the Negro said gently. "I'm from Rivard Plantation on Bayou Teche. Near St. Martinville. I only come to play piano to earn money for Rivard. I grow sugar cane. Our family works five hundred acres. We have tenants who work for a share of the profits. I tell you this so you won't be so afraid of me."

He'd noticed her fear. And he owned a plantation! Five hundred acres—that sounded as big as the world. Secretly now, Pearl watched his face as he played, his eyes half-closed again.

He was so very black, so very big, but he looked kind. She couldn't imagine those great hands, so loving on the ivory keys, ever gripping a strap and beating another human being or even a mule that wouldn't go. If he truly was as gentle as his music, then he had in him more gentleness than anyone in the world, except Ma.

Ben played on and on. He felt sorry for the beautiful, frightened girl whose father had brought her to work in a sporting house against her will.

He wished there was some way he could help her. She was utterly friendless. And terrified. And probably burning from the pain of the beating her father had given her. He wondered if she even understood where she was and what she would be expected to do.

He kept playing, one of his own compositions now, and studying her through his half-closed eyes. She was exquisitely beautiful. She had a delicate, perfect form, and that wondrous platinum hair. Her eyes were silver, her features fine and dainty. Her lips, which quivered now and then, were pink and shapely. Her skin was so white and looked so soft he wished he dared touch it, just with his fingertips. Her voice was soft and pretty, even though she was scared and in pain and desperate.

She was very young. Amazed that he should speak so

boldly to a white girl, Ben asked, "How old are you, miss?"

She looked frightened. "S-seventeen."

Right then, the thought struck him. Maybe he could help her someway. Somebody had to. It was unthinkable to stand aside and let Josie—even kind Josie—force that innocent, shrinking young body into the arms of some passion-inflamed man. Gently, still playing the piano, he asked her name, feeling his way as in a dream.

"Pearl," she said. "Pearl Babin."

"Pearl," he mused, as if the name meant something special. "Pearl. One pearl."

"My ma . . . she liked that name."

Three couples came gaily into the room, the rustle of taffeta and satin sounding softly against the music. The girls' voices were bright and laughing; the men spoke in deeper tones, but jovial, too. They were dressed as Pearl had never seen men dressed before, wearing fine, dark suits and elegant silk shirts. The girls' dresses were low-cut, showing their bosoms, and the hems revealed their ankles, enticing in silk stockings. Waves of heady perfume came from the girls, and their lips were painted.

They all looked so happy, even the girls. Especially the girls. They were young, but the men were older. One looked to be in his thirties, another in his forties, and the third one was at least sixty and had a flushed red face and a big stomach. The youngest girl of the three was clinging to his arm, squealing at every word he spoke, telling him he should be on the stage, his jokes were so hilarious.

"Ben," sang out one girl, "Sammy wants to hear some jazz. Come out of your dreams!"

Pearl saw Ben nod, and he began to play a strange kind of music, a kind Pearl had never heard and didn't like. The couples began to dance.

Pearl shrank into her sofa. She'd never be able to dance

like that. Maybe when Josie found she couldn't dance at
all, she'd turn her loose; maybe Josie'd think it was too
much trouble to try to teach her the steps.

Watching, praying that none of them would notice her,
Pearl could hardly believe that these men paid money to
be with the girls, to go upstairs with them. They seemed
so proper and polite.

Two more couples drifted in. One man was quite handsome, the other extremely fat. Both girls were very pretty.

The fat man demanded to hear boogie-woogie, and the
music and the dancing changed again. At the end of a
number, Josie herself came in, one arm around a very thin
man of forty or so, the other around the prettiest girl Pearl
had seen yet, a very slender, white-skinned nymphet with
hair the color of butter.

"Cissy!" cried a black-haired girl. "Here you are, and
here's Ben, and here's the piano! Sing for us, do! And after
that, I'll pick up my skirts way high and dance!"

"Oh, you goose!" said Cissy with a laugh. "All right, I'll
sing. But you'll be sor-ry!"

Cissy's voice was startlingly deep, and she sang a gospel
hymn Pearl remembered from church when Pa let them
go. All joined in the refrain, clapped their hands to the
rhythm, and then the black-haired girl danced, kicking
and showing her legs to the thigh.

Pearl, willing fiercely that she not be noticed, stared as
the men and girls frolicked. She hardly dared to breathe,
she was so afraid one of them would spy her hiding on the
sofa.

But someone did. It was the black-haired girl. As she
finished her madcap dance, she flung herself onto the sofa
beside Pearl. She stared at Pearl, her surprise went to
laughter, and she put a hand on Pearl's hair to feel it. Pearl
shrank, and the girl smiled.

"Now, lovely," she soothed. "Don't be afraid. Don't you

know you've got million-dollar hair?" She looked across the room, then motioned to the fat man. "Come here, Billy. Look what I found!"

He waddled to the sofa, stood spraddled in front of Pearl and gaped. "What you doing here alone, pretty thing?" his voice grated. The piano music rose angrily in volume, and Billy had to raise his voice. "Josie," he called, "who's this one?"

Josie was there right away. "This is Pearl," she said. "She just got here tonight. She can't take part because she's been whipped by her pa and has to heal up. Come on, all of you, can't you see you're scaring her? She just wants to listen to the music. Have any of you been upstairs yet? I'm serving a repast after you come down. Wine is on the house tonight!"

Josie lingered after the couples had departed. "You ready to go up now and have those cuts treated?" she asked kindly. "They must hurt like hell."

Pearl shook her head numbly. The only place she felt safe at all was here with the piano. With the music. With Ben.

Josie shrugged, told Ben to play softly, and went into the parlors. Pearl heard voices and realized that still more girls and gentlemen were in there and that more gentlemen would arrive.

Ben had noted Pearl's reaction to the singing and dancing, to the way all the men had looked at her, and had seen her fright of the fat man. He continued playing his music softly. He asked, "Do you know the bayou country?"

"Only Lafourche...La Vie. I don't know where the Teche is, and I never heard of St. Martinville."

"St. Martinville is very old. It was settled by Acadians from Nova Scotia, which is far to the north of here, very far."

"Acadians . . . I never heard of them either. Just of Cajuns, us on Lafourche and around."

"The Acadians at first lived in France, across the ocean. Long, long ago they fished in Nova Scotia, then took their catch the far distance back to France to sell."

"That was hard work."

"Indeed it was. And too long a voyage. So, gradually, the Acadians stayed in Nova Scotia, made their homes there."

"How did they do that?"

"There were great, primeval forests in Nova Scotia. The Acadians cut down tremendous trees, and using these trees and native rock, too, they built sturdy houses and stables to keep out the fierce winter cold. They raised cattle and grew crops, and they prospered. They had large families because their land was rich and beautiful and there was enough for all. But it didn't last."

"What happened?"

"England got control of Nova Scotia from France. England took the farms and cattle and crops and kept them. She deported all Acadians, tore families apart, separated them forever, loaded them onto different ships—even put smallpox-infested blankets on some ships so Acadians would sicken and die—and sent them to American colonies. Some of the Acadians, after hard and dangerous travel, reached Louisiana and the bayou country and were given land grants in return for developing the land. Which they did—the Acadians loved the bayous then, love them today, and call themselves Cajuns."

Pearl, quivering less now, for she was no longer so frightened, gazed at Ben in wonder. "Are you Acadian?" she asked.

He shook his head, his fingers lightly playing the keys. "Acadians were French, remember. I'm colored. The Acadians brought in Negro slaves to help them farm. One of the biggest plantations on the Teche is L'Acadie, which the Leblancs established. Twelve thousand acres and more than one fine house. They're still the leading family."

"Then they've had an easy time."

"No. Not easy at all. They've had trouble and scandal. One Leblanc woman lost her mind, murdered her child and her husband, and later died in a rage over a jeweled dagger she'd lost. The Leblancs have had to live down a second murder done by a Leblanc wife, a murder done with that same dagger the first one couldn't find. They've also stood up against gossip that there's Negro blood in the family."

"But you didn't have bad things happen to you?" she asked Ben. "You've got a plantation—five hundred acres!"

"Rivard was bought by my ancestor," he said. "We've managed to keep it through the Civil War, through Reconstruction, and even now in this war with Germany. We aim to keep it as long as there is one member of the Rivard family alive."

All the while as Ben talked, his long, strong fingers had been playing, stroking the ivories. Pearl watched those fingers and marveled anew that they could be so big, yet make such tender music.

"I've never lived anywhere but on Lafourche," she said. "On the houseboat. It's little and crowded. Pa and my two biggest brothers go shrimping every day, and I used to go, too. I suppose that ain't like a plantation at all."

Not believing his own words until he heard them float to her on the music, Ben said, "You don't have to run away alone. My job here ends in a week. I've got a room on the waterfront. You can hide there. I'll see if I can find you a job as a maid, though most ladies have colored girls for that. And if I can't find you a job, you can go to Rivard with me. Nobody will think of looking for you there. Then you can decide what you want to do. You can hunt for a job yourself. Josie'll just think you ran. She won't make any trouble."

Pearl gazed across the room into his big, so big, brown eyes.

"Or," he added, "you can just tell Josie you don't want to work here. She's a good woman; she'd never try to keep you by force."

Josie, who had come into the room quietly, heard Ben's last words. She crossed to the sofa, settled on the edge of it, and looked kindly at Pearl.

"Is that true, my dear?" she asked. "You don't want to work here?"

Heart in her throat, Pearl managed to shake her head. "I . . . it was Pa who wanted it," she whispered. "Not me . . . not Ma."

Josie frowned. "Can you go home?"

"I . . . Pa . . . no."

"What can you do then?"

"I . . . I'll find a job."

"They're not that easy to find, Pearl. Why don't you stay here and be a part of my establishment? Or at least work on yourself until you become reconciled to it. Do you think you can at least do that much?"

"I . . . no, ma'am . . . no."

"You're upset, and you hurt from the strap," Josie reasoned. "I'd insist that you stay here, but you'd have to be at least reconciled to the life if you're to be any good to me. How about it, want to spend the night in my attic room and think it over? The life isn't too bad, really. You saw how free and easy my girls are. I treat them good, pay them good. And I screen the customers—only the best gentlemen in New Orleans are permitted to patronize my house. In fact, I think you'd better stay and heal up. Then try it for one week—one short week—and find out."

"N-no, please!" Pearl choked out. "I don't mean to be

stubborn, but I don't even want to spend the night in this house, nice as you are!"

Josie gave her a searching look, then shrugged. "I don't like to just put you out on the street in the middle of the night," she said. She dipped her fingers into the bodice of her blood-red gown and pulled out some money. "Here's two dollars for a start. With my best wishes." She proffered the bills.

Pearl drew back. "I couldn't," she protested. "My ma says never to take money unless I've earned it."

"Take it, miss," said Ben, from the piano. "If you'll excuse me for putting in my word, Miss Josie."

Josie flashed a smile at him as she pushed the bills into Pearl's trembling hand. "Try restaurants," she advised. "They might hire you as dishwasher."

"Thank you, ma'am. I'll do that." Pearl tried to stand up to leave, but fell back weakly.

"Go when you're a bit more rested," Josie told her. "And good luck."

Pearl wondered what Josie would say if she knew about Ben's offer.

"My offer stands," Ben said, as he continued to play. "Two dollars won't last forever. And if your back is cut up bad, you're in no shape to wash dishes or do any kind of work. You'll do well if you can even walk out of here tonight."

"Y-you'll walk with me when I go?" she asked, suddenly frightened that she might collapse and be forced to stay here, not just to heal, but to repay Miss Josie, to whom she was already in debt.

Ben shook his head. "It wouldn't do. White and black don't mix, even in Storyville. No, I can't walk out that door with you. I have another hour to play, anyhow. But tell you what."

He paused, and Pearl waited, her eyes on his.

"I suggest," he continued, still playing the piano, "that if you decide to accept my help, you sit here another half hour—you can see the hall clock—and then leave. Go along the banquette to Basin Street; it's only a short way. Turn to your right. Go to the first corner. Turn right again, and you'll find a bench hidden by bushes. Sit on the bench, and wait there for me. I'll come when my hour's up."

Pearl didn't reply. He asked gently, "Understand? You'll be safe. I promise."

Suppose he tried to do what Miss Josie's white gentlemen were doing upstairs right now? Suppose some man on the street grabbed her? Her teeth chattered, but finally she got words out.

"I'll go with you," she said.

V

On the night Pearl Babin ran away from Josie's sporting house, Pièrre Leblanc was dressing for his wedding.

He was thinking back on his childhood, of riding his horse across the vast reaches of L'Acadie, the great, twelve-thousand-acre plantation. He thought anew with gratitude of his father, René Leblanc. He recalled school at St. Martinville and his many friends there. He thought of the lessons with Monsieur Duval, the tutor with the crippled leg who had come to live and teach him the advanced subjects.

"But Monsieur," he'd argue, "what's the sense of Latin for me? Pa's teaching me how to raise sugar cane because that's how we make our living. But Latin and Greek and history and how other countries are governed—it's a waste of time!"

Monsieur would always smile. "It's to train your mind, to make it keen."

Then pupil and tutor would plunge into the intricacies of algebra and physics. Pierre had honed his mind until he'd covered all the subjects, and Monsieur Duval had moved on to another bayou plantation to teach three brothers.

All Pierre did then was talk of enlisting in the Army. He was determined to do his part to put down the Kaiser.

"You can help just as much by growing crops for the Army," René said. "That's what the Leblancs have always done when there's a war."

Pierre insisted and offered himself to the Army, but he was rejected because of flat feet. He was angry and disappointed. He worked the fields, but he was restless and not at all his usual eager self.

It worried his father, and one evening after the two of them had finished dinner, Pierre brought up the subject. He'd never known his mother, who had disappeared from his life when he was an infant and now, suddenly, he boldly asked to know of her. René studied him for a moment, then began to speak, sadness and regret in his tone.

"Your mother went to jail for murder," he said bluntly. "She died there."

"What murder? Why did she do it?"

"She was a lovely but very jealous woman. She found out that I'd fathered a near-white child on a black girl, Tansey Rivard. As Tansey was about to give birth in a cornfield, your mother killed her with a knife, a dagger, to be exact. Riel Rivard, master of Rivard Plantation, smothered the child at birth because he was determined that all Rivards should be black. It was a great scandal, swept the

bayous like wildfire, but gradually, in time, it died down.
Especially after Ramona . . . your mother . . . died."

"Is that why we've always been so close, you and I?"
asked Pierre, a trembling in him for his mother but for his
father, as well. René must have suffered greatly over what
he had done, and regretted.

Now René leaned back in his armchair. His brown hair
matched the leather exactly except for the streaks of white
at the temples; his light brown eyes and handsome face
were somber.

"You're unhappy, son," he said quietly, "about the Army
and now—about your mother."

"Sad, rather . . . about you and my mother. But I feel no
anger toward you, no blame."

"You're unhappy, though. About the Army, too."

"Not exactly unhappy about the Army . . . just . . ."

"Restless?"

Pierre considered. "Yes, sir. That's the word."

"And you find it hard to settle down to farming?"

"That's it," Pierre admitted. "I must be selfish, to
almost resent farming when I know it's a help in the war."

"Not selfishness, son—youth. You're not quite twenty-
one, and you've been tied to L'Acadie all your life. The
Army would have given you the change you need. Well,
you still need the change."

"I don't see any way to get it, sir."

"I've a suggestion. Duval reported to me on your studies, as you know. Your final course was in geography—he
said learning about St. Louis and the rivers there was
exciting to you."

Pierre smiled, and his voice quickened as he spoke.
"It's the wilderness, sir. The trapping and the excitement
of the Missouri River, which is a brute. I'd give anything
to—" He broke off. "But that's impossible."

"Why impossible?"

"I'd be leaving you shorthanded, and there's the money it'd take."

"We've a bit laid aside, a cushion. I can think of no better use than to send you to St. Louis. The work here can be done without you. You'll work all the harder when you get back."

"I can repay you with what I make trapping!" Pierre exclaimed eagerly. "I can more than pay you back! The fur market is good. I've watched the papers!"

"So you have been thinking of a trip," smiled René. "It's settled." He held up his hand before Pierre could protest. "I want you to have the adventure, son. You'll come back a mature man, watch and see!"

A week later, Pierre was boarding the great, puffing, noisy train. He'd never been on a train before, and he walked down the aisle of the car holding his suitcase endwise, bumping his knees, and made for a seat. The car was filled with people in the high-backed green plush seats and luggage in the overhead racks. The conductor called, "All a-board," and the train began to move.

The train sped past farmlands and villages faster than any horse or even any automobile. It stopped at small, hot, and dusty depots, where people got off and others got on, but the seat beside Pierre remained empty, and for this he was glad, because he wanted to look and see, not talk.

St. Louis, which Pierre had pictured as a quiet fur-trading post, was actually a big city bristling with activity. The streets were filled with automobiles, streetcars, and hundreds of people. Shops of every description lined the mainstreets—grocers, clothiers, drapers, furniture, and hardware dealers.

Away from the waterfront were the fur-trading establishments Pierre sought. The aisles were filled with bales of fur—bearskins, buffalo hides, wolf skins, pelts of marten, beaver, otter, and others he didn't recognize. The peltries smelled musty yet fresh; he found the odors invigorating and knew that he had chosen right to come here for a taste of life.

He saw shelves of traps, neat rows of rifles, and even Indian bows, each with a quiver of arrows. He decided these must be for an occasional white man, because any Indian would fashion his own bow and make his own arrows.

A small, faded clerk with sideburns approached and asked if he could be of help. Pierre smiled at him. "I need a place for room and board," he said. "After that, I want to join up with trappers and go into the wilds."

The clerk smiled at Pierre's enthusiasm. "The widow Estess lets rooms, sets a fine table. You'll see her house at the end of Front Street. It's one of the oldest houses in town, got five rooms."

Pierre found the place without trouble. He knocked on the door.

The door was opened by a beautiful dark-skinned girl in a yellow dress. Her body was small, but shapely and strong, and she was very young. Suddenly he realized that she was an Indian. Her skin was brown and her dark eyes almond-shaped. The way she held her head with its coronet of black braid was regal. He wondered what she was doing here.

"Mrs. Estess?" he managed to ask. "I'd like a room."

"She's gone to nurse the little Griggs girls," she said. There was a soft touch of French in her fluent English and a hint of something else—her Indian tongue, perhaps.

"Can you rent me the room?" he asked.

The brown eyes assessed him slowly. She studied his face and his brown hair. He hoped she'd not object to the red in it or how deeply blue his eyes were; her eyes were so brown. She seemed to note his height and strong build with approval.

"I'm sure Mrs. Estess won't mind, monsieur," she said. "May I take your valise?"

He shook his head. That she, so tiny, should carry his suitcase was unthinkable. "Thank you, no," he said, "just show me the way. Do you live here too?" he asked.

"While school is in session, monsieur, I work here. I teach in the mission school. When the trapping starts, they let me go home to the reservation. I've never been anywhere but here and with my people, the Osage."

He noted her gentle, confident lips and told her why he had come to St. Louis.

"I live in a highly civilized world—Louisiana," he explained. "I go to New Orleans, which is a big city, but not at all like St. Louis. I want to trap in the wilderness, taste a different sort of life."

She smiled up at him and was radiant. "You're in time to make the upriver boat trip to the village of my people," she said. "In a month, we go deep into the country at the time the beaver and otter and all the fur-bearing creatures have on their fine, glossy, winter coats. We bring our peltries here to sell."

"How can I join your people for the hunt?" Pierre asked eagerly.

"I need only to speak to my father, Wild Eagle. He is the chief."

"You'd do that for me, a perfect stranger?"

She stopped at the open door of a bedroom, and he was aware of a rough-hewn bed, a bright coverlet, rag carpeting, and the glint of mirror above a washstand. There was a fresh scent of soap.

"Some people remain strangers always," she replied. "Others . . . We have a month to get acquainted. And then

I will know. And if you're to be trusted, I'll speak to my father."

"You're so kind," he murmured. "And you don't even know my name. I'm Pierre Leblanc."

"And I am Yellow Flower, only daughter of Wild Eagle."

"Princess?"

"Yes."

"Why are you called Yellow Flower?"

"With the Osage, it is the custom for the new father to take the new baby outside the lodge and the first thing he sees that pleases him becomes the baby's name. Wild Eagle saw a beautiful yellow flower."

"You come from the wilderness," he mused.

"Yes, monsieur."

"Pierre."

"Pierre, then. Originally, it was vast wilderness. Now it is the reservation, but it is still vast. I come from the sweet and spreading land the Great Father permits the Osage and other Indian nations and even the white man to use."

"My own land spreads far, too," Pierre said, wanting to have something in common with her. "Only it belongs to me, to the Leblanc family. It is no loan."

"All land, all life is a loan from the Great Father," she said gently. "People die and leave the land, and the land remains loaned to those who come next. So it is treasured and used carefully by the Osage. We take from it only what we must, to live."

"What do you think of the white trappers?"

"They are greedy. They would strip the land to get much, much money. Is that what you do on the land you have, Pierre? Do you strip it?"

"No," he said, struck by the wisdom of this girl, this Yellow Flower. "We tend our land and plant crops."

She nodded solemnly. "I shall tell Wild Eagle that you

are the same as Osage toward the land. He will respect and honor you for it."

When she left him, he felt strangely lonely. She was beautiful in her own Indian way, and she was well educated. She was a marvel of wild Indian and civilized white. He unpacked, thinking of her, and then he went out to see what he could of this bustling, strange city.

Mrs. Estess was at home when he returned. She was squarely built, had steel-gray hair arranged in a knot and a kind face. She accepted Pierre's rent money matter-of-factly.

"I know it's a bit high," she said. "But it's clean here, and we set the best table in town. Yellow Flower cooks as well as I do. She's a jewel, one I'm afraid I can't keep much longer because an important Osage brave wants her for his number one wife. So far, thank goodness, he hasn't gotten an answer from her. You make yourself at home now. There's magazines in the living room, if you want to read, and a Victor machine, if you want music. And there's a streetcar line a square away, if you want to sightsee. I'm staying nights with the Griggs girls. They got penumonia and take a heap of nursing."

Yellow Flower served his supper, but for some reason wouldn't talk, though Pierre made several efforts to start a conversation. She seemed to be making up her mind about something, and he wondered if it was that brave in her tribe; for some reason, Pierre didn't like the idea.

Like a blow, the thought hit him. She might be afraid to sleep in the same house alone with him, afraid he'd take advantage of her. He flushed at the idea. He wished there was some way he could tell her that he'd never slept with a girl yet.

"What are you thinking about?" he finally asked.

"Osage thoughts, Pierre. The thoughts of an Osage girl,

who's been educated and who knows the ways of the white man."

After that, he couldn't get a word out of her. Downcast, he went into his room, undressed, got into his nightshirt, and lay watching shadows grow into blackness until he fell asleep.

Mrs. Estess was there for breakfast. Yellow Flower said good morning to Pierre as if last night had never happened, and when the older woman suggested that she take Pierre sight-seeing, she smiled and looked at him shyly.

"I could," she said. "I teach only part-time. Do you want to go?" she asked.

"Of course," he said quickly. He'd meant to ride street-cars, walk, see what he could. But Yellow Flower could point out things, tell him what they were, and he'd get a much better grasp of the city. Besides, she intrigued him.

"We can go as soon as I wash dishes," she said.

He drew a breath of relief. If she had been afraid he'd molest her in the night, she knew better now. He wondered if most white men tried to get into an Indian girl's bed. He supposed a lot of them did, so he'd be extra gentle with Yellow Flower. He liked her and wanted to be friends, wanted her to feel at ease with him.

She wore a different dress today. It was yellow, too, but softer looking. She insisted that he sit next to the window in the streetcar, and she leaned forward to draw his attention to the courthouse and other sights along the route. After a while they changed streetcars and rode along streets lined with fine, beautiful houses, some of which looked French.

He bought her a hamburger at a stand, ate one himself, and they each had a bottle of soda pop. She said strawberry was her favorite. She told him about concerts given in the opera house every winter and said she'd like to go once. He wondered how much it cost, but knew that he couldn't afford it now, even if there were a concert playing tonight.

They began to spend more time together. One afternoon they went to a picture show. A skinny man sitting near the screen played the piano while the picture flickered on and on, and when the cowboys chased the Indians, the piano thundered until it seemed they could hear the horses' hoofs.

Yellow Flower began to laugh during the most exciting part. Pierre knew she was laughing, because she had her hand clamped over her lips and her shoulders were shaking.

Coming out of the dark movie house into the glare of sunlight, Yellow Flower was wiping away tears of laughter.

"What was so funny in there?" Pierre asked.

She laughed softly. "Those Indians! They didn't know how to ride! They rode the way white men think Indians ride, not the way Indians really do. In real life, why, every one of those Indians would be dead. But in the picture show, they all got away from the cowboys alive!"

Every Sunday they went to Mass. She wore a very pale yellow dress with ruffles and a pale yellow scarf. She also wore white lace gloves. No Indian this woman, Pierre thought, kneeling and rising in the rituals of worship. She's like any girl of the Teche, he thought. She . . . she's wonderful! He wanted, then and there, to take her in his arms, to kiss her. He'd never kissed a girl before, but he wanted to kiss Yellow Flower on the lips, to hold that sweet Osage body close and feel her warmth. He wondered if he might be on the verge of falling in love with her.

The morning finally came when she went with him to help him buy traps. She was leaving on the steamboat next day to join her people, and it was settled that he was to go along.

She was silent and thoughtful at supper that night.

"Is something wrong?" he asked.

"Nothing is wrong, Pierre," she replied.

"More of that Osage girl thinking?" he teased. He looked at her lips, wished he dared get up, go around the table and kiss her. His heart grew warm. He didn't know if this was love or not, but it was certainly confusing.

They went for a walk after supper, and she let him hold her arm when they crossed the streets. They didn't talk much, and that was mostly about his traps. She suggested that he could resell them at the end of the season, because she knew that he didn't have much money.

That night he couldn't go to sleep for thinking of her. He lay watching the light patch the window in his room made. He didn't hear the door open and close. The first he knew, Yellow Flower was standing at the foot of his bed.

He sat up fast, his loins on fire with that Leblanc hunger. He tried to speak and couldn't. And she didn't speak.

Slowly she unbuttoned her gown, slid it off her shoulders, letting it fall down her body to the floor, then stepped out of it. The window light showed her to be exquisitely formed. Where her legs met, a small, thick patch of black jutted forward, offering itself.

"Yellow Flower!" he whispered at last.

There was a smile in her voice. "It's what I've been deciding ever since I first saw you, Pierre. Never have I lain with a white man or a brave—once I almost did with Stalking Wolf, then did not. Since I also go trapping, I choose to be with you. Like this."

He felt a wildness for her and a tenderness. He felt a gentle concern and an overwhelming eagerness. And when her body was under his, with his own clumsy virginity he soon broke hers. Then they moved together, ever faster, ever nearer to explosion, and his hunger grew. At the last, when they were swept to glory, he knew that this girl was priceless and he would love her forever.

He lay holding her, picturing how she would be as mistress of L'Acadie. He decided that though she might, at first, seem different to the bayou folk, her love for land and her gentleness would make her the perfect mistress. He could see her teaching their sons to treasure L'Acadie, nurturing them in the Osage manner.

He drew her closer, loved her again, long and with tender passion, and then he asked her to marry him.

"In the white man way or the Osage, Pierre?"

"Both, if you want it."

"You'd stay here, live with my people, live Osage?"

"I can't, my little Yellow Flower. I have to go back to L'Acadie and take care of it. You would go along and help me. I love you now; I'll love you always."

She was silent. "I have eternal love for you," she finally said, "but I must stay here, where I can live both Osage and white. You could live both ways here, too. Would not all the vast Osage reservation, stretching from sky to sky, be enough for you, Pierre? Must you be at this L'Acadie, which is less in size, which keeps you penned in as the Great Father never intended?"

"If we can't marry, we can't make love, Yellow Flower."

"Why not?"

"It isn't fair to you. I have no right to you without marriage. If your father had any idea—"

She kissed his lips softly. "Wild Eagle will bless what I do. At the Osage camp and trapping, we will be as here, this moment. It is Osage custom for the chief to provide a visiting white man or brave with a woman, one of his own wives, even his favorite. It is a courtesy."

"But he's your father, not your husband. He'll—"

"Let me do as I wish. Please, Pierre! No marriage is needed between us, unless..."

"That's the one thing I can't do, lovely Yellow Flower. I must go back, want to go back, and I want to take you with me."

Time passed like a dream as the steamboat carried them up the Missouri. Pierre saw spot after spot where the tall banks at the edges of the perpetually angry, powerful river had caved in, leaving the earth raw, trees still clinging, roots bare.

Pierre, astounded by the pitiless fury of the surging, leaping water, listened as Yellow Flower explained the Missouri to him. She told him how the white trappers and rivermen cursed and damned it for a devil river.

"The white trappers and the Indians use dugouts to bring the peltries downstream to St. Louis," she told him. "This we will also do. The Missouri is no plain river running its bed, but an outlaw that cuts crooked through the land."

Pierre whistled, marveling. "Go on. Tell all."

"The river grabs the dugout and whirls it and tries to suck it down and swallow it, pelts and all. And men and braves, too. It's too deep for poles, too swift for oars, too crooked for sails. It rises suddenly, lifts logs off a hundred bars, yanks out strong trees, hurls them all downstream. And when the waters fall, it lodges the trees on bars, piles them, mats them with fast-growing roots, forms rafts and islands overnight."

Pierre began to sweat at the prospect. Yet he thrilled at it, too.

"And that's not all! It lays traps, the rivermen say, and it does, Pierre! I see it every year! It wedges logs in its mud bottom so they stick up, leaning downstream, sometimes breaking water, but mostly hidden. They're called snags because they pierce a boat or rip it. It even anchors the roots and branches of logs in its mud, and these move back and forth in the water, surging up on the current, falling under, jumping up again. These are the sawyers, the most dangerous of all; they can destroy the strongest dugout. Then, in deep pockets, the Missouri hides its quicksands. Oh, it's a real adventure to come down this river, one you'll never forget!"

Nights on the steamboat were wondrous. Yellow Flower would slip from belowdecks, where Indians had to travel, and into Pierre's cabin, where he wooed her with words and with his body, aching with the need to win her for life. And she, in turn, wooed him with words of love and with her body, wanting the same thing.

It was late afternoon when they got off the boat. The Osage village was located far from the treacherous shoreline. It was filled with lodges, barking dogs, playing children, and women at work. Tall men squatted in groups, talking, playing some kind of game with short sticks, twigs almost, and small stones.

Pierre gazed about the village, estimating there must be two hundred lodges.

"Some of the lodges are so big," he remarked. "Why is that?"

"Each one," Yellow Flower replied, "holds one Osage family. An Osage with three wives must provide a fireplace for each wife. She keeps her clothes and cooking equipment around her own fireplace."

"Then there's no quarreling," said Pierre with a smile.

"Not among the wives. But they quarrel at their men, urging them to greater feats so they, through him, will be important in the village."

"This," she said, stopping at one of the biggest lodges, "is where Wild Eagle, my father, lives with his four wives. We'll make our greeting to him first."

She pushed aside the blanket which hung over the door opening and went in. Pierre followed.

It was warm inside, which was welcome after the crisp autumn cold, and it smelled of food. There were four cookfires, with children and women at each. The floor was covered with buffalo robes and bearskins, and there were hunting accessories, wooden saddles, cooking utensils, and clothing along the sides of the lodge.

A tall man rose from the first fire and stood looking at Pierre. And at Yellow Flower.

VI

The tall, powerful Indian held out his arms to Yellow Flower, and she went into them. For an instant she remained there, cheek against his chest, then moved to stand proudly beside him.

"Wild Eagle, my father," she said, speaking English, "I have brought a fine man to share my blanket. I have brought Pierre Leblanc from far away to the south."

Wild Eagle's hair was glittering black like Yellow Flower's and hung in two heavy braids over his chest. His features were noble, bronze in color; his black eyes were lustrous, and they searched Pierre's face.

"You marry Yellow Flower?" he asked in careful English.

"I wish to," Pierre replied, "but she does not."

The black eyes rested on Yellow Flower. "Why, daughter?"

"He will not live in Osage country. And I will not go to faraway south, for I am Osage. All Osage. His pride and mine are alike, and we do not agree to marry. But we wish to share a blanket."

Wild Eagle frowned. Yellow Flower laid her cheek against his chest again. "This I want, Wild Eagle, my father. I ask it of you."

The father held the daughter's shoulders, peered into
her eyes. At last he nodded. "Spread your blanket near
your mother's fire. Tomorrow night, when we have started
our trip, you can build your own lodge."

Smiling, Yellow Flower drew forward a lovely, deerskin-
clad woman. "This is my mother, Cooing Dove," she said.
"She speaks no English. "Those boys are her sons, my full
brothers. Cooing Dove is number one wife."

Next Yellow Flower took Pierre to meet Wild Eagle's
other wives, then led him outside. The braves were tall
and bronze and powerful and handsome; the women and
girls they met were comely and smiling.

They stopped before a muscular brave who stood at
least four inches over six feet. Neither the faltering light of
day nor the deerskin garments he wore concealed the fact
that he was without doubt the most powerful, the mighti-
est brave in the tribe. His head was shaven except for the
gleaming black scalp lock. He had the tall forehead of his
race, the width at the temples, and a bold, aquiline nose.
His upper lip was flat with a more jutting lower lip, and
his mouth was straight and not gentle.

"You have come," he said sternly to Yellow Flower. He
spoke English as though it were filth; he glowered at
Pierre. "With a man. As I knew you would one day come.
All say you are not his wife."

How, Pierre wondered, had this information spread?
And then he realized the source. Wild Eagle had announced
it proudly and with authority.

"Pierre," Yellow Flower said, "this is Stalking Wolf." To
the brave she said, "This is Pierre Leblanc. He is accepted
by my father."

"You are back. You will be Stalking Wolf's number one
wife."

"I've come back before. I'm not ready to be your wife."

"You will be. After Pierre goes."

"Have you lost your pride, Stalking Wolf? Do you wish to take me for your wife, a girl who has lain with another man?"

"It is Osage way for Osage brave to give his favorite wife to any man who visits. When this man goes, it will be as before. Stalking Wolf will have you for his own then."

The warrior eyes met Pierre's eyes with hatred. Pierre glared back, every nerve crying out to order the brave to stop tormenting Yellow Flower. Instead, to avoid breaking any Osage custom, he stood rigid, holding his fists to his sides.

"All Indians know," Stalking Wolf said, "that the white man comes where he is not wanted, that he takes what is not his. You have taken Stalking Wolf's number one wife, but you will not be allowed to keep her."

He turned and strode majestically away.

"What did he mean by all that?" Pierre asked. "If he wants to fight, I'm ready for him. I take threats from no man."

"He is a man of honor," Yellow Flower replied. "He will not plot, and he will not fight easily. Though he is arrogant, he is patient because he respects Wild Eagle."

In the morning there was unbelievable activity as the Osage village got ready to leave for the overland trip up the Missouri. Every living thing in camp was moving—babies, children, dogs, horses, women, hunters.

As braves charged about on horses, the little bells fastened to the horses' manes made a silver music. The braves bared their chests to the cold after painting themselves red and green. They were more handsome than ever in fine blankets fastened at the shoulder, which moved and lifted behind them in the wind, showing their brown, painted bodies and waving the eagle feathers in their scalp locks.

In the village the lodges were taken apart, and the women loaded the parts onto packhorses and buried things not needed on the trip, such as extra cooking pots.

When the village was lined up, each family waited in place with its horses, with those who would walk and with those who would ride. Soon a young brave, at a signal from Wild Eagle, came charging down the line, bells tinkling, blanket billowing, shouting, "All make ready to move!" over and over again. "Stalking Wolf, leader of the trappers, says the time has come!"

The women were already in the forked-stick saddles, with small children tied in amongst the bundles. The babies in wooden cradles were tied onto the saddles; some were asleep, some squalling, and a few watched the activity, wide-eyed and solemn.

The line of Osage moved ploddingly out for the long trek to the trapping river, a small stream which emptied into the Missouri. One group of braves rode far behind to make certain no one fell out of line or died or was lost.

All looked forward to the long journey, but no one more than Pierre.

Pierre threw back his head. "It's a wonderful life!" he cried. He felt a new freedom in his veins, exulted in the fact that his lodge would stand in a new spot each night. And every night, in each new place, he would make love to Yellow Flower, wooing her ardently, drawing her into the fastness of his love so that she would never part from him.

The first night, and all the nights, they touched glory in their new wilderness home. "Do you love me more to-night than last night?" he asked. And she murmured that she did. And she wooed him in turn, then asked, "Do you like this spot better than last night's spot? Do you like new home after new home?" And he said honestly that he did. He knew her hope was that the wilderness would creep into him with the love she had for him, and he would live Osage.

Three weeks after the start of the trek, Pierre sensed a change in the Osage. Yesterday their voices had been subdued, this morning they sparkled. Everybody was alert. The dogs barked excitedly. The horses pranced. Even the babies on the papoose boards laughed.

"Soon we'll be at the site of our trapping village," Yellow Flower explained. "Our lodges will stand there all the weeks of trapping as the braves go up the wooded, hilly banks of the peaceful little river. It is a lovely river, we call it Small Stream, and each year the Osage take from it only enough peltries to bring money needed until the next year, plus a few skins for our daily use."

Pierre rode beside her, filled with questions, but not asking them. Let each day bring its surprise, each night its delight of their mutual courtship; he was content. He was thrilled by the wildness of this northern country—the fierce, rampaging Missouri and now, just ahead, the small and placid river.

At dawn the men loaded themselves with traps, bows and arrows, rifles and knives, and set off up the new river. They went in pairs, each pair prepared to establish a trapline that would stretch for miles. They would walk it each day, removing the catch, resetting the trap, going on to the next. The women would follow; their duty was to skin the animals.

Stalking Wolf named Pierre to be his partner. Tight-lipped, speaking as little as possible, Stalking Wolf showed Pierre how to set the traps, how to hide the traps, and how to remove the beaver and otter and marten and mink from the traps so as not to damage the valuable fur.

In their lodge that night, Pierre said to Yellow Flower, "I don't understand a certain matter."

"What is that, my Pierre?" she murmured.

"Why did Stalking Wolf take me as partner?"

"Because my father told him to."

"Why would he do that?"

"He knows that you and Stalking Wolf are equal men. It is his wish that you not be enemies. He knows that you will recognize each other's worth, that you will become friends."

Pierre reflected. He failed to see how he and Stalking Wolf could ever become friends with both of them wanting to marry Yellow Flower. He gathered her into his arms, sank his body into hers, and they knew a greater rapture than ever before.

He almost brought up the subject of marriage again, then decided to wait, to let the wilderness help him win her. Yellow Flower snuggled to him, but bit her lips. It was too soon to ask him again to live Osage.

One week slid into another, into a month, two months, three. Still Yellow Flower and Pierre gloried in their lodge at night; in the days Stalking Wolf and Pierre were still silent as they worked together. They spoke only of traps, of where to leave the animals for Yellow Flower to dress. Their attitude toward each other grew more tense in spite of Yellow Flower's efforts to get them to talk.

"The women," she ventured, "want to have a skinning contest. A tournament."

Pierre saw her glance from himself to Stalking Wolf, who scowled. "It is not for women to push themselves forward," the Osage said. "Contests are for men. Women are for the lodge."

"I don't see why women shouldn't have a contest," Pierre said carefully. "It could even help some of the slower ones perfect their skill and thus benefit everyone."

"Wild Eagle will never permit women to be so bold," Stalking Wolf said coldly.

Pierre saw disappointment on Yellow Flower's face. She looked unhappily down at a particularly fine mink Stalking Wolf had dropped at her feet. Pierre burned. Such a simple demand. Yet he knew Osage custom would not permit such a contest even though she was Wild Eagle's daughter, his favorite child. A white man he would grant her; a contest he would deny her and the others because they were women.

"Show us," Pierre said to Yellow Flower to erase her unhappiness, "show us how fast you can skin this mink." She flashed a smile, dropped to her knees, set to work. He watched her swift, sure hands as they plied the knife.

First she slit the fur at the throat of the mink, then cut swiftly down the stomach to the tail in one motion. Then she slit the fur down the inside of each leg, one after another. Finally she pulled and spread back the pelt, separating it from the bare, skinned creature.

She stood. She was breathing a little fast. "That was faster than I ever did it before," she said, and smiled. "Do you think, Stalking Wolf, that I might be the fastest skinner . . . if such a contest could be held?"

"You'd win," Pierre declared.

Stalking Wolf said, "The only reason a woman needs to be fast is to get the work done. Add the pelt to your bundle. We still have much trapline to run this day."

Pierre hid his distaste as Yellow Flower shouldered the growing load of pelts. Twice he'd tried to carry them for her, but she wouldn't allow it.

"This is Osage way," she said. "The men set the traps and empty them. The women do the skinning and carry the pelts."

Stalking Wolf became even more aloof. After two overtures were ignored, Pierre stopped trying to establish even a cool relationship with the Osage brave. Even so, he admired Stalking Wolf.

As the trapping season neared an end, both men were busy with traps when Pierre suddenly spied an enormous bear only twenty yards away. He wheeled, grabbed his rifle, and suddenly remembered it wasn't loaded because he'd just shot down a rabbit.

Stalking Wolf was behind him some yards; Yellow Flower, still farther behind was skinning. Pierre dropped into a crouch. He had to take cover, but there was no cover but trees, and the bear could climb a tree. He looked at the river, but its bank wasn't more than three feet high and he couldn't hide there.

Shouting to warn the others, he tried to retreat at a walk, quickening his pace as the bear ambled toward him. The instant he turned to run, Pierre knew, the animal would rush him.

Now he heard Yellow Flower's cry, and suddenly the animal halted, then crashed to the ground. Pierre stared. An arrow quivered where it had gone through the bear's eye and into its brain.

Stalking Wolf strode to it, yanked the arrow free, and kicked the carcass. Yellow Flower, looking pale, made certain Pierre was unhurt, then dropped to her knees and began to skin the bear.

Pierre spoke as soon as he got his breath. "I owe my life to you, Stalking Wolf. Thanks."

The Osage met Pierre's eyes, his face impassive. He said something in Osage, then went on upstream toward the next trap and Pierre followed, loading his rifle as he went.

The day came when Stalking Wolf decreed that the village had collected enough peltries. Wild Eagle agreed, and the traps were cleaned and oiled, the dugouts were loaded with furs, and the Indians prepared to leave.

Yellow Flower rode in the same dugout with Stalking

Wolf and Pierre. Wild Eagle hadn't wanted her to, and
Stalking Wolf had spoken against it. But Yellow Flower
had laid her cheek against Wild Eagle's chest.

"This one time in my life, my father!" she pleaded.

"Sir," Pierre said quietly, "she has earned the trip."

Yellow Flower kept her cheek against her father's chest,
and he reluctantly gave his consent. Pierre felt a thrill of
joy. He wanted Yellow Flower with them, dangerous though
the trip would be. Stalking Wolf went rigid, his face like
rock, and he would not speak to Yellow Flower as she
loaded the furs.

"He will recover," she whispered to Pierre. "The trip is
fierce and rugged. He will give orders, and then he will
speak."

Four dugouts plunged down the Missouri. All were on
the lookout for snags and sawyers and devilish twists in the
current. These twists frequently sent all four boats traveling sidewise until the river changed and let them go
straight for a distance.

They hit bad water every few minutes. Stalking Wolf
snapped out orders as they worked the poles. They fought
through one stretch, then came full toward one of the
Missouri's wickedest rafts. It was made of logs and willow
shoots, and just in front of it was a sawyer whipping brutally
back and forth in the tide. The sawyer hit them broadside,
overturning the dugout.

Pierre went down and down in the water where chunks
of ice still floated. When he surfaced, gasping, he saw
Yellow Flower swimming toward the overturned dugout
from one side, and Stalking Wolf stroking mightily toward
it from the other. Pierre swam for it, too, aware that all
their peltries had been dumped into the river.

The other dugouts passed, but their crews were unable
to help. They were fighting to prevent the same disaster
from happening to themselves.

"The pelts!" yelled Stalking Wolf. "On the raft!"

Pierre thought the pelts had sunk, but now he saw them being tossed and upended and slammed against the raft by the raging waters. Swimming strongly, despite pain and his heavy, wet deerskin clothes, he made it to the raft. He grabbed some willow shoots and pulled himself onto the raft.

As soon as he turned, he saw Stalking Wolf in the water at the edge of the raft holding a bale of pelts. Between them, they fought the bale onto the raft, and then the Osage swam for the next one. Yellow Flower was already at the edge of the raft with another bale to be manhandled out of the water. On the far side, that vicious sawyer kept up its relentless, brutal sweep.

Finally they got all their furs out of the water, and the three of them swam to free the dugout. It had been sucked a third of the way under the raft. His breath an icy, slicing knife, Pierre swam underwater, struggling to move the dugout into the clear. Stalking Wolf and Yellow Flower swam with him, pushing, lifting, straining.

Suddenly it seemed the river decided to sport, for the dugout was yanked from their hands and flipped right side up atop the raging water. Stalking Wolf clambered into it. He flung the rope to Pierre, who tied it around two strong saplings of the raft.

Not daring to catch their breaths, they loaded the soaked furs back into the dugout. When it was done, Stalking Wolf turned his rocklike face to Yellow Flower and gave her a shove.

"Woman bring bad luck," he growled. "The bear. Now this. Osage woman and white man make bad medicine."

With all his remaining might, Pierre drove his fist into Stalking Wolf's eye. The Osage staggered backward. The raft, surging mightily on the river's evil breast, threw them both down. Stalking Wolf was on his feet first, going for Pierre's knees as he struggled up, but Pierre caught

the Indian under the jaw. Suddenly a mighty bucking of
the raft sent both of them into the water, but they
continued to fight.

They got their hands around each other's throats, keeping afloat by kicking. Pierre heard Yellow Flower calling,
pleading, but he fought on, his outrage at Stalking Wolf's
insult of the girl consuming him, knowing that Stalking
Wolf meant to kill him first.

Unexpectedly, Stalking Wolf appeared to stand as if he
were on the riverbed, and then he began to sink. Yellow
Flower cried out. "Quicksand! He's in quicksand!"

She jumped into the water to help, but Pierre grabbed
Stalking Wolf under the arms. Using his last remaining
strength, Pierre pulled him out, inch by inch, and boosted
him into the pitching dugout. Somehow Pierre helped
Yellow Flower aboard, too, then he himself managed to
climb aboard. Panting deeply, he sank onto a bale of
sodden furs.

Pierre and Stalking Wolf stared into each other's eyes,
panting. Stalking Wolf had saved Pierre from the bear.
Now Pierre had saved Stalking Wolf from the quicksand.

Yellow Flower put it into words, knowing that neither of
them would. "You've saved each other's lives," she gasped.
"You can't be enemies! Not now!"

The two men let their eyes speak. You are man . . . real
man . . . their eyes said. And Yellow Flower glowed, because she could read the language of eyes.

They untied the wildly pitching dugout and started back
down the treacherous river which could do them no harm,
for they could deal with it.

In St. Louis, Pierre and Yellow Flower made love. It
was like a homecoming, this love, and again, as always, it
was the best love of all. They lay in each other's arms.
Pierre was now ready to batter down all her defenses, to
make her his wife and take her home.

Yellow Flower rested in his arms, almost trembling. She had something to say, and suddenly she was frightened to say it. She lay half-breathing, seeking courage.

Pierre sensed her fear. "What is it?" he asked. "What's wrong?"

"You have said you love me. Every night, you have said it. Since the beginning."

"Because it's the truth. I want you for always."

Her breath caught. "You have seen my land. Could you love it, too?"

"I love it now."

"As much as . . . L'Acadie?"

His heart went heavy. And then it raced. And he remembered with pain how they had wooed each other nightly all these months, and knew that he must speak.

"I can marry you Osage way only, Pierre," she said before he got out the first sound.

"Why are you still so sure of that? We belong together. We . . . fit."

"In my body lies your son," she whispered. "He must grow up Osage, true to his heritage."

Stunned, Pierre rose up on his elbow. His pulse thundered with surprise and with outrage. "But his heritage is also mine—and he is heir to L'Acadie!"

"Osage comes first," she said, her voice trembling. "Wild Eagle will so decree, and I must heed. He will order that you no longer share my blanket if you'll not be Osage."

"You know I can't do that, and you know why."

"Then L'Acadie comes first? Before your son?"

"That isn't fair, Yellow Flower! L'Acadie waits for my son. Please, marry me both ways, but come back to L'Acadie with me, come to a land even more beautiful than your own!"

"No, Pierre," she whispered, weeping, but giving not

an inch. "It's wrong for me and for my son! Stalking Wolf will marry me, and we will raise my son Osage. My son will inherit from us, even on the reservation, more than he would at your L'Acadie."

All night they went over and over their problem. Yellow Flower would raise her son Osage; Pierre would raise his son on Bayou Teche.

"You will leave us here, Pierre," she said with a finality which he had to accept. "Go home to your small piece of land. Marry a white girl in the white man's way. Bring up your white son to inherit your small piece of land."

"Twelve thousand acres isn't small!"

"It is, compared to the land of the reservation."

Pierre was shattered. There was no persuading her. And he had to return to L'Acadie. He'd been away for a year. René needed him on the land and needed the money from his furs. Suddenly Pierre wanted to leave, to be gone before his Osage son was born. He didn't want to see him if he couldn't keep him.

Yellow Flower left for the reservation next morning, knowing she'd marry Stalking Wolf at once. They parted sadly, but mixed into her sadness was the future of her child. And mixed into Pierre's sadness was the knowledge that the son he would never know would be a good Osage. Yellow Flower would educate him and love him, and Stalking Wolf would teach him to be a man.

With Yellow Flower gone, Pierre decided to look over the girls in St. Louis. He was a man. He needed a wife. Thus, on the rebound and knowing he was on the rebound, he lingered, went to parties and met many a pretty, bright girl. But none of them appealed to him.

He decided on one thing. He had to have more than just a wife. There must be attraction on both sides. The girl he married must be ready and eager to marry him at the drop of a hat.

Disgruntled, cross with the world, Pierre packed his suitcase and took passage to New Orleans on one of the last steamboats plying the Mississippi, a sternwheeler called *Maebelle*. Suddenly he was anxious to get back to the bayous.

VII

They sailed at dark. The *Maebelle* sparkled with lights, and bright, lively music from the three fiddlers she carried drifted out over the moonlit Mississippi. Pierre felt his sadness drop away and a feeling of his old self surged through his veins.

He did still wish Yellow Flower were at his side, but she wasn't here. He had to reconcile himself to that. She'd never be at his side. Even now she was married to Stalking Wolf, the child within her now belonging to the Osage brave forever, no part of Pierre except by the accident of blood.

He frowned at the lights. It was no easy thing to give up an heir. He wasn't fond of children, but he would have loved his own baby. Pierre would have trained his son to run L'Acadie, to return it to the heights it had enjoyed before the war between the states.

Yellow Flower. The farther the *Maebelle* edged into the current, the less difficult it was to think of Yellow Flower belonging to Stalking Wolf. Bold and ruthless as he was, the Osage brave was what she wanted, and he'd be decent toward her in the Osage manner. She would be happier living Osage than living L'Acadie, for that was her own choice.

The captain, wearing a blue uniform, stood beside Pierre

at the rail. "Lovely night, lovely night," Jebediah Horne said. He was white-haired with a white goatee, and Pierre had made friends with him soon after boarding.

"It's good to be headed for New Orleans, good to be on the way home," said the captain. "Do you feel that way, or did you want to linger in the wilderness?"

"I've already adventured enough, sir. It's time I went home."

"The bayous, yes, ah, the bayous! I plan to take my daughter into them. She's with us this trip—been visiting in St. Louis while I voyaged to New Orleans and back again. She wanted to stay, begged in her prettiest manner, but now she's happy as a lark to be back aboard the *Maebelle*, happy as a lark."

"Where is she now, sir?" asked Pierre making polite conversation. He was tired of inspecting girls, but the captain's voice quivered with such pride that courtesy demanded at least an idle question.

"She's yonder." He waved a hand toward the forward end of the sternwheeler.

Pierre gazed past the dark forms of passengers toward the bright lights at the prow. The moon laid a path on the water ahead, and the moonpath extended backwards onto the deck.

At the rail, spotlighted by the moon, stood a girl. She wore a thin white dress which moved in the breeze, stirring and folding back on itself just below midcalf.

"Come, you must meet her," the captain said. "You must meet my Maebelle."

Pierre's breathing almost stopped. She was so beautiful in the moonlight that he couldn't believe it. Her figure was delicately curved; her hair was so completely red it just escaped being flashy, and her features were fine-drawn and animated.

"Maebelle, honey," Captain Horne said, "this is Pierre Leblanc from Bayou Teche."

She looked up at Pierre, and he could see that her eyes were very blue.

"Mr. Leblanc . . . I'm delighted!" Her voice was light, sweet, breathless. She held out a tiny hand, and he took it carefully, not wanting to hurt it, and pressed lightly.

He wondered how he'd ever missed her in St. Louis. All those parties. Now, touching her, that fiery, overwhelming beauty put all thoughts of Yellow Flower out of his mind. Maebelle laughed, and a tingle went down his spine. Reluctantly he let go of her hand.

"It's an honor to meet you," he said. "I see you admire the beauty of the river at night as much as I do."

She laughed deliciously. "I made Daddy introduce us!" she confessed. "I watched you board the *Maebelle*."

Pierre, speechless, managed to smile at her as he made a wordless bow.

Maebelle, shyness suddenly flooding her, was filled with the clamor of her pulse. She'd never seen such a handsome man before. She was glad she'd told the truth about their meeting, because she was sure there was more than just flirtation between them. If not, she couldn't bear it. She'd turned down so many suitors, and now . . . out of the moonlight . . . loomed Pierre Leblanc, and she had to have him.

"Don't let my daughter fool you." The captain smiled. "She's not one of your bold minxes. She's spent her life traveling with me, understand, always traveling, and she is accustomed to being on speaking terms with all the passengers."

"But I 'specially wanted to meet you," she told Pierre, her voice unsteady.

In that instant, he had a fleeting picture of her on the front steps of L'Acadie. For if ever a fine plantation house

and a delicate beauty with fire in her hair had been
created for each other, Maebelle and L'Acadie were the
ones. He felt his own face burn and held out his hand
again, and she put hers into it trustingly.

Pierre was unaware that the captain had left them. He
heard the big wheel at the stern turning, turning, pushing
the luxury steamboat along the water toward New Orleans.
And in the shower of moonlight, in the soft light of
lanterns, not caring if any saw, he bent and gently kissed
Maebelle on the lips. And she, rocked with wonder, kissed
gently back, and both of them knew that everything was
settled.

VIII

She looked stunning—Maebelle had to admit that—as
she stood in her wedding dress of white georgette, ankle-
length. The shoulder-length veil was trimmed with bands
of fragile lace. She turned to the bevy of bayou girls who
had watched the maids dress her.

"Shoo!" she cried happily. "Send me my daddy! I want
to see him alone before I go and marry anybody, even
Pierre!"

Laughing, they fled.

Captain Jebediah Horne entered Maebelle's suite. He
was handsome in a white suit. His flowing hair and
perfectly trimmed goatee were snow-white and glossy. His
eyes were blue, like hers, and his lips were pink and
smiling with tenderness.

When the door closed, father and daughter stood admiring each other. Then she flew into his arms, and they

embraced with pure affection. She stood back while he admired her and told her what a beautiful bride she was.

"And I'll keep on being beautiful with the trousseau you bought me, the scads of dresses and *piles* of lingerie! I teased you out of them, but you managed, didn't you, Daddy?"

"I managed."

"How did you manage?"

"I borrowed. The *Maebelle* trips will pay it back."

"Will you have to scrounge and scrimp? Will you be hungry, Daddy?"

A smile stirred his lips. "I may be a bit threadbare, but you know the food on the *Maebelle*. . . . Don't worry, honey, don't worry. You've been a joy to me from the time your mama died."

"Have I been selfish, Daddy, wanting tons of clothes? Have I?"

"No more than is natural, no more than is natural. And now especially is your time to have things, as a bride, a Leblanc bride. You couldn't go to Pierre without a proper trousseau."

"I've already told Pierre that I want jewels, too, Daddy! Jewels to match every outfit! Diamonds and pearls and rubies and emeralds and sapphires—and jet, so smart with black or white. I want a jet brooch and earrings and twin bracelets and a ring! Pierre'll get them for me, you'll see, Daddy!"

"You're sure you love him, certain sure? It happened so fast. I don't want my little girl to make a mistake."

"Oh, I do love him, Daddy! And having it happen so fast is the best part! Why, just knowing that I'll see him in a few minutes for the first time today sets my heart to pounding! Every time I'm away from him, the minute I see him again, it pounds like crazy! I know inside myself that I'll be crazy about him every day of my life, even when I'm an old lady!"

"Marriage is for a lifetime, honey, a long lifetime. Sometimes love just can't last."

"Ours will! I'm grown; I'm twenty-one! And Pierre was full man when he went to St. Louis. If you only knew how we feel when we've been apart, how excited we are to be together again!"

The captain nodded almost sadly. "The excitement will settle down, honey, it'll settle down. It has to, sweetheart, to give love a chance to grow. Be prepared for that, be prepared and treasure it, for it will enrich your lives."

She hugged him, half-believing, for her daddy had never told her wrong about anything. But she was so madly in love with Pierre, she simply knew the excitement would last. And she knew her daddy was going to miss her after she was married as he took the *Maebelle* upriver and downriver and she wasn't aboard. She hugged him again, stood back, made her promise.

"I'll come to visit on the *Maebelle* when she's docked in New Orleans, Daddy. I'll bring Pierre if he'll come, and he will, I swear it! Because he's perfect! Our life is going to be absolutely perfect . . . like a fairy tale!"

Smiling, the captain produced a jeweler's box, opened it, took out a pearl and diamond ring. Maebelle gasped and held out her right hand. He slipped the jewel onto her ring finger, and she turned her hand this way and that, admiring it.

"Daddy, I don't know what to say! How did you ever pay for it?"

"A wedding present, honey. To last all your life. I was tired of my stickpin, and the jeweler made me an even trade. It's perfect for you, and it will be the start of the jewel collection Pierre will give you."

Music began to float up to them. The wedding march

started. Maebelle picked up her bouquet of white roses in one hand and held it lovingly, then tucked the other hand into her daddy's arm and descended the curving stairway into her future.

PART I

1918–1920

IX

Terrified, Pearl sat on the edge of the bench, waiting, wondering if this was the right spot. Night sounds here were so different from the frog sounds on Lafourche. Here, it was the clip-clop of horses' hoofs on the street, the sound of carriage wheels, the occasional throaty laugh of a woman.

At last Ben appeared.

He moved closer, and she shrank.

"Don't be afraid of me, little miss. Please trust me. Come, we must be on our way."

On trembling legs she walked with him in silence. They met no one else, it was so late. At the waterfront, she recognized the crib the soldier had gone into earlier. She shivered, wondering if there was a soldier in there now or in the other cribs lining the banquette.

Ben stopped at a tiny house; a street light shone on Pearl's white face. He'd felt her fear every step of the way, and now he saw the fear and wanted only to free her of it.

"I told you," he said, "not to be afraid of me. That is a true thing. My pa taught me not to lie, and I never have. My intentions toward you are only good, so you can believe that and relax."

Pearl, standing with him outside the tiny house, searched his face. Slowly she came almost to believe that she really could trust him, at least for now. But the fear which lingered warned her to be watchful.

He unlocked the door, and as if in a dream, she followed him inside the house, down a dark hallway. They entered

a dark room. She heard the door click shut and a key turn
in the lock.

"That's so nobody can open the door and see you here,"
he said. "It's for your safety. It wouldn't do for a white girl
to be found in a colored man's room."

She stood against the locked door while he lit a plain
glass lamp. By its flickering light, she saw that the room
was small, square, plain. There was a wooden floor, a
wooden table with two chairs, and some shelves with
things on them in neat rows. There was an iron bed,
tightly made up, and a dresser with a few toilet articles
arranged on it.

A starched brown curtain covered the window. The
room was like a clean, neat box, but it frightened her and
she felt unsafe. She wished that he would speak again; his
velvet voice was a strength to lean upon.

"Couldn't we go to your plantation now, tonight?" she
asked. "If Pa finds out I've run away, if he knows I'm still
in New Orleans . . ."

"He won't come back until you've had time to heal and
earn. He won't know about you until then. We'll be at
Rivard long before that. Anyway, I've got to finish out my
last week at Miss Josie's. I promised her, and we need the
money for boat fare."

Soothed by the velvet sound of his voice more than by
his words, she felt, well, almost safe. But then she looked
full at Ben, at his blackness and his size, and she was
frightened anew. She moved restlessly, and her bloody
chemise stuck to her back, and she hurt miserably. Ben
was looking at her when the flicker of pain crossed her
face, and she knew he saw it.

"Sit here," he said, taking her arm and leading her to
one of the chairs at the table. Knees weak, she sank onto
the hard wooden seat. Her back flamed so painfully, she
wished to cry out, but could not, not before Ben and his

kindness. Gently he took hold of her other arm and turned her so that she sat sidewise on the chair.

"Unbutton your dress," he said.

She clutched the buttons, shrinking away.

"It's so I can treat your back," he explained. "While you're unbuttoning, I'll fix soap and water and ointment. You can hold these"—he produced clean, thin towels—"in front of yourself. I'll stand behind you, see only your back. You can't reach it, little miss. I'll wash and anoint your back so it will heal. You can tend your front and the welt on your arm."

"That's all you'll do? Just that?"

"Indeed it is."

Burning with soreness and shame, she loosened her dress as he collected what he needed, his back always properly to her. She let her dress fall to her waist.

She sat still while he soaped and rinsed the wounds on her back and shoulders, patted them dry, smoothed on ointment. His touch was so gentle it scarcely hurt, even in the worst places. There was bloody water in the tin basin now. He placed a clean towel across her shoulders and kept his back turned while she cleansed and treated her breasts. After she'd pinned a clean towel in the front of her dress and pulled it back up and rebuttoned it, he removed the bloody water and towels.

"You'll have scars for only a while," he told her. "Now may I treat that cut on your arm?"

She nodded, he got fresh water, and she gave her arm into his keeping. He'd noticed at Miss Josie's that when he talked, she didn't seem to be so afraid of him. He talked quietly now, explaining that the ointment had been created by his beautiful great-grandmother, Olive Rivard.

Pearl murmured, wondering what would come next, her fear building. Would he try to get into bed with her? Would he expect her to do the things the girls at Josie's did? Was that to be his price for helping her? She went so weak she was about to topple off the chair.

She tried, but couldn't fight him as he lifted her and carried her to the bed.

X

"No need to be scared," he said quietly, in that velvet voice. "I'll sleep on a pallet in the corner. I'll not touch you."

And he didn't. She lay rigid as he finished tidying the room and made up a pallet. He took one pillow from the bed, leaving the other one for her. He stretched out on his pallet, and presently she heard his deep, regular breathing. Soon she sank into the safety of it, and she felt herself drifting off to sleep, despite fear and weakness and a raging hunger.

In the morning, he treated her back again, and while he went out for food, she treated her breasts and tidied the room.

He returned with an oversize mug of coffee and a double portion of sweet rolls. Her hands shook as she took a roll and bit hungrily into it.

He watched, dismayed. "How long since you ate?"

"Not at all yesterday. I ate supper the night before."

"I'll bring you all you can eat," he promised. "The restaurant where I go asks no questions—the man's colored. If he notices I'm buying double, he may guess I've got a girl, but he'll never dream it's someone like you."

Pearl nodded, eating hungrily.

"I'll get you a set of clothes so you'll have a change. You want white, or a color?"

Her instinct was to refuse clothing from him, but reason dictated that she couldn't wash the white voile and go naked while it dried. "B-blue," she said. "I've never had a blue dress."

"You understand you need to stay hidden until we leave for Rivard? It'd cause trouble, me having a white girl here."

She nodded. "I understand. But what can I do to repay you?"

"I don't want pay, except to see you safe."

Yet, as he was buying her a blue dress and a chemise, guessing at her size, being careful of what he spent, he knew he was being inexorably drawn to her. He knew, as well, that she was a bit less afraid of him, though she was still repelled by his huge size and his blackness.

He bought her a newspaper so she'd have something to read and fill some time. He brought in two more meals, and then he went to work.

While he was gone, Pearl wept for the first time. She wept because she would never see her ma again, or her brothers or the twins. She wept because she missed the motion of the houseboat under her as she lay on the bed.

It took all of Ben's money to pay the boat fare to the Teche. They traveled as strangers. "You'll have to travel with the white folks," he explained. "And me, I'll be with the colored."

"But what will I do? How should I act?"

"Act like the lady you are. Look at the boat itself all you wish; it'll seem strange and new and fine to you. But keep to yourself. Be pleasant, but not over friendly, especially with men." She caught a man-look in his eye as he gazed at her, and she blushed.

Aboard the steamboat, she was awed by everything; it was so grand and beautiful. And all the ladies and gentlemen were dressed so fine, and they were laughing and gay. She dropped her eyes and hurried on each time a young man so much as glanced at her. One or two tried to engage her in conversation, but she pretended not to hear and walked away from them as fast as she could.

She didn't see Ben once until the boat docked at St. Martinville. She moved with the other white passengers onto the little wharf. Looking about for Ben, she saw clusters of people greeting passengers who had arrived, heard the happy voices, the laughter.

The colored folk disembarked last. Ben came directly to her, carrying his straw suitcase. He had guided her only a short distance from the crowd when a squarely built mulatto of forty, clad in neat work clothes, hurried toward Ben. He took over the suitcase with his left hand and grabbed Ben's right hand with his own.

"Glad to have you back, boy!" he said, his dark eyes asparkle, his grin making creases in his cheek. "Rivard ain't the same without you!"

Ben grinned happily, slapped the fellow on the shoulder, turned him to face Pearl. "This is Hank Moss, my overseer," he told her. "Hank, this is Miss Pearl Babin, come to stay at Rivard for a while."

Hank blinked, then caught himself, and kept smiling. He gave Pearl a small bow. "It's an honor, Miss Babin. We'll do all we can to make you comfortable. Shall we go now, Ben?"

Ben nodded, and Hank led them to a pirogue. Once in it, Hank oaring, Ben said to Pearl, "You can trust Hank and his wife, Bessie, and daughter, Christa. You can trust everybody at Rivard."

Numb with sudden, fresh terror, Pearl managed a nod. How could she trust these people? They were all Negroes. Rivard was a Negro plantation. And Pa said all niggers were dirty and diseased and no-account. How could she be safe with them? Why, oh why, had she come here?

XI

"Miss Pearl," Ben told Hank quietly, "was being forced into working at Josie's house. By her pa. So I'm bringing her to Rivard until she decides what life she can follow. For now, it's vital that we let no one on the Teche know she's with us."

Hank looked grim. "It'd sure stir up talk."

"With the Mercers leading the pack," Ben agreed. He explained to Pearl. "The Mercers are white trash. They've worked every evil trick they know, trying to force us to sell them Rivard. They even burned down our plantation house once."

Pearl felt a sweep of concern for Ben. "If they find out about me, will it make trouble for you?" she asked.

"They'd try to buy us out first, that's certain. They really want Rivard because it adjoins property they own to the north. For that matter, they want all the bayou property they can get."

"How did they get so rich?"

"The stock market."

"What's the stock market?"

"It's where people buy and sell shares in business. Silas Mercer's son, Silas junior, has got a head for figures and a nose that guides him. He always knows when to buy and when to sell. On the side, they buy every parcel of Teche land they can get, and pay cash. They may want to own the whole bayou, but they'll never get Rivard!"

As the pirogue nosed in at the landing and Hank tied up, Pearl stared at the big plantation house. It was a misty, weather-beaten silver and had a row of fat pillars across the front. She knew, in that first glance, that she'd never, in all her life, seen a house that looked so beautiful.

Back from the house was a street of tidy cabins, and at one cabin children played near an old woman who was watching over them. The stable and other buildings spread away from the cabins and the fields began, and in the fields Negroes were working; Pearl could hear them singing.

"The big house," Ben told her with pride, "is built of cypress grown at Rivard. It's never been painted. We like it silvery. See how it blends into the great cypresses around it."

"It's the prettiest house I ever saw," Pearl breathed. She gazed at the mansion. For some unknown reason, it looked like home to her, she who had never lived in anything but the little houseboat on Lafourche.

As Hank led the way and she and Ben followed, Pearl saw that all the Negroes weren't in the fields. They met a wiry man with a hoe, bound for what looked to be a kitchen garden, and Ben stopped and introduced him to Pearl.

"This is Darcy," he said. "Darcy, this is Miss Pearl, though I think it'll be safer for everybody to call her just Pearl. The folks on the bayous aren't to know she's at Rivard."

Darcy, eyes bugging, squeaked, "I git it, Ben. Hello, Pearl. I'll tell Betts—she's my woman—to tell the othahs to keep it hushed up. The children won't notice nothin'. They don't pay no mind to colah."

Hank left Ben's suitcase on the back gallery of the big house, then turned toward the Quarters. "You aim for Pearl to stay with Bessie and me?" he asked.

"If you don't mind, yes."

"Happy to have her. We got the room. Christa'll go crazy, havin' a girl her own age, you wait and see."

Pearl walked along, feeling her pulse slamming. She felt like she was coming home, and yet, she felt like an outcast. Who was she to show up so unexpectedly, to be in their way, to create a secret they must keep? Dejected, she kept up with the other two, never forgetting that they were colored and foreign to her.

"This is the Quarters," Ben said. "It's where our tenants live."

Pearl gazed at the cabins. Each one was bigger than the houseboat.

"Three good rooms in every one," Ben explained, trying to make her feel comfortable. "Hank has the overseer's house—six rooms. The land beyond and on all sides, farther than you can see from here, is Rivard land. We raise sugar cane and feed crops and vegetables for the market."

She gazed at the wealth of land, awed. She gazed at horses and cows and chickens, the stable, the pig pen with grunting pigs in it, the blacksmith shop.

Now Hank led them out of the Quarters toward another grove of cypresses. There stood a sprawling, weather-beaten cottage. Hank opened the back door of the cottage, and Pearl found herself in a big, square, well-scrubbed kitchen. A woman, lighter skinned than Hank, with big soft curls, looked up. She was plump and soft, and a smile came readily to her pretty oval face.

Hank did the introducing and the explaining. "Pearl needs help, Bessie," he finished, "and Ben's going to see to it that she gets it."

Bessie's face showed sympathetic concern. She came to Pearl and put her arms around her, and Pearl winced, because this hurt her back.

Bessie murmured, "First thing you got to do, honey, is forget we're all colored and you're the only white. We're folks, just like you, and we'll be your friends."

Instinctively Pearl relaxed in Bessie's arms. She was sort of like Ma, even if she was colored. Ma would help a girl in trouble this same way. She began to feel that Bessie really was a person, not a Negro, and a quick liking for the motherly woman rooted itself in her.

A girl of about seventeen ran into the room and stopped, staring at Pearl. She looked as Bessie must have looked years ago, except for her skin, which was shades lighter than that of either parent.

Hank put his arm around the girl. "This is Christa, our daughter. Christa, this is Pearl. She needs friends, so Ben brought her to Rivard."

"She in trouble?" asked Christa.

"Christa," warned Bessie, "don't be forward. You'll find out all you need to know. The most important thing is that Pearl's being at Rivard be kept secret."

"But why?"

"Because she's white and we're not. There could be trouble."

"Oh, that. I won't tell, I swear it."

Bessie let her arms fall from Pearl. "We'd be honored if you'd stay in our extra bedroom as long as you please," she said.

Hesitant, taken aback by such kindness, Pearl glanced at Ben, uncertain what she should do.

He smiled. "I told you Rivard folk are kind," he said. "Accept, and make Christa happy. She'd like a chum right in her own house."

"Do stay!" urged Christa. "We've all this room, and it'd be wonderful to have you right in the house!"

Hesitantly, gratefully, Pearl accepted the offer. Her heart shook; these people were so kind. Even though they were colored and she felt strange to be with them, their kindness radiated from them, and she felt the start of deep liking, especially for Bessie and Christa.

Christa showed the rest of the house to Pearl. "This is our dining room, and we eat in it," she said as they entered the next room. It had a big round table with armchairs and a heavy sideboard which displayed a pewter coffee service.

"That's Mama's and Papa's room," Christa continued as they passed a sunny room with hand-hewn furniture, then passed through a living room which had real carpet, a leather couch and hand-hewn rocking chairs. A big clock-shaped radio stood on a table, and Christa snapped it on and danced a few steps to the music which flooded out, then snapped it off. "Papa worked extra to buy it," she explained. "There's one in the big house, too." Next, they paused in Christa's room; there were blue curtains at the window and a blue cover on the wooden bed, which was made of inch-thick walnut.

"And this is yours," Christa announced, leading Pearl into a small, square room. It was sturdily furnished with a walnut bed like Christa's and was sparkling clean like the rest of the cottage.

"Like it?" demanded Christa. "Mama let me fix it up."

"It's . . . lovely!" breathed Pearl. The bed was covered with a white quilt. At the two windows, thin white curtains, smelling of starch and sun, moved in the breeze.

"And we're allowed to play the radio and dance!" laughed Christa. "We'll have fun!" She perched on a chair, indicating that Pearl should sit in the rocker. She laughed, then sobered.

"Did you come to Rivard because you had to?" she asked.

Pearl nodded.

"I'm glad you're here, just the same. Someone my own age . . . I'm seventeen."

"So am I."

"Then we can be best friends!" squealed Christa. Abruptly, she looked doubtful. "Unless—"

"Unless what?"

"You being white and me colored, maybe you won't want to be chums."

The woeful look on Christa's face touched Pearl. She felt the sting of tears. "The color doesn't matter, not between us," she said, and meant it.

"Oh, goody!" Christa flew to Pearl, embraced her, kneeling beside the rocker. Timidly, she ran her hand along Pearl's hair. "It's so beautiful. And you're so beautiful, like an angel!"

"Oh, no," protested Pearl. "Pa always said I look washed out."

"He was crazy! You've got the most beautiful silver hair, and light silver eyes and white, white skin and pink lips! I'll bet you're the most beautiful girl in the world!"

Pearl smiled shyly, blushing. "I think you're beautiful, too," she said. "I'm proud to be your chum."

"Chums tell each other everything. They share secrets."

"I've never had a chum before. But the secret part sounds right."

Christa giggled happily. "I'll go first," she declared. "Mama and Papa never had any baby but me. I'm spoiled, used to getting my own way. But Papa says, what chance do I have *not* to be a little bit spoiled, with no brother or sister to give in to."

"I have four brothers, all younger," Pearl smiled. "That meant lots of giving in."

"Why did you leave home?"

"Pa got me a job in New Orleans."

"Didn't you want to work?"

"Not at that place."

"What place was it?"

"A madam's sportin' house. Pa said I'd make a lot of

money. Ma said I'd have to do nasty things, wrong things."

"What nasty wrong things?"

"Pa said gentlemen come to the madam's house to meet girls to go to bed with. I don't know exactly what they do, but Ma says it's nasty and wrong."

"You're supposed to be married if you go to bed with a man. I know that much."

Pearl nodded wordlessly.

"Did Ben get you away before any of those men . . . ?"

"Yes, he did. He was good to me. I know that, even if he does scare me sometimes."

Christa gasped. "Ben Rivard scares you? Why, he gives work to more than twenty tenant families. That's crazy, you bein' scared. He's the kindest master that ever lived. Look how he helped you, a white girl, a runaway, just like in slavery when white folks helped slaves escape!"

"You called him master. I thought slavery was ended."

"Oh, that! We call him master because he owns Rivard. Pierre Leblanc of L'Acadie, the biggest plantation of all, has got thirty tenant families, and he's called master, same way! It don't mean slavery! It's just respect."

"I see."

"Any girl gets Ben is the luckiest girl in the world! I don't know what he wants, but it ain't me!"

XII

Ben made the rounds of Rivard and spoke to every soul, getting each to swear to keep Pearl's presence a secret. The women assured him earnestly; the men said, "Got you, Ben. It's a deal. Whatever you want."

Ben knew what he really wanted. Not to be black. He had wanted it, always.

Now, going about his field work, he recalled that day when he was six and his pa, Beau Rivard, had taken him to St. Martinville for an outing.

Scrubbed, hair shorn, he had danced along the street with Pa. St. Martinville looked big and exciting. To the boy, it was the biggest place in the world, with stores and people walking along, and over there, two horses pulling a carriage with people in it.

He spied some boys his size playing ball. Excited, he asked Pa, "Can I go play, Pa, can I?"

Pa looked serious. He seemed about to speak, hesitated, looked more serious still. "Yes, son," he said finally, "you can try. I'll be sitting on the bench after I look in the store windows."

Ben raced to where the boys were playing tag. There were four of them, and they paid no attention to him, just kept on with their game.

Finally, one of them noticed Ben. "See the tar baby!" he yelled, and the others began to laugh and yell, "Tar baby! Tar baby!"

Ben laughed too, thinking he was accepted, but they turned on him, hitting him. "Go away, tar baby, we don't want you!" One boy socked him in the eye, and it hurt. Another boy kicked him in the leg, and that hurt, too.

Pa came over, took Ben's arm and drew him to the bench. The boys started to play ball again. Ben was crying, bewildered. "Why they do that?" he sobbed. "I'm no baby! I'm big enough to play!"

Pa held him close, stared at the jeweler's window, opposite the bench. He looked angry and sad, looked like he didn't know what to do.

"They did it because you're colored, Ben," he said,

"and they're white. White boys don't play with colored boys except at home on the plantation."

"Why not?"

"Because long ago, white men owned Negroes the way we own our horses, and the Negroes had to work very hard. The white men got so they thought they were better than the colored men."

"I don't want to be colored! I want to play!"

"You're not colored all the way through. You've got a drop of white blood hidden in you, deep down."

"Where deep down—here?" He rubbed his stomach.

Carefully, Beau tried to explain. "Your Grandpa Rivard was a white man with just a few drops of black blood."

"Where is he?"

"Dead, son."

"Dead?"

"That's right. He decided that all Rivards must be colored, like you. He wanted them to be very black, so he married a real black girl, Deedee. She was my ma, your grandma. And I was this color—brown. And then he wanted *me* to marry a coal black girl, too, and I did. I married Tansey because I wanted her. Tansey was your ma."

"My dead ma?"

"That's right. And you were blackest of all. Like your Grandpa Riel wanted."

Ben pouted. "I want my drop of white blood. I want to see it."

Beau sighed, took his son to a jeweler's window. "I can't show you the very drop of blood, son," he said, "it's too mixed in with the others. But I'll show you something like it."

In the window was a display of pearls. In front was a ring with a single, lustrous pearl set on prongs, large and gleaming and rich. Beau pointed it out.

"Your drop of white blood is like that pearl. Pure and strong."

Ben clutched his middle. "I want to get it out!"

"No!" Beau said sharply. "Your Grandpa Riel ruined his life making the Rivards black! You're not to ruin your life by trying to—"

Suddenly Ben was tired of the subject. "I want my candy!" he cried. "You promised!"

Sadly, Beau took him to a shop and bought a big sack of peppermint sticks. Watching Ben blissfully licking a peppermint stick, Beau went into a cold sweat.

God forbid that Ben be like Pa! Hell-bent to breed the Rivards black, Riel had done it at incredible cost. It would be madness to reverse the process and stubbornly breed back to white.

Years later Beau told the older, understanding Ben of that last day when Riel, to insure the success of his life's obsession, had strangled the light-skinned baby that Beau's first, faithless wife Tansey—Ben's mother—had just borne. Beau was to relate how Riel then killed his own mother, Olive, because she was nearly white and Riel would have no white on Rivard, crying out that he himself, who could pass for white, would be executed for murder. And Beau explained that Riel had felt no remorse, only exultation that at last he had won his life-long battle.

"I prayed to God," Beau later told Ben, "that you'd really take to music, take to sugar cane. That you'd become a contented black master of Rivard."

Ben, wielding his hoe all these years later, thought his Grandpa Riel must have been insane there at the end to murder the light-skinned baby, to murder his own mother, to insure his own death at the hands of the law.

All so Rivard could be black.

XIII

The day after her arrival, Pearl was still in a daze. Never
had she known such splendor. She had never seen people
eat so neatly or discuss things at table. Here the mother
and father discussed the war, the Kaiser, spoke of letters
three of the young Rivard tenants had written home. Pearl
hadn't known what the war was about, but she learned
from the discussion that the Kaiser was bad and the
Americans were going to beat the Germans and make
them behave. Especially the Kaiser.

She listened, she watched how the others ate, and she
copied them. On the houseboat, Pa grabbed his food and
the boys did, too. Pa ate very fast, choking down his
meals, and Pearl had done the same, as best she could.
Here it was different, and she liked to eat slowly and hear
the talk, even if it was about war and guns.

"Christa," Hank said finally, "suppose you show Pearl
around Rivard, help her decide what chores she'll do
while she's here."

"She can't work... her back!"

"It's healing fast," Bessie said. "She can do light work;
it'll be good for her."

"I'll need to be taught," Pearl said. "I know nothing
about a farm."

"Christa will show you," Hank said kindly. "Everybody
at Rivard works—especially Ben. He got a deferment from
the army so he could head things up right here and train
me to take his place if need be. You'll find that everybody
at Rivard works—they work the land as well as doing

regular chores like milking and churning and cabin cleaning
and cooking. Bessie, overseer's wife or not, takes care of
this house, and with Christa, she cleans Ben's big house.
Besides which, Bessie works in the cane, and so do I."

"My main work is gardening," Christa said eagerly. "We
raise all the vegetables for everybody. What we don't eat,
we put in glass jars. That's hard work, too, but it's fun.
The green beans look so pretty, and the beets—we pickle
them—are prettiest of all. I'd show you the jars, but we
ate all the vegetables during the winter. We're eating
straight from the garden now. I hope you choose garden
work so we can be together!" she finished with a sparkling
smile.

Later, they went into the fresh, rosy, dewy dawn.
People were emerging from their cabins, calling out greetings, bound for their chores, mothers leaving toddlers and
infants with Granny and young Jade to look after. Nursing
mothers would come to feed their babies, then return to
the field, Christa said.

She introduced Pearl to still more tenants, and each had
a smile and a murmured welcome for her. Pearl found
herself smiling back, murmuring back, but she clung to
Christa's hand, feeling strange and out of place.

Ben, passing them, paused in midstride, then walked
on, saying only, "Good morning, girls."

Christa laughed and sang out a cheerful greeting, but
Pearl could only murmur. Seeing Ben, knowing him to be
master, her feeling of strangeness grew.

What am I doing here? she wondered. I'm the only
white among them. Where can I go, what can I do? She
kept murmuring the polite responses to each tenant she
met, and gradually their kindness began to dull her sharp
feeling of strangeness. She could easily believe that these
people did feel kindly toward her, and she tried half-
heartedly to return the feeling.

First Christa showed her the barns, the cows and chickens and pigs, and the blacksmith shop. Then she asked, "Want to try working in the garden with me?"

"Of course," agreed Pearl, for she did want to. It sounded like interesting work, growing vegetables for the table, knowing that every soul on the plantation would eat the fruits of her labors.

Christa introduced her to the garden workers, then led her off to a far corner. "This is where I've been working," she explained. "I've planted carrots and turnips. Cabbage, too. We got to weed carrots today—think you'll take to that and your back can stand it?"

"My back feels lots better." Pearl looked at the vast garden, saw beauty in the straight rows of fast-growing sweet corn with its pretty, green stalks, in the climbing bean vines hung with new green pods, in the squash plants dotted with yellow. She knew that this was, indeed, where she wanted to work.

Christa went to her knees between rows. Carefully, Pearl did the same. Christa showed her the weeds they were to pull. She dug her strong hands into the soil, going deep to the roots, pulling out the unwanted growth, and tossing it to the uncultivated space.

"We'll gather up all the weeds later," she said, "and feed the hogs and chickens what they'll eat. Ben has us put the rest in a mulch pile, and when all the stuff dries and mixes in together, we spread it on the garden to feed the dirt. Ben don't waste a thing."

Pearl, at ease with Christa and eager to do her part, dug her own fingers around a lacey green weed, probed deep, and pulled it out. Startled, she cried, "Oh, Christa! Look!" At the end of the lacey top dangled a half-grown carrot.

Christa giggled, then doubled over with laughter. "That's the exact same thing I did first time!" she said.

After supper, Ben came to see Pearl. Hank motioned his

family out of the living room, leaving Ben and Pearl together.

"How did you get along today?" he asked.

"Fine. I weeded carrots and learned the difference between a carrot top and a weed." She smiled ruefully.

Ben grinned, then sobered. "Is your back very sore?"

"Some, not too much."

"I mean from working—stooping."

"I think working helped it. That and the sun."

"Limbered it up," he agreed. "Do you want to work in the garden a few more days before you go looking for a job?"

She considered. She had barely started to overcome her feeling of utter strangeness at Rivard. She dreaded meeting more strangers, even though they'd be white.

"If I could just work here a week," she murmured. "I . . . seem to need the time."

"Good idea," he agreed. "In a week, Hank can take you to St. Martinville, and you can go to houses and ask to be housemaid. Don't tell that you're staying at Rivard. It'd go against you."

"Y-you won't be with me?"

"Can't be. It'd never do for a Negro to take a white girl to white people's houses, asking for work. It'll be hard enough, you going alone."

And hard it was, the days she went. Neatly dressed in the blue dress Ben had bought in New Orleans, she went to back door after back door. All day, every day, she tried, but failed to get work. There was only one door left in the town, and she knocked on it, head up, chin determinedly steady.

This lady was quite fat and had a pretty face. She was also kinder than most. "I do my own work," she said, "send my washing out. And all the ladies I know who have help, they hire nigra girls. There isn't a white housemaid in town. You're wasting your time, my dear. And there aren't any jobs in stores for you—the stores hire only men. The few who hire women . . . well, they're full up."

"What," Pearl asked desperately, "do the white girls do to make a living?"

"They live at home until they marry."

When Pearl got back to Rivard, she told Ben of her complete failure. "What can I do?" she asked, looking into his face, which showed kindness and concern.

"Stay here. How long you stay doesn't matter. There's plenty of work—you'll earn your keep."

"But that could go on for years!"

"It won't, Pearl. Something will work out. Relax and heal and enjoy whatever you can of Rivard."

"Do you think Pa'll quit looking for me? Could I go back to New Orleans and get a job?"

"I think your father will stop trying to find you, yes. As to getting a job—you'll find that the New Orleans ladies, too, all have colored maids. And I know for a fact that shopkeepers who do hire women take older women, or else their wives work behind the counter. I thought there might be a chance for you to find work in St. Martinville or I wouldn't have sent you there. But New Orleans . . ." He shook his head.

"You're saying it's hopeless! I'll never get a job!"

"You have one now," he reminded her. "Keep it until you can do better. And you will do better, of that I'm convinced."

"I will, then," she murmured, and forced a smile. She saw that his eyes glowed as he smiled back.

Bessie decided to really clean Ben's house. "Top to bottom," she declared at breakfast. "Windows, too. Everything. Christa, Pearl, you're both to help. And you, too, Hank."

Pearl was excited at the prospect; she hadn't yet seen inside the plantation house. Ben made a point of talking to her every day, and she found conversation with him ever easier. But he had never invited her into the big house, and she wouldn't ask.

When she first stepped inside, the beauty stunned her. On the main floor, there was a big, well-equipped kitchen, a dining room, and a big double parlor. The kitchen had hand-hewn pine furnishings; the other rooms had mahogany furnishings, polished until they shone like glass. There was an entrance hall with a walnut-railed stairway curling upward into a big hallway which ran the length of the second floor. Upstairs, there was a large bedroom with its own sitting-room and bath, and two other bedrooms, all furnished with the glistening mahogany—"made by hand," Bessie said proudly.

Ben's clothes were in the master suite, his books on shelves in the sitting room. There were white curtains at every window in the house.

Ben, coming in while Pearl and Christa were polishing the plated silver, asked Pearl how she liked the house.

"It's beautiful!" she breathed.

"It was built after the fire. It's exactly like the original house," he said. He hesitated. "How would you like the job as housekeeper-cook? The way things are now, the women have to take turns looking after my needs."

Pearl was shocked. His offer caught her completely by surprise. This was another reverse situation, she realized. A Negro was hiring a white housekeeper instead of the other way around. But she knew she couldn't turn it down, knew she had to have it.

"I . . . I'd like the job!" she gasped.

XIV

There was, of course, no money attached to the job, that was understood. Pearl tended the big house, cooked, and worked the rest of the time in the garden with Christa.

Ben enjoyed Pearl's cooking. At first she cooked as her mother had taught her, then she learned bayou cooking from Bessie, and Ben found himself with a varied and delicious table.

He'd never been so satisfied. The house shone, the china was brighter, the silver gleamed like jewelry. His bedroom suite was perfection and had a clean, sweet smell it had not had before. Every day he found himself looking forward to supper, which he insisted Pearl eat with him.

At meals, they talked. She told him about life on Bayou Lafourche, and he explained how sugar cane was grown and processed into sugar. Their minds met, but he never forgot that she was white and beautiful.

After six weeks, the memory of the pearl and his father's words strong in him, Ben came to realize that he no longer pitied Pearl, and he allowed himself to glory in her beauty. Every night, he walked her to her room in the overseer's house.

Gradually he realized that he had fallen in love with her. Impossible! was his first reaction. Not to be thought of! He reminded himself, deep down, she's afraid of you. Nonetheless, her allure for him grew, and he pondered, weighed, measured, considered.

After supper one night, she asked again about New

Orleans, if she might find some elderly gentleman in need of a housekeeper there. And Ben heard himself saying things he'd decided he could never say. Even to his own ears, his voice was very deep, and everything he said was impossible.

"Pearl," he replied to her question, "such gentlemen have colored help. Besides, you can't leave Rivard. I'm in love with you."

She stared, drying the last piece of silver. Her pulse hurt. What was he saying? What was she to do? With reluctance she asked, "Isn't that bad . . . evil? For colored and white to love?"

"I don't see how love could ever be evil, Pearl."

She kept staring at him. He was so very black. But the look on his face was infinitely gentle.

"I won't ask if you love me," he said.

She swallowed audibly.

"I will ask if you're still afraid of me."

How had he known she was afraid? How could he tell?

"I . . . at first . . . not now."

"Are you as . . . repulsed . . . by my blackness as you once were?"

She felt herself blush. He'd known, then. And he'd been so kind. Numbly, she shook her head.

"Exactly how do you feel now?"

It was an honest question. She gave an honest answer.

"It doesn't bother me. Not any more."

"I'll not ask if you could ever love me."

"I . . ." She swallowed again.

"If I were white or if you were colored, I'd ask you to marry me. But as things stand, the law won't permit marriage between us. I've been to an attorney, however, and there's no law that says you can't live at Rivard. Or that you can't be very close . . . and dear to me."

She bowed her head, overwhelmed, understanding his motive, and feeling the warmth of his sincerity.

"We've explored your situation," he said. "There's no work for you . . . except at Josie's."

She stood clutching the dish towel and a silver fork.

"But there is a place for you where you're wanted," he continued. "I offer myself, Pearl, for life. I offer you Rivard."

Her pulse rioted in her veins. "What do you m-mean?" she asked.

"I mean that we take our vows before the tenants, that we live as man and wife. I want you as mistress of Rivard . . . if you can . . . tolerate me." He finished, his chin hard.

She gazed at him, speechless. She drew a sobbing breath. Her mind flashed between New Orleans and Rivard. There was no other place she could go, no other thing she could do. She couldn't continue on the present basis, not after what he had said, and what he had offered her.

"Do you feel toward me as a friend?" he asked.

"Y-yes . . . or I could. Maybe I'm your friend now, or I wouldn't be here in your house. I'd be running to . . . nowhere."

"Do you respect me?"

"Oh, yes! So very much!"

Carefully he drew her rigid body into his arms, and she felt not repelled but curiously safe. He stroked her hair, her cheek, her shoulder, his touch more gentle than when he had anointed her with ointment. Finally she relaxed against him. This was Ben, good, helpful Ben, and he was asking her to be his wife in the only possible way he could. What he wanted was unthinkable, yet she had to think about it because he *was* Ben, not some black, sweating Negro like those in New Orleans.

His fingertips traced her cheeks; he made no move to kiss her. Her breath stabbed as she spoke, but the words came out almost naturally. "You've never told me a wrong thing to do," she said. "So . . . I'll do what you want now."

She would always like him this much, of course she would. But love—that would have to come from his side, not hers, and she told him so honestly.

"The love will all have to be from you," she said.

He touched her lips with his finger. "I thank you for the privilege," he said softly, "and vow that through no act of mine will you ever regret this."

XV

Pearl fled straight to Christa's room. Christa looked up in surprise at Pearl's obvious excitement. "What is it? What's wrong?" she asked.

"Ben asked me to marry him. I said yes."

Christa's pretty face was an instant mixture of delight and doubt. "Ooh," she squealed, "how wonderful! But I thought it was against the law for—"

"Ben says it is. But its not against the law for me to live with him. He's going to write vows for us to take, and he says we'll be married that way, in spite of the law."

"That means you'll live at Rivard, be mistress, and we can be best friends forever and ever!"

"Unless you marry and move away."

"Not me! I'm not leaving Rivard and Ma and Pa and now you! I'll marry a Rivard boy! I can take my pick any time, just don't want to yet!" She tossed her curls. Then she danced over to Pearl and hugged her fiercely.

"When's the vow-taking to be?"

"Tomorrow night," Pearl said faintly. That was so soon, so very soon!

"That means everybody'll have to work like mad to get ready! Just think—a wedding!"

"It's not to be a wedding, Christa. This is different. Ben just wants everybody to see us take our vows. He's going to fix a paper, saying how things are."

Christa hugged Pearl again, then insisted that she lend Pearl a dress for the occasion. "You haven't got but that blue dress, and it won't do!" she declared. "And there isn't time for Mama to make you another one! Come on, let's see which one looks best!"

Reluctantly Pearl turned to Christa's wardrobe and a respectable array of dresses. With Christa chattering and helping, the girls looked through them, made their selection.

While the girls were thus occupied, Ben faced Hank and Bessie and the others in the church house where he had summoned them, and revealed his plan. The men and women listened soberly. Some showed the beginning of pleasure, others were deeply serious, and a few showed open concern.

"Speak out," Ben said when he had finished. "Say what is in your minds."

Hank spoke first. "Pearl is a lovely young woman," he said. "She'd make any man a wife he could be proud of. The thing is, when word gets out that you are living with her, there'll be scandal on the Teche. Maybe some white trash will try to get even."

"If you mean the Mercers," Ben said, "I can deal with them."

"What about Pearl?" asked Bessie. "Can she deal with them?"

Ben nodded confidently. "She's not had an easy life. It's toughened her a bit, and with all of us at Rivard standing behind her, she'll have the strength she needs. And that strength will grow as she matures."

Finally they all assured Ben that they would uphold him. "And we'll look on Pearl as mistress of Rivard," they all agreed.

The next night, the plantation house was crammed with Rivard people, dressed in their best and bursting with excitement. Ben had given them the day off from work, and they had spent it preparing for the occasion.

Pearl was in the master bedroom, dressed and ready. She wore a sheer, white-dotted dress with a wide silver sash. Christa had braided Pearl's platinum hair and wound it around her head in a coronet.

"You're beautiful, so beautiful!" Christa breathed, pretty as a picture herself in blue. "I think Ben's mean not to let me stand up with you. My dress would look lovely beside yours!"

"He isn't being mean, Christa," Pearl said loyally. "This is the only kind of marrying we can do, and he doesn't want it to be an imitation of a regular wedding. He wants it plain and honest."

Now Bessie appeared, saying that everybody was waiting and Ben was on his way upstairs. Even as she spoke, Ben came into the room wearing his good black suit, his face solemn. In his hand he carried a framed paper with writing on it.

He came straight to Pearl. His eyes glowed as he looked at her in Christa's dress. "Are you ready? And still willing?" he asked.

Wordless, she nodded. What else could she do, where else could she turn?

"Then we'll go marry ourselves," he said. He took her hand and led her down the stairway. They moved to one of the two big fireplaces of the double parlor and faced the people. There were no flowers, at Ben's request. And there would be no illegal wedding ring.

Pearl, trembling, felt an impulse to pull away from Ben, but she noted how warmly he held her hand, and did not. She had promised, and she would keep her promise.

Ben felt the quiver in her and silently willed that she be strong in these moments. He pressed her hand, and the quivering lessened.

"Folks," he said to the waiting people, "we're ready." He lifted the framed paper in his free hand. "Here is what we have to say." And he began to read aloud.

"We two, Ben Rivard and Pearl Babin, promise:

"To live our lives as man and wife.

"To respect and honor each other.

"To be as one in all we do, forever."

He turned, offering the framed words to Pearl, and she held them as a bride would hold a bouquet.

"Pearl," Ben asked, "do you agree to do what I have read?"

Filled with the honesty of his words, she met his eyes. "I agree, Ben," she said quietly.

"I, Ben, agree also. With pride and love."

And then he took the framed document from her, turned, and hung it on a tiny nail above the mantelpiece. "This is our pact for the world to see," he said. "Pearl Rivard is now mistress of Rivard, and we thank you all for coming to witness our vows."

A sound went through the massed crowd, a signal of approval and pleasure. Some of the women were weeping and smiling and blowing their noses.

"Thank you all for coming," Ben told them. "It's ended now. You can do what you please."

Bessie stepped forward, eyes flashing. "You mean we can go home! You blind or something? Think we worked in our kitchens all day and hung lanterns in the Quarters and got all dressed up to stand here for the vows, then rush away? You told us to do what we please, and what we please is to have a celebration!"

Ben protested. "We wanted this different, Bessie."

"Every girl's got a right to a party when she promises her whole life to a man! You'll cheat Pearl if you get stubborn, and you'll cheat all of us! We want cake and music and dancing!"

Ben, speechless, looked unconvinced. Hank spoke up. "Your vows, Ben. One was to do everything together, as one person. Have you even asked Pearl whether she wants the party?"

Ben, abruptly ashamed, looked down into Pearl's silvery eyes.

"They want it so, Ben," she whispered. "Please!"

His resistance melted. Maybe Pearl was reluctant to be alone with him in the bedroom, afraid even. Maybe music and dancing and laughter and a bit of wine would make it easier for her.

He grinned. "Let's have a party!" he shouted. "Let's have fun!"

The parlors and all the rooms of the house filled with cheers. The people moved slowly outside. The men started to put up makeshift tables, and the women provided cloths to cover them as well as special dishes by the dozen.

At the same time, every man stopped long enough to shake Ben's hand and clap his shoulder and touch Pearl's cold fingers and wish her happiness. And every woman and girl kissed Ben and embraced Pearl until her hairpins loosened and her braid fell, and Christa had to rewind it around her head.

The spirit of merriment crept into Pearl, and she laughed because the others were so happy. She saw that the paper lanterns hanging from the trees were lighted, and she loved the golden glow they cast. One lantern had been hung directly over the tall white cake in the center of the longest table. Pearl momentarily forgot that she was an alien in a new world, and then she remembered and wondered if she'd done wrong, but Christa chose that moment to hug her and dance a few steps with her, and Pearl forgot everything but the celebration.

Hank poured the wine, a bit for each person present, even the children, and he proposed a toast. "To the master and mistress of Rivard!" he sang out, and everybody drank, and then someone began to play the piano, which had been moved out from the church house.

Bessie led Pearl to the cake, put a knife into her hand, and laughingly ordered her to cut it. This she did, making the slices small so it would go around, and it was eaten at once, even before the merrymakers filled their plates with food. And the plates were from cabins, not Rivard, for this time the people were entertaining.

Dancing came last. Pearl and Ben were allowed the first dance together, then both were captured by new partners, dance after dance. Ben danced with every woman and girl, even Granny, and Pearl danced with every man and boy, including one who proudly announced he'd be ten next birthday.

Swept along by the music, the dance, and the happiness, Pearl enjoyed herself, though mostly because she recognized this party as an expression of love for Ben. Warmth glowed in her for the people because of this, and before the party ended, she had again almost completely forgotten that everybody but herself was black.

XVI

When the party ended, Ben took Pearl upstairs to their bedroom. Trembling suddenly, deeply frightened now that she was alone with him, she began to undress for what was yet to come.

She kept her back to him; he did likewise. The lamp threw light and shadow over them as they removed their wedding clothes.

This was the moment Pearl had feared, had pushed out of her mind. It was the moment which Ben had looked forward to, had prayed to God that he could carry through without terrifying her. He thought of her beauty, her goodness, her purity; she thought of trusting him. He'd been trustworthy always, even though he was so big, so black.

"Don't be scared," he said quietly, his voice coming from directly behind her. "I'm scared myself."

"You . . . scared?" The words caught in her throat.

"Afraid I'll scare you. Afraid I'll hurt you. I'll be gentle. I vow it. You've trusted me until now. Trust me further."

"I . . . will, Ben. I'll trust you," she whispered.

Still trembling, she put on the white nightgown he had bought her in New Orleans when she shared his room, felt it slide over her head and down her body to her ankles.

He stepped around in front of her. He wore a white nightshirt. Solemnly, he took the pins out of her hair, put them aside, unbraided the coronet, and spread her hair so it flowed gloriously about her face and over her shoulders and down her back. She looked like an angel to him.

"There," he whispered, "this is how I've dreamed of seeing you. You're so beautiful, my Pearl, my darling."

He looked enormous, looming so black in his nightshirt. "May I kiss you?" he asked.

"I . . . yes, Ben." It was Ben. A kiss was to be expected. Reverently, he placed his hands on her shoulders, slowly touched his lips to her brow. It was a brief, tender kiss, over before she had time to stiffen, and she realized that this was Ben, kind and gentle Ben, and that his kiss had been, not repulsive, but pleasant.

She let him guide her to the bed, help her to lie back on her pillow, make certain that she was comfortable. He felt her almost tighten, and he lay beside her, not touching, knowing how easy it would be to frighten her, to ruin their union before it had begun.

Yet he must make the next move. His body was ready, was clamoring, but she didn't even know what happened between man and woman. He must lead her carefully, as reverently as he would an angel from heaven; he must lead her down the path which could bring her to love and away from the one which would repulse and sicken her.

First, he must show her that there was no danger, that he was no animal. "I'm going to slip my arm under your shoulders," he said quietly. "Let me know when you're comfortable."

Her throat closed. This was it. This came next. And after this there would be more, but she must face it, she must trust him. She nodded.

He saw the nod and carefully slid one arm under her, then moved his other arm over her, so that he was holding her. When she almost stiffened, he murmured assurance, and she responded to his gentleness, laying against him, waiting.

He stroked her hair, murmuring, "My Pearl . . . my wife." He kissed her cheek, her chin, her brow, but never her lips, for he was afraid the thickness of his own lips would be repugnant. He stroked her eyebrows, her nose, then let his hand wander until it held one breast, covered by the gown. She began to tremble, but didn't push away.

"Beloved," he whispered, and kissed her neck, and for some reason unknown to herself, this soothed her, and she ceased to tremble as she waited for him to kiss her neck again.

"Trust me, darling," he said softly. "Trust me all the way." Swiftly he lifted her gown and his own garment and took her quickly, but with reverence and deep passion. She sensed his reverence after the one flash of pain, and she felt his passion as it flowed into her, and she felt . . . yes . . . comforted.

And he, lost in bliss, thought of her as divine, and he was awed and proud that he was rendering to her his one drop of white blood.

They lay in lamplight, entwined, and he said, "I worship you, Pearl . . . worship you!" Then, softly, "Did I scare you, darling?"

"Not really."

"Did I hurt you at the first?"

"Some."

"It's supposed to hurt a little the first time. Because you were a virgin. It won't happen again."

They remained entwined. Their breaths mingled softly.

"Ben," she murmured.

"Yes, my darling?"

"What you . . . what I . . . what we did . . ."

"It's the natural thing for man and wife, my Pearl."

"Is it what those men do to the girls at Josie's and pay them money for?"

"Yes," he replied softly, stroking her hair. "But it's . . . different . . . at Josie's."

"How is it different?"

"The men—they don't love the girls. They want only sex. It's pretty wild and rough, and the girls have to stand it because of the money."

Her breath quivered. Her hand came to lie on his arm. "Thank you, Ben," she whispered. "Thank you for making it different from Josie's. Will it always be like tonight between us?"

"That depends. Did you feel even the least bit of . . . pleasure?"

She lay very still. "At the end," she whispered, "it was . . . warm . . . even felt . . . good."

"In that case," he whispered back, "it will get better for you. I'll show you, teach you. You can trust me." She snuggled to him and he ached to take her again, but dared not risk frightening her. There would be tomorrow night and all the nights. He felt her grow heavier against him and knew that she was falling asleep.

He'd never mentioned children to her, but he'd thought of them. Though their children, his and Pearl's, would be half white, adding greatly to his one drop, Ben had no intention of breeding the Rivards back to white. If I could accomplish something far-reaching, he thought, it would be to mix all the peoples of the world, to have one people and one only.

Still holding Pearl, he felt himself drift into sleep.

XVII

Last night, Pearl thought, dressing along with Ben, is what happens to the girls at Josie's house. Only those girls have to lie with any man who will pay, stranger or not. And with more than one man a night. She shuddered at the fate she had escaped, knew she was lucky it was Ben, who treated her as if she were holy, with whom she must sleep. She'd made him happy last night. Afterward, she'd felt at peace; what he'd done after that one pain had felt . . . good. . . .

She glanced at him, and he smiled. She smiled back. "You okay?" he asked, and she nodded, smiling again at his thoughtfulness. They went downstairs, and he set the table while she cooked.

He left her washing dishes and made for the cane field. She arrived at the garden for her day's work; the garden crew always arrived together. Today the women smiled at her and spoke warmly, and she managed to smile back, her face burning, because, of course, they all knew what she and Ben had done in bed.

Christa, as usual, was outspoken.

"How was it?" she asked when they were alone.

"How was what?" Pearl quibbled, cheeks flaming.

"You know . . . with Ben. Being married and alone. Was he easy and kind, or so anxious he got . . . rough?"

"He was . . . like always," Pearl said, wishing she could hide her face.

Christa hugged her. "I thought he'd be easy on you! You can thank your stars! Ma says that some of the easiest-going men turn into studs in bed." She smiled at the stunned look Pearl gave her. "Yes, Ma talks to me about man-woman things. She don't want me to marry blind. Her and Pa would've liked for me to marry Ben, but I never had a chance, not even before he saw you."

The day wore on, and the days that followed. The tenants accepted Pearl as mistress, and she entered into a deliberate period of adjustment, learning to be mistress of Rivard, learning to be a wife. This included night and Ben and bed.

Gradually, gently, he taught her the pleasures of love.

Soon she began to experience a feeling of desire as soon as he entered her, and always, at the end, she was carried into pure and utter delight and Ben was, too, though he never made love to her without the reverence.

Soon he was instructing her how to move, and she did what he said, and her pleasure increased. When he told her to move as her own body dictated, he set her free. She moved wildly and embraced him as he did her, glorying in the words of love he uttered, holding them in her memory. In these exquisite moments she forgot that he was Negro. She found herself taking joy in his daily company. Almost every night they danced to the music of the big radio in the front parlor, and more than once she knew she had found more happiness here than she'd ever had on the bayou.

And every night after love-making, she would be filled with peace and the memory of him. "I love you, my Pearl. I adore you," he would whisper, his velvet voice laying for her a pathway into sleep.

Bessie approached Pearl one day. "Ben asked me to teach you how to run Rivard as mistress," she said. "He mention it to you?"

"Just barely."

"I told him I've already taught you everything I know, even to setting the table for the supper parties he wants to give."

This alarmed Pearl, and she showed it.

Bessie chuckled. "Not for white folks, dear. For tenants from the plantations up and down the bayou. What little you haven't learned, I told Ben, you will now as I help you get ready for the first party."

"Are you sure?" Pearl asked. "I wouldn't want to do anything wrong. I want it perfect for Ben."

Bessie smiled. "Ben wants Rivard run the way his great-grandmother, Olive, ran it."

"I've heard about her," Pearl said. "She was very beautiful and passed for white, and Rivard was one of the loveliest plantations on the Teche. But she didn't entertain. She kept to herself because of the colored blood in her."

In a week, Pearl served as hostess at her first dinner party. Bessie helped, but declared Pearl wouldn't need special help in the future, and indeed, as her confidence grew and she realized these guests were people like Ben's tenants, her pleasure in entertaining grew, and there was much merriment at Rivard.

It became known on the Teche that Ben Rivard had a white woman at his plantation and was living with her. All the white inhabitants on the Teche were scandalized.

As did the others, Pablo and Clio Sanchez of Sanchez Sugar, and Anton and Felice LeFleur of Three Oaks, dining at the Sanchez table, could talk of nothing else.

Pablo, who had run to fat and was nearly bald, scowled when the subject was first mentioned. "Think we should discuss it?" he asked Anton, who was blade-thin and whose hair was like the gleaming silver on the table. "We have ladies present."

"Oh, piffle!" cried Clio, black-haired and black-eyed. "It's more than just gossip. It's a fact! My Mandy went there on a personal errand, and she *saw* this white woman ev'rybody's talkin' about! So it isn't just gossip—it's gospel! There is a white woman livin' at Rivard, and she was in the plantation house, sitting in a rocker and doing needlework and singing!"

"My dear!" gasped the blond, blue-eyed Felice, whose beauty, though fading, lingered charmingly on. "What did this woman look like?"

"She's just a girl, younger than Mandy, 'cause Mandy asked her friends there at Rivard. She's only seventeen! She's got hair the color of silver—platinum, if you please— and eyes the same! And she's a raving beauty!"

Pablo and Anton listened intently.

"How did she ever get to Rivard?" gasped Clio. "Why, it's almost not to be believed!"

"Ben Rivard brought her from New Orleans is all Mandy could find out. Seems the nigras at Rivard really like the girl. But she lives in the big house with Ben, mind you, with Ben Rivard, and you know what that means!"

Felice shook her head wonderingly. "It can't be! No white girl would lowah herself that way!"

"How else can it be explained?"

"Simple," Pablo put in at last. "The girl is bound to be a white nigra . . . a light-skinned wench who can pass. An albino, even. It's the only possible explanation."

Clio was adamant. "She's white, I tell you! Mandy got a look at her fingernails, and they're the nails of a white person. And skin whiter than anybody Mandy ever saw!"

And so the talk went through the Teche and St. Martinville and all the bayou country. The majority opinion was that Pearl had a bit of Negro in her, that she was nothing but a light-skinned or albino wench. But none of them could figure out why she'd take up with a nigra as black as Ben except to get her hands on Rivard. Even the ex-slaves, surprised at Pearl's being at Rivard, couldn't figure it out.

Inside a month, Silas Mercer, Jr., took it upon himself to visit Rivard. Cocksure, just twenty-three, he drove up to Ben who was off on one side of a cane field. Silas let the wheels of his new automobile crush a swath of cane.

He braked sharply, glared at Ben with wire-colored eyes, his unruly hair the usual Mercer dirty tan, features sharp. "Didn't you see me comin'?" he demanded in a brittle voice.

Ben, who was chopping weeds, leaned on his hoe. He wiped sweat off his face and chest. "Let us say," he responded, "that I was aware that an automobile was crushing my cane."

"Hell, what harm I done don't matter! It grows back."

Ben said nothing, simply waited. Silas junior got out of the car, his polished black boots breaking more cane. He glanced carelessly at the flattened path his car wheels had made along the edge of the field to this spot.

Some of Ben's tenants looked his way and began to approach, but Ben motioned them back. They resumed their chopping, but still watched.

"There's talk about you on the Teche," Mercer said.

"That's no surprise. There's been gossip about Rivard always."

"This gossip is jucier than most." Silas junior grinned evilly, then pulled his scanty brows into a scowl. "Talk is you're livin' in sin with a white woman."

Again Ben waited.

"That the truth, Rivard?"

"Whether it is or not is no affair of yours," Ben said tightly.

"Happens to be a concern to me, just the same. A concern of ev'ry decent plantation owner on the Teche."

"I repeat, Rivard is used to gossip. We do nothing to hurt others. Be content with that."

"You got a white woman in your bed or not?" demanded Silas junior, glaring in an ugly, menacing mood.

Ben's impulse was to hit him, but he refrained. Slavery had ended, but it still wasn't tolerated for a colored man to strike a white man.

"Have you got a white woman or not?" snarled Silas junior.

"I have a white girl," Ben said from behind his teeth. He'd not deny Pearl, for she was his heart. "And I'm keeping her. There's no law against it."

"You marry her some cheatin' way?"

Ben set his jaw, met the other man's eyes. He wouldn't sully Pearl by discussing her further with this white trash.

"I advise you, Ben Rivard, to get rid of her, or take her away if you can't do without her. You do that, take her away, and I'm the man to make it possible. Us Mercers been wantin' to buy Rivard for years. Name me a price I'm willin' to meet, and you can keep your white woman, maybe in New Orleans. You might get away with it there."

"The answer to selling Rivard is the same as ever." Ben gritted his teeth. "Rivard is not for sale. Not at any price or for any reason. It is family property and will go down the generations as Rivard property. Not Mercer property, never Mercer. And that is final."

Silas junior got into his open, two-seater car, glared from behind the steering wheel. He'd left the motor running, so didn't have to crank it. "You'll suffer for that insult," he threatened angrily. "Us Mercers have stood enough from you Rivards. The whole bayou will rise up and drive you out if you don't move your white whore away!"

He set the car to moving, turned it, drove it fast toward the little road that led back to his own property, crushing another wide swath through the sugar cane. Ben began to clear the damage and ready that part of the field for replanting, and some of his men came and silently helped, shaking their heads.

That night the entire field was flattened. It took two days to clear away the broken stalks, ready the soil, plant anew. Then Ben and his crew returned to their regular tasks, working twice as hard to make up for lost time.

Every one of them knew they had no recourse; they had to silently accept what the Mercers had done and hope they wouldn't return.

Hank, however, was angry. "You going to put up with this, Ben?" he demanded. "You know the Mercers done it."

"I won't lower Rivard to retaliate, Hank. You know it'd be useless to report it. If we let it lay, it'll pass. And no one else will molest us."

But Ben thought as he worked, and quietly made a decision.

In bed, after their nightly closeness, he told Pearl what he was going to do. She knew about Silas junior's visit, knew the Mercers had ruined the cane field. Now she must be told the rest.

"The Mercers have got to have time to cool off," Ben said. "If they don't, and with you still at Rivard, they'll be up to more mischief, worse than the cane. We've got to trick them into letting up on Rivard."

"Oh Ben, I've brought you trouble! I'll leave, and there'll be no reason—"

"You can't leave. You're my wife. But I've figured out a way to handle it."

"How, Ben?"

"The war."

She was bewildered. "The war?" she asked. It seemed so remote, so far away it didn't seem real, though she'd heard Ben speak of it and knew he kept up with its progress. And she'd seen those soldiers in New Orleans.

"I'm going to enlist in the Army," Ben said quietly.

She pressed into his arms. "You can't go away!" she whispered. "Besides, with you gone, won't the Mercers get worse than ever?"

"They want to buy Rivard, and with me gone, they can't even try. And they won't have cause to torment anyone here. A black man won't be living with a white woman, you see. They'll calm down since they won't have our living together to keep them stirred up. Over the years, they've found excuses to molest us, and now they won't have any. And I can do my part for our country, which is an obligation I've put off too long now."

"But when you come back, what then?"

"Our living together will be old business to them. They like something new to make trouble about. Besides, while I'm gone, they can hope I'll be killed in battle so they can somehow buy Rivard from the estate."

"What estate, Ben?"

"I'll make a will before I go, leaving Rivard to you. If you inherit, the Mercers will be at you to sell, but don't do it. They wouldn't be able to get too ugly because the black man/white woman situation would no longer exist. Put Hank in charge, do what he says. In the future you could marry. Marry a white man, and your son could be my heir. That's the best way I can figure it out."

She began to cry, pleading with him not to enlist, but he wouldn't give up the plan. "It's the best course, darling, and I'm going to pursue it," he told her.

She sobbed herself to sleep in his arms.

He had one comfort. Whatever happened, Rivard would be her home. She'd always have a place to live and work she loved to do.

XVIII

Before Ben dressed in his uniform that last morning, he kissed Pearl on the cheek. "If you don't mind, my darling, please wait with the others in the back. I want everybody to see me at the same time, get it over with."

She looked into his eyes, and what she saw there helped her to smile teasingly, though she was in no teasing mood. "I do believe, Ben Rivard," she chided lightly, "that you're shy about getting all dressed up in a uniform!"

"Know what?" he grinned. "You're more than beautiful—you're also smart!"

She kissed his cheek, then went to join the others, gathered on the packed earth near the back gallery. They didn't speak, just nodded, and she nodded back.

She sucked in her breath when he appeared on the gallery, erect and fine. He looked taller in uniform, more powerful and more handsome. Yes, he was handsome, and the realization brought the sting of tears.

Pearl didn't want him to go, to leave her. Yet she had to say good-bye with a smile and keep secret her belief that she was pregnant. This she couldn't tell him, not now. She couldn't put a tinge of sadness on Ben's proud, smiling face, even though the sadness would be mixed with wonder and joy.

"Here I am, folks," he said. "Off to war. There's time only to say good-bye. Got a boat to catch, then a train."

He descended to the ground, put his arms around Pearl, kissed her forehead. He'd never kissed her lips. She forced a smile, and he kissed her cheek. Then he turned away, shaking hands with every man, hugging every woman and child, coming back frequently to Pearl. She followed him about, a set smile on her lips, unshed tears behind her eyes, her whole being filled with a truth which was clawing, tearing at her to be recognized.

At the very last, he kissed her tenderly on the bridge of her nose, and it was then she knew what was tormenting her. Tears burst forth and she cried out hoarsely, "Ben, you can't go! You can't! I love you . . . want you . . . need. . . ."

He grabbed her into his arms, lowered his thick, trembling lips to her upturned, quivering lips, and for the first time they really kissed, drinking each other's tears.

"Life is perfect now, my Pearl," he said, through tears. "All I need is your love to bring me home again. But I've got to go. I've signed up, and the government's tough about these things." He kissed her again on the lips, gently but firmly put away her clinging hands, and turned to the overseer. "Let's go," he said gruffly, and went striding away.

Ben wrote her from the army camp. When the first letter came, she ran to their bedroom to read it. Christa, who had come to live with her for the duration, was working in the garden.

Pearl opened the envelope with care. She would keep it perfect always. She already had a shoebox in which to keep Ben's letters, and she knew there would be many, for he had promised to write every day if he could.

"My Pearl, my beloved and precious wife,

"I miss you every moment of the day and night, feel your lips on mine, remember how it is to make love to you, and thank God on my knees that you have come to love me.

"Your beautiful eyes would open wide if you could see my living quarters here. No nice bedroom, no starched curtains, not even a window. Several dozen of us live in a barracks—a long tent with a row of canvas cots down each side. My cot, like the others, has a black wool blanket and a pillow, and I have a footlocker to keep my clothes and your letters in. When they come, I'll read them over and over, then tie them in a bundle to read again when I am lonesome for you, which is all the time.

"The training they give us here is tough. Some of the fellows are so sore they groan in their sleep. I can understand now why Pierre Leblanc was turned down because of flat feet. The marching makes even my feet feel flat. I'm lucky I worked so hard at Rivard, for I'm already tough, so the training doesn't bother me.

"What I don't like is learning to handle a gun the army way. I have used guns all my life for hunting, but I don't enjoy target practice because in battle the target will be a breathing, living man. The officers tell us we can't afford to think of the enemy that way, that it's them or us, which is true, but it's hard to think of carrying out orders to kill.

"Don't be scared, my Pearl. If my company gets sent overseas and into battle, we'll be in trenches. A trench gives a soldier good protection, and if he's a good shot, he has top chance of not even being wounded. So draw an easy breath, my darling. I'm the best marksman in my company, and I mean to improve. I'll come home to you safe. Believe that, for it is true.

"Evenings we play cards, using matches for money. As to real money, I'm sending my army pay to you, so be expecting it and use it as you see fit.

"Don't forget me while I'm gone. With every day that passes, I see your loveliness in my mind like a picture. Please write to me.

                                        "I love you,

                                            Ben"

Pearl read and reread this letter, and all the letters he wrote until the pages were limp. Ben wrote to Hank, too, and these letters the overseer read to the assembled tenants, so all would know what was happening with Ben. Pearl missed Ben, really missed him, and she'd lay aside his letters with the educated words on them and strive to make her own penmanship and language good enough that he wouldn't be ashamed for her.

The first one was the hardest.

"Dear Ben,

"I got your first letter and have read it a lot of times. I miss you, too. Christa stays in the front bedroom, like you said, and she is good company. But I am still lonesome for you.

"The barracks sound ugly, and you are used to Rivard, which is so pretty. I know you will be glad to see it when you come back. And I hope your feet quit hurting.

"I have got a secret I haven't even told Christa, because you would want to be the first to know. I am going to have a baby! I think I am more than two months along. I hope you will be glad to hear this. It scared me a little bit at first, and then I remembered how cute my baby brothers were, and I think this baby will be as cute.

"Please let me know what you think about the baby.

"With best wishes,

Pearl

"P.S. What you said about trenches scares me, because I love you so. They don't sound safe with no tops. Can't they build them out of rock that would stop bullets?"

The answer came by return mail.

"My darling wife,

"Other than having you for my own, and having

your love, nothing could make me happier than our
baby. I have told the men in my company, and they
keep congratulating me.

"Now, please darling, tell Bessie about the baby at
once. Tell everybody. Put yourself in Bessie's hands
until the baby comes, and do what she says.

"Work in the house and garden only as much as
Bessie thinks you should. And have the doctor come
to Rivard when the baby is born. If I'm still in this
country, I'll try to get a furlough so I can be with you.

"Walk carefully, especially on the stairs. I'll wait
anxiously for your next letter and hope you'll agree
with all I've written here.

"Don't worry about the trenches. They're pretty deep.

"My heart is bursting because I am to be father and
you, my sweet Pearl, are to be mother to our child.

"Your adoring husband,

Ben"

At night, alone in the wide bed, Pearl searched for what
had caused her to fall in love with Ben, a Negro, so big,
black, foreign. She could find but one answer. She had
fled Pa's brutality, his evil, and had found safety in Ben's
gentleness, his tenderness, his selfless love. She loved
him. Simply and truly did. The only barrier left was that
sometimes the contrast of color startled her anew. Yet, in
spite of it, she felt comfort in him only and wanted him at
home again.

Christa was delighted about the baby. She chattered
about how it would look. "It might be white, or it might
be black!" she proclaimed.

"Maybe the colors will mix," Pearl speculated.

"Y-yes . . . they usually do."

This disturbed Pearl, for she secretly wanted her baby
to be white, but she told herself that Ben had a right for it

to be black. She wondered what he wanted, but refrained from asking in her letters. These she filled with details of her pregnancy and assured him that she was in perfect health, which was true. She was in glorious health, and Hank assured her that he, too, had written this information to Ben.

Hank subscribed to the local newspaper, and Pearl avidly read every word about the war. She stared at the long lists of American soldiers killed or wounded in battle and was relieved that Ben was safe in training camp. She prayed nightly that he would not be sent overseas. She studied the accounts of battles, tried to understand them, but gathered only that the enemy soldiers were killing Americans and that Americans were killing enemy soldiers.

At the last of October, when she was heavy with the baby, the newspaper ran tall, black headlines: THE WAR IS OVER! AMERICAN, GERMAN GENERALS DECLARE TRUCE! ARMISTICE TO BE SIGNED!

Pearl read the front page over and over, her heart racing. This meant that Ben would come home, that they'd never be parted again! He was safe, would always be safe!

At last she surrendered the paper to Hank, who read it to the tenants crowded into his house. Many of them wept through smiles. The men clapped each other on the back; the women let their tears stream and hugged one another. At the end, all knelt and Hank prayed earnestly to God, thanking Him for saving Ben, their master, and for saving all the other soldiers as well, both American and enemy.

After the prayer, they started making plans for a celebration to welcome Ben home. Pearl thought repeatedly, thank you, God, thank you for making it so Ben can be home when the baby comes!

The very next day the newspaper crushed the elation

and joy at Rivard and stunned Pearl so that she couldn't so
much as weep.

FALSE ARMISTICE! the headlines read. WAR CON-
TINUES!

Pearl tried to read the account, could not. She knew
what it meant—that Ben wouldn't be coming home, that
he would have to stay in training camp. She tried to thank
God for that blessing, could not. She'd counted so on
feeling Ben's arms again, on his being home when the
baby was born! They'd never let him out on furlough with
the war hotter than ever, over there.

Four endless days passed and still she hadn't been able
to weep, to cleanse her grief and give it a chance to heal.
No letters came from Ben, and this added to her unhappiness. She wondered if the Army had put a ban on letters.
On the fifth day one of the familiar envelopes arrived. Her
name was on it—Pearl Babin—the way he always sent
them, bold and neat and so beautifully inscribed, it was
like a caress.

She fled to the bedroom with it, opened it with shaking,
yet careful hands. Ben would know better than the news-
papers what was happening, because he was a soldier and
a part of this war.

She read it faster than she'd ever read one of his letters,
crammed his words into herself through her eyes. Then,
her heart pounding, she read it again, numbly, slowly,
taking in its full meaning.

"My Darling Wife,

"For one day it seemed I'd never have to write this
letter to you, but things have changed. We got very
excited here in the barracks at news of the supposed
armistice, and there was awful disappointment when
we found out it was a false armistice, a rumor. I do
find one ray of hope in it, sweetheart. If such a rumor

got printed, there must be truth hidden in it somewhere, and before long, there'll be a real armistice.

"Cling to that thought, darling. It will help you
until I can come home. But now, the bad news—my
company is being sent overseas soon. We don't know
where we're being sent, but we'll be fighting, and we
won't be allowed to write home.

"Be brave for me, honey. Take care of our baby now
and until I get home. Because I will get home, I feel
it in my bones. I'll do my share of fighting and more.
If I would get wounded, I'd be sent to the hospital to
mend and then probably would be sent home. This is
the worst that can happen, I promise.

"But if I'm forced to break that promise, raise our
baby to be master or mistress of Rivard. You know
what that will take on your part. Chin up at all times,
from the beginning on, which you will do because
you love me and because our child will have to
depend on you.

"I write the bad as well as the good to help you, my
darling. Keep one thought, one prayer, in mind—that
the war will end soon and I'll come home in one piece
and we'll be happy forever after.

"Take care of your sweet self, take care of our baby,
wait for me. For if any man in this army is determined to come home, Ben Rivard is that man. I'm
kissing the paper on which I write and if you kiss it,
too, it will be long-distance love-making.

"God bless you and help you, my Pearl,

                              "Your husband forever,

                    Ben"

Trembling, she kissed the paper Ben had kissed, kissed
every inch of it. She read the letter again, and it fright-

ened her. The possibility that he'd never return terrified her, yet she understood it with her heart.

That night the tears came in a storm. She held the letter to her breasts; she laid it on her abdomen so it would be near his child which moved within her; she sobbed her heart away. She thought of the lists of the thousands of dead and wounded in the paper every day. Now she would be searching those lists for Ben's name, holding her breath, praying that she wouldn't find it.

In the dark of night, sodden by tears, she imagined what a whole life without him would be. Her tears flowed into agony, then terror. When morning came they had ceased, but hadn't eased her, had only built a terror that he would be killed in battle.

Hank had got a letter, too, and read it to all the people, and they went about their work with tears and sadness. They tried to encourage each other that, of course, Ben would come home, and they tried to encourage Pearl, who forced herself to smile and thank them.

She couldn't answer Ben's letter because he wouldn't get it. She couldn't tell him that she loved him and would do what he said. Days dragged by like centuries. The movements of the baby were her only comfort; it was a part of Ben no war could take from her.

The weeks dragged heavily on. She prayed constantly.

When Hank came running to her on November 11, 1918, which she'd marked off on her calendar as being one day closer for the baby, she almost didn't listen to what he was shouting, his voice hoarse and breaking.

"Pearl!" he screamed. "The war's over! Really over! There's a real Armistice! They've signed the paper! It's no mistake this time! You can believe in it!"

It was then, for the first time in her life, that Pearl fainted.

* * *

When Ben returned to Rivard, still in uniform, Pearl
went into his arms, the gathered tenants cheering and
weeping. She realized anew how much she had missed
him. Tears streamed down her cheeks. "Don't ever leave
me again!" she sobbed.

"I won't," he vowed, putting his cheek against hers. She
was so swollen with child, it was impossible for him to
hold her close. "You're beautiful," he whispered, "lovely
with our child!"

"Y-your plans about the Mercers worked," she said.
"They haven't been near or done a thing."

"They won't now," he predicted. "They'll be too busy
making money out of the end of the war. There'll be land
they can buy cheap, so they won't consider spending a
good price to get Rivard, not for a long time, anyway."

Delighted to see him, Pearl kissed him full on his lips
for all to see. Filled with awe, he kissed her in return, and
then they walked together around the Quarters, stopping
every few steps for greetings and consenting to a celebration tonight.

And after the celebration, with no love-making possible
because of her size, Pearl took comfort in seeing Ben's
black head on the white pillow beside her. And her breath
quivered in happy relief, and soon she slept.

XIX

Maebelle, a blushing, tremulous bride, toured all the
houses at L'Acadie the morning after the wedding. Pierre's
arm was around her and his head was bent to catch every
matchless word she spoke. She continued to blush and he
to adore, and each knew there had never lived a happier

bride and groom. And all on L'Acadie let them wander and
marvel, keeping their distance, feeling privileged to witness from afar such wedded bliss.

"We'll walk to L'Acadie, the plantation house, first,"
Pierre said. And Maebelle, quivering with joy, agreed and
so they toured, on and on.

Leading from the bayou to the great, lovely, white main
house was a long, grassy driveway, lined on each side by a
double row of moss-festooned giant oaks. Another identical driveway led to the big, unpainted Old House, and
Maebelle caught her breath at the sight of such magnifi-
cent twin driveways and such big, graceful houses. Out
from the ends of both houses stood twin octagonal towers,
and at the rear of both houses on a line with the towers
were dovecotes, alive with cooing birds.

They wandered about the giant rose garden which
surrounded the two great houses and another, smaller
dwelling—Honeymoon House—where they were to live
for the present. They ended up in Grape House. This
structure, made of vine and purple grapes covering a
wooden frame, was square. It had door and window
openings and was furnished with white wooden chairs
from which one could gaze out over the distant bayou.

They sat here on a bench holding hands, Maebelle's
wedding ring casting a rich golden glow. She looked at it,
pleased that it had more than eighteen carats of gold in it.

I need a diamond, too, she thought wistfully. The
thought grew, filled her mind, throbbed. She'd wondered
why Pierre hadn't given her one before their marriage,
then had decided he intended it for a wedding present,
but now the wedding was over. It was already the next
morning, and still she had no diamond. She had waited
eagerly, reluctant to suggest it herself, but she still had
only the pearl and diamond ring her daddy had given her.
She loved it, but it was a disappointment that her very

own bridegroom hadn't given her a diamond, too. Her happy quivering ceased, and she frowned. This didn't fit her dream of marriage, didn't fit at all, and she didn't know what to do about it. All she knew was that she longed for a diamond.

"Do you mind that my daddy didn't have a dowry for me?" she ventured, determined somehow to turn the conversation to diamonds.

Pierre chuckled. "Dowry! That's a thing of the past, sweetheart. I want you, not money!"

"That's what Daddy said. He hasn't got anything but the *Maebelle*, honest and true! And by the time he had bought my trousseau and linens..." She flung her hands out daintily, the wedding band glowing on one, the pearl and diamond ring gleaming on the other. "Because he spent so much on me, he won't make a profit this year. Or next year, or maybe the next!"

Pierre kissed the corner of her lips. "What does a lovely creature like you know about profits?"

"Daddy told me. He said you make a profit at L'Acadie."

Pierre chuckled. "Precious little!"

"Why not? With twelve thousand acres, you've got to be rich."

"We're far from rich, honey."

She drooped. It wasn't that she'd married Pierre for L'Acadie. She was so crazy about him she'd have married him if he'd been a bank clerk. "It's just that L'Acadie's so big, it's bound to make money," she pressed in a gentle, teasing manner.

"Not so, love. We're barely solvent."

"It was sweet that your pa gave it to you for our wedding present."

"In spite of that, I'll pay heed to what he says about running it. I need experience before I take over."

"How do you run it, darling?"

"We raise a fair crop of sugar cane and cattle feed. And food, of course. We have thirty-two Negro families who work as many acres as possible each. In return, each gets a cabin, a garden patch, a ration of milk and eggs, time off to hunt and fish, and after harvest, an equal share of the cash profit from the cane."

"You mean, every nigra family gets as big a share as you and your pa do?" She heard the consternation in her voice, but couldn't hold it out.

"Precisely. It's common practice on the bayous."

"But the other plantations aren't big, like L'Acadie!"

"A couple are. But we have to depend on our families. We could use dozens more. We'll make it, eventually. Our descendants—"

"But that'll take your lifetime and mine!"

"And then some. But L'Acadie will, in the end, be restored."

"That scares me! Makes me think I can't fix things up! That I can't even have a few dresses . . . or a diamond ring . . . ever! And ev'ry woman has a diamond ring!"

"You'll have all those things, darling. I'll get you what you want."

She wept a bit. He held her. She snuggled. A diamond. Of course, he thought. All the bayou ladies had at least one diamond, some had more. He thought of the Leblanc jewels, which had belonged to the murdering beauty who had lost her mind. His father had declared them stained by blood, had sold them, and had given the money to charity. Maebelle was a treasure more precious than L'Acadie itself. He kissed her tenderly and promised her a diamond. She smiled through her tears, and he saw her love for him in her wet eyes, saw the love and adoration.

That afternoon he cornered René, who was thirty-nine but seemed older. Pa was looking sad. He'd had a sad look ever since Pierre could remember. His voice and features

were sharp, his brown hair shot with gray, his light-brown
eyes brooding, but he still worked hard in the cane. René
was pleased over Pierre's marriage, because he wanted a
new heir for L'Acadie, someone to take Pierre's place
when the time came.

"I need to talk to you, Pa," Pierre said.

"Anything wrong? Maebelle?"

"It has to do with Maebelle, sir. She didn't exactly say
so, but I believe she's deeply hurt that I haven't given her
a diamond ring. She says all the other women have them."

René looked thoughtful. "Every girl wants a diamond. I
don't suppose you have any money left."

"A hundred dollars. It would leave me broke."

"And would buy a decent stone, but if I put a hundred
with it, she could have a stone she'd be proud of all her
life."

"Can you afford it, Pa?"

"No, but I will. It'll leave me with nearly a hundred,
and our shares from the cane will come a month from now.
Maebelle's worth it, son."

Enthralled by the large blue-white diamond set in gold
prongs, Maebelle wept from sheer delight. She stood
holding her hand out, watching the flash and glitter of her
new ring. She told Pierre and René they were angels and
darlings and she'd always wear the diamond with her
wedding ring.

Her flashing mind held as many thoughts as the facets of
the diamond held fire. Pierre must have more money than
he realized—the Leblancs had always been so rich that
probably what they had left seemed like nothing to them,
but to her it would be a fortune. That had to be the way it
was. Her next objective leapt into mind at that second,
and she lost no time getting Pierre in the proper mood to
listen to it.

At bedtime, she waited until he was in bed. Then she stepped behind the folding screen, took off all her clothes, hung them over the top of the screen, peeled off her silk stockings, and tucked them into her discarded slippers.

Her fiery hair a nimbus that reached her shoulders, her skin gleaming white, she stepped naked from behind the screen and strolled toward the bed.

The effect on Pierre was instantaneous. He'd never dreamed she'd do a thing like this. He shot up in bed, fought his way out of the pajamas. "You devilish little imp!" he whispered, his arms out. "I never thought . . . a girl like you . . . how did you get so bold?"

Maebelle smiled enticingly, ran her slim hands up his arms, stirring the hair, tickling. She pressed against his naked body with her own, fitting her fiery patch at the center so that it drove him nearly crazy.

"It's you, silly!" she teased. "You make me want to tempt you. I want you to make love to me ev'ry night! What's holding you back?"

"Not a damn thing!" he groaned and bore her down upon the bed and took her fiercely, glorying in fierceness which she returned. It's the red hair, he thought numbly, there isn't anything to beat red hair!

Afterward, as they lay naked in each other's arms, she proceeded with her scheme. "I'm going to redecorate L'Acadie, darling," she murmured. "Top to bottom. And we're going to move in with your pa and take care of him!"

Pierre chuckled indulgently. "What do you plan to use for money?"

"Whatever you give me, of course! I've made plans to completely do over ev'ry single room! In Old House, too, and even here, in Honeymoon House! I'm going to have ev'ry house wired for electricity!"

"Maebelle . . . sweetheart . . . you're teasing."

"It's you that's the tease! Like with the diamond! You're still rich, but you just don't re'lize it!"

He sat up in bed. "Honey, we're not rich. Pa helped me buy your ring. I'm flat broke, and he's got less than a hundred dollars left."

"But when you sell the cane, then there'll be money!"

"A few hundred, hopefully. And that's all until next year."

She sat up in bed, too. "There's a way, darling! It's kind of new, but easy! You pay on time!"

He stared at her. "How the hell—"

"You pay a little bit of money down to make the deal and buy what you want. Then, while you're using it, you pay some ev'ry week, until it's paid for!"

"No!" he shouted. "The Leblancs pay cash, only cash! No debts!"

She began to weep desperately. "Then the ring was a bribe! A pacifier to keep me quiet! You know L'Acadie needs doing over because I told you so, and you agreed!"

"I still agree. We simply don't have the money now."

It wasn't until he promised to let her redo all the buildings the instant there was money that she stopped weeping. Then he made love to her again in that way that set her afire, and after that, she said no more about redecorating for weeks, and Pierre thought she had reconciled herself to waiting.

Suddenly, she was pregnant. She was sick all the time, wanting everything Pierre said they couldn't afford, sobbing her heart out. Being so sick, throwing up all day, she refused to believe that they didn't have some money to make a down payment at least so she could make L'Acadie beautiful again.

She spent hours in tears and reproachful scenes with both Pierre and his father. Their share of profit was low this year, less than five hundred dollars, but to calm

Maebelle a bit, René gave her a hundred dollars to
convert one of the rooms at L'Acadie into a nursery and
outfit the baby with clothes.

XX

Silas Mercer, Jr., dressed in a fine tan suit, showed up at
L'Acadie. Pierre, watching him bring his shiny automobile
to an arrogant stop, hated the very sight of him.

Mercer knocked just as Pierre, Maebelle, and René
were finishing breakfast. Pierre opened the door in the
great hallway, managing to keep a scowl off his face.

"I hope I ain't intruding so early," Silas junior said in his
thin voice. "But there's a matter my pa and me have been
mulling over for quite a spell, and we can't go no further
without your ideas."

He stood looking at Pierre, then at René and Maebelle
who had joined them at the door.

Maebelle touched Pierre's arm. "I don't believe I've
met this gentleman, darling," she said quietly.

"Silas Mercer, Junior," Pierre responded, "my wife."
Maebelle inclined her head, and when she lifted it, saw
with surprise that Pierre was angry.

Silas junior made a jerky bow. "Pleased, ma'am. Us
Mercers date back to Reconstruction days. And proud of
it."

To Maebelle's bewilderment, neither Leblanc invited
the caller to enter. It was obvious they didn't like him, and
she wondered why. He didn't have the Leblanc polish, but
surely they didn't expect that from every man they met.

"I got a business matter to talk over with you," Mercer
said.

Pierre hesitated, then said coldly, "Come into the library."

"Lead the way," Mercer responded with a grin.

When Pierre turned to excuse himself to Maebelle, she tucked his arm into hers and smiled. "These days," she said, referring to her pregnancy, "I do as I please. Remember?" Pierre frowned, but let her go into the library with them.

Maebelle was somewhat excited, curious to learn what Mercer had on his mind. She sensed that money was involved, and she was excited over the vague prospect of getting money from Mercer, yet disturbed at the prospect of having to pay him some debt she knew nothing about.

Pierre closed the door. "We may as well sit down, since a lady is present," he said, and they all settled into chairs and on the sofa. Mercer sat in his chair as if he were a king. He boldly looked the room over, assessing it openly.

Pierre broke the silence. "What do you have on your mind?" he asked.

Mercer leaned forward. "First, I need to tell you the Mercer histr'y since we came to the Teche."

"I think we know it well enough," René said sharply.

"Still, I aim to refresh you. We came as carpetbaggers, and we was proud of it. We scouted around, learnt to trade on the stock market. He's a sharp man, my pa, and I take after him." Silas junior paused, as if expecting comment, but when none came, plunged on.

"Pa didn't want all his cash money tied up in the market 'cause it busts, so he smelt out what was open and decided to buy land, bayou land. It was sellin' cheap after the Civil War, and he bought because land'll always climb back up to its value."

"We know," Pierre said coldly. "He bought two plantations right on the Teche."

"And he's in the market for more."

"Why tell us?" René demanded icily. "We don't know of anyone who wants to sell."

"Right, right. But my pa, he's set on buyin' one of the really big Teche plantations. Dead set on it."

"What are you doing here?" breathed René, face red.

"To make you Leblancs first offer. Pa's got a hankering to buy L'Acadie, the whole twelve thousand acres, and he's makin' a flat-out offer of a hundred dollars a acre." Mercer sat back, triumphant.

René's redness deepened. Pierre's face was stony. Maebelle held her breath, her mind whirling.

"The . . . gall!" Pierre said at last. "First you aspire to get your filthy hands on L'Acadie, and then you dare to make an offer!" He stood. "I order you to leave!"

Mercer didn't move. "The offer comes to over a million dollars," he said. "You'd be nigger rich, and the Mercers'd be land poor. Until I work the stock market some more."

"Get off our land!" René whispered, even his neck red. He stood, swaying slightly.

"My understandin' is that L'Acadie belongs to you, Pierre. Right?"

"Yes," Pierre snapped. "But it so happens I agree with my father. The answer is a flat no."

"If you won't sell the whole plantation," Mercer said, getting easily to his feet, "we got a second proposition. We'll settle for the two thousand acres at the south edge of L'Acadie where it joins Rivard. That means twenty thousand in your pocket."

Maebelle could stand her own eagerness no longer. "Why not," she cried. "Pierre? Papa René?" She was on the verge of tears. "Twenty thousand dollars, and you'd still have ten thousand acres! And we'd have money for everything. We could refurbish all the houses and buy scads of things—even a diamond pendant! And there'd be money to hire people to work the land and raise loads more cane! Please, Pierre... please, darling!"

Pierre held his pleading wife to him. He was in an untenable spot. He didn't want to sell an acre, an inch. René caught his eye and scowled. Pierre knew how his pa felt. He also knew what this meant to Maebelle, how sensible it was to her, how grief-stricken she would be if he refused to sell.

She pulled back so she could look abjectly into his face. "I understand why you don't want to sell, darling," she said with tenderness. "But twenty thousand dollars! Think of how you can improve the land, even buy modern machinery, and don't forget how much more sugar cane you could raise! You'd make scads more money with machinery!"

He shook his head. "This is L'Acadie. To sell one acre is unthinkable, darling."

"You don't farm that two thousand acres anyway! Think how many years it'll be before you can farm it!"

"There's horse sense in what the little lady says," Mercer put in slyly. "We'd put the land right to cane, and you'd have the satisfaction of seein' them acres filled with cane, like they ought to be."

"He's right, Pierre darling. Papa René, he's right! It's plain as day!"

They both shook their heads.

"Them two thousand acres ain't helpin' you none," urged Mercer.

"They certainly aren't!" cried Maebelle. "Even I can see that! It just lies fallow. It's silly for us to live poor and work and struggle when we could have twenty thousand dollars to invest! Pierre, do the right thing and sell just that one little piece of land! I'm going to be the mother of the future heir, and you know I'd never do anything that would take from him!"

"She's got a point, Pa," Pierre said unwillingly.

"L'Acadie is not to be sold!" shouted René, very red and greatly agitated. "Pierre, I'm astounded that you'd even listen to this madness, much less consider it!"

"Why shouldn't I at least consider it?" Pierre demanded, suddenly irritated at being pulled in this direction and that. "I own L'Acadie. It's for me to say what will and will not be done!"

René turned purple. He was trembling, and could hear himself shouting, saying wild, hurtful things. "I tell you, Pierre," he said, "taking money for this land, any part of it, is the same as taking blood out of Leblanc veins! And all for a girl—a girl who hasn't lived long enough yet to appreciate the true values!"

"It's not for her alone, Pa. We could buy modern machinery and improve L'Acadie a great deal with that money. We could make the ten thousand acres earn much, much more than the twelve thousand acres earn now. Surely you see that."

"I can see that you've turned against me, your own father, against L'Acadie itself. If you agree to this preposterous suggestion, it will be over my dead body!"

"Can I have your answer now?" Mercer asked Pierre.

He shook his head. "I must think it through. When my father is calm, I want to discuss it item by item with him before coming to a decision."

"Twenty-four hours, then. I'll come back tomorrow with my pa. And with the cash."

He waited for someone to speak, and when no one did, he arrogantly left the room. He closed the door smartly.

The three Leblancs collapsed into chairs. Maebelle was no longer weeping, but trembling... praying... with anticipation and hope. If Pierre didn't take the Mercer offer, her life would be a shambles.

Voice quivering, she restated her case. "I won't be greedy. I swear it! I'll take whatever you give me and fix up all the houses and make L'Acadie like it used to be. And you'll buy scads of machinery, Pierre, and raise oodles more sugar cane! Why, we can even hold out some of the money and put it in the bank! Am I wrong, Pierre? Am I?"

René answered. Surprisingly, he agreed that every word Maebelle spoke was true. Regardless, they should not sell the land.

"Why not?" she wailed, bewildered. "If it's a solid move, why don't we make it?"

"Because," René told her, his face ashen now, "L'Acadie was granted to the first Leblanc who came here from Nova Scotia, homeless and penniless. Because he and every Leblanc after him has labored, really labored, to keep the plantation intact. We made it through the Civil War, through Reconstruction days. We can't give up now. We can't sell any part of our birthright no matter how it might benefit us."

"The benefit would be permanent," Pierre said.

"Promises. If Mercer gets some of our land now, he'll never give up trying to get more. The Mercer gang is like a pack of wolves getting their fangs into the throats of their prey. They'll nibble and eat, buying until they get all of L'Acadie. I regret that I signed it over to you, Pierre, so soon. If you were older, the importance of keeping it untouched would be engrained in you, and you'd never sell. You'd never so much as consider it."

Maebelle's tears spilled over. "You did right, Papa Leblanc, to sign L'Acadie over! Pierre will be sensible, you know he will! Think of me a little, think of my condition! I want to give L'Acadie a healthy heir, not a sickly one from all this quarreling! I mustn't be forced to mark my baby!"

"I'd be robbing my grandchild if I agreed to sell," René told her flatly. "Pierre, you know the hard times we had during this past war."

"That I do, and me gone trapping up the Missouri, leaving you with the load on your shoulders."

"I wanted you to go to make up for missing college. And you know how we work now to maintain L'Acadie."

"All true, Pa."

Maebelle's tears increased, running down her cheeks and onto her neck. "You can make your choice, Pierre Leblanc," she cried heartbrokenly. "Sell the land so we can prosper, or I'll go home to Daddy. I'll have my baby there and live on the *Maebelle*! I don't want to g-go, but if I do, you won't have an heir, either one of you, and that's a solemn vow!"

Pierre, wanting to be loyal to his father, frantic with love for Maebelle, mulling over what was best for the plantation, spent a sleepless night. Over and over, the facts ran through his head, and he became more and more miserable as the hours passed.

The Mercer men, father and son, arrived at eight the next evening. Pierre, with a wan Maebelle clinging to his arm, led them and a tight-lipped, pale René into the library. In total silence they all sat.

Silas junior wore the same tan suit. His father wore a black suit, impeccably brushed. Silas senior was taller than his son, but with the same coarse features. He sat grinning, his graying hair tousled, his heavy body planted in the chair. His sly intelligence was apparent in his fierce brown eyes. "Good morning, folks," he said tauntingly in a heavy, coarse voice.

Silas junior spoke next. "Pa'll be in charge of what we got to say," he announced.

Maebelle turned her eyes on the elder Mercer and waited, holding her breath. René stared straight ahead unblinkingly, his face slowly growing red. Pierre was expressionless.

"I figure," Mercer said at last, "my boy here done enough talkin' yesterday that you got it clear in your heads what the deal is." He turned his burning brown eyes on Pierre, asked harshly, "The answer's up to you, ain't it?"

Pierre, his mind as stony as his expression, nodded. He couldn't think, couldn't decide. He was on the sofa and felt Maebelle snuggle to him, holding his arm, her body swelling with child. He felt her soft, sweet breath on his cheek as she leaned close, felt the swift, loving brush of her lips. He dared not glance at his father.

"We'll sell the two thousand acres," he heard himself say to the Mercers in an absolutely toneless voice.

The Mercers stood, elated, their hands out, but Pierre ignored their hands. He disengaged himself from the quivering Maebelle and went to the big desk.

"I'll make out a bill of sale," he told the Mercers, "and give it to you after you pay me."

Mercer senior worked a wad of bank notes out of his pocket. "Twenty thousand dollars!" he chortled. "In fine new bills... count 'em!"

"I'll take your word for it," Pierre said, ignoring the money. He sat at the desk, picked up paper and pen, dipped the pen into the ink. He glanced at his pa.

René sat frozen, his face purple. He scarcely seemed to breathe.

Pierre wrote swiftly, blotted, handed the paper and pen to Mercer senior. Grinning hugely, Mercer added his signature.

"Count the money," Silas senior insisted, returning the pen, rolling up the bill of sale. "So's you'll know the Mercers deal fair and square."

Maebelle, trembling with relief and excitement, stared at the money as Pierre reluctantly counted it. Her heart kept fluttering; she felt the baby move and was overjoyed. Everything was going to be so wonderful now!

The money counted, the Mercers left.

"Pa," Pierre said, after he'd put the twenty thousand dollars into the library safe, "will you go to New Orleans with me to buy the machinery?"

René, ashen again, refused. "I'm keeping out of it, son. I trust your judgment. This deal today was against my every instinct, but at least now you're capable of buying machinery and running the plantation without my help."

Two mornings later, René died in his bed of a heart attack. Pierre immediately blamed himself and the sale of the land for his father's death.

Maebelle, her countenance stark white but tearless, thought she was the one responsible. "If I hadn't carried on so," she told Pierre, "if I hadn't got hysterical and threatened to go home to Daddy, you never would have sold the land! And if you hadn't sold, Papa René would be alive this minute!"

They buried René simply, putting his cypress tomb beside that of Ramona, his dead wife. Maebelle, her heart sore, wondered if René and Ramona were together now, and supposed not. For a murderess surely goes to hell, she reasoned, and a good man like Papa René goes to heaven.

Pierre delayed his trip to New Orleans because Maebelle, although she did not weep, still went about listlessly, blaming herself. At last he summoned the doctor, and with an uncaring Maebelle present, explained her self-censure and behavior.

"She blames herself for Pa's heart attack, because she urged me to sell the land," he concluded. "Was this the case, doctor? Would the sale of the land against my father's wishes have caused his death?"

"As I told you earlier," said the graying doctor, "René has been under treatment for a heart condition the past five years. He could have gone in his sleep after the most

peaceful day. The sale of the land may have hastened his
death, true, but even so, I don't think he would have lived
to have seen his first grandchild. Don't blame yourself, my
dear," he said kindly to Maebelle. "It's bad for you, bad
for the baby. René thought a lot of you, boasted about how
fine you are. Once he said you liked money, then laughed
and asked what beautiful young woman doesn't like money. Believe me, he'd be most unhappy for you to feel even
a scrap of guilt, now or ever."

After he left, Maebelle's tears broke, and she wept an
entire day and night. Just as Pierre threatened to call the
doctor again to give her something for weeping, she blew
her nose, washed her swollen face in cold water, and came
into his arms.

"I still love money," she confessed, "but now I know it
isn't the most important thing in the world. People are."
She paused. "How much did you say you deposited to my
account?"

"Five thousand dollars," he answered, and smiled. She'd
matured a bit, but she was still his same sweet, greedy
Maebelle. He determined anew to rebuild L'Acadie, to
wrest from it a fortune for her and for the child she
carried.

Soon she was selecting fabrics and wall coverings, ordering
a blue linen rug for the nursery, refurbishing all the
furniture in all the houses. L'Acadie began to bloom again,
and Maebelle bloomed with it, especially after Pierre
promised her a diamond pendant when the baby was
born.

PART II

1920–1960

XXI

Ben Rivard was happier than he had known it was possible to be. The baby was due soon. He and Pearl had worked out a way for making love despite her swollen body, and he felt her come fully alive in his arms every night.

"You're my treasure," he told her, kissing her cheeks, her nose, her brow, her lips, then lying back in joy to let her kiss him the same way. He murmured, "You're my love, my delight. Our baby will make us complete."

Strangely, a thought of Pierre Leblanc crossed his mind. Pierre had an heir, Gabriel, born November 15th, and rumor had it Pierre was exceedingly proud. And L'Acadie had begun to flourish after the sale of the land to the Mercers.

Ben hoped the Mercers were satisfied, that they'd not approach him again about buying Rivard. Pearl mentioned the fact that they hadn't come to Rivard since Ben got home.

"Do you think your being gone has calmed them down?" she asked.

"That, and the Leblancs selling them land."

"Why did they sell, Ben?"

"Wanted the money, I guess."

"Does that mean they'll forget about Rivard?"

"Hopefully. If they can get their hands on more L'Acadie land . . . nothing compares to that."

"Are the Mercers planting the land?"

"They're busy at it."

"Then they're too busy to bother you."

"And you, my darling."

"Why me?"

"They won't give Rivard more than a passing thought. They'll be too busy to gossip about my harboring a white woman. I hear they now claim I've taken a light-skinned wench and did or did not marry her, they don't care which. I'd say the edge of their anger is dulled."

Still, unknown to Ben at the moment, all the bayou elite were gossiping. "To think," exclaimed the ladies, "that the Leblancs of all people sold land to those carpetbaggers! It was bad enough that the Mercers got their filthy hands on two smaller plantations, but this! What is the world coming to?"

Pearl's labor began suddenly on a November afternoon with long, steady pains. The house was taken over by Bessie, Granny and the doctor. Ben tried to stand where he could see and not be in the way, but refused to leave the room, even when Granny tried to shoo him out.

Pearl endured the long, excruciating pains without a moan. She knew Ben was there, and she didn't want him to get the idea that the pains were his fault. They would end sometime, surely they would, and she'd have a baby that was part Ben, part herself. Now with pain upon pain riding her, she never even wondered if the baby would be black or if it would be white. All she wanted was to be rid of the agony, of this endless sweating. It would be so much easier to give in to the pain and let out her screams.

At last she heard Dr. Gordon say, "Here it comes!" and then he was shoving the newborn at Bessie, almost shouting, "There's another one . . . it's twins!" He caught the second baby deftly as it shot out, and Ben, stupefied, watched Bessie and Granny and the doctor work on the squalling infants.

Pearl felt Ben take her hand. Spent and nearly swooning, she couldn't see her babies, surrounded as they were by excited adults. She heard the doctor say, "Identical to the last toenail! You'll never be able to tell them apart! This one with the string around his wrist was born first."

"Ribbon . . . not string," Pearl murmured weakly. "Blue ribbon . . . nothing on the other."

Bessie and Granny diapered, then swaddled the twins in blankets, and laid them in the crook of Pearl's arm. She took her first look at her sons. They were mulatto color, and this was a shock, but they were handsome, and pride surged in her. She began to love them, so perfect and helpless.

"Names," she whispered. "The first one . . . Fred. The other . . . Floyd . . . for my little twin brothers."

Tears stood momentarily in her eyes. For the hundredth time she mourned that she'd never be able to see her mother again. How proud her mother would be.

Ben stopped, touched the string on Fred's tiny wrist. "Fred's the heir," he said. "He's first born and I think he should be the main heir. But Floyd's so close to being heir, we've got to raise them so there'll be no jealousy."

Unaware that Pearl yearned to have a white baby, one like herself, Ben was pleased with his children's color. In bed one night, he told Pearl this.

"It's a comfort to me," he added, "that although they'll be called colored, they can never rightfully be called tar baby."

"What are you talking about?" Pearl asked.

Only now did he tell her the story of his one drop of white blood, and his grandfather's obsession to breed the Rivards black. When he finished, Pearl was silent for a moment.

Then she said, "And now we've ruined his life's work."

"The work was misguided, my dearest. He tried to play

God. Our descendants must be free to marry as they choose because they all have black blood."

Pearl agreed with all he said because she wanted him to be content. But still she hoped to bear just one white baby. To have just one member of her new family like herself.

Maebelle bore Elizabeth, a tiny, red-haired replica of herself, one year after Gabriel and another son, Lee, wiry and active, a year after Elizabeth. At Lee's baptism Pierre declared that they had a large enough family; their task now was to educate them.

The Leblanc children attended school in St. Martinville. If there'd been enough money left from the twenty thousand, they would have gone to college in New Orleans, but they were instead tutored by Pierre. Even Elizabeth, beautiful and protesting, had to learn Latin and Greek.

Gabriel had been a leader in the St. Martinville school. Auburn-haired and handsome, he charmed them all. His two most devoted followers were his brother Lee, brown-haired and almost handsome, and Diana Foxe, with golden hair and delicate features. Orphaned, she lived with two elderly relatives.

On the fringes of the group was Francie Warner. She had very red hair and a temper to go with it. She also had pretty, piquant features and knew it, and a spiteful nature inherited from her grandmother, crazy Phrony Warner. She lived with Phrony and long ago had learned how to get her way with the old woman, no matter what she had to do. Her pa was a drayman. What he said didn't count, and besides, he was so afraid crazy Phrony'd go into one of her tantrums that he rarely spoke.

All the children knew about Francie's family, but they played with her because she was bright and quick and fun. And if they caught her cheating in their games, which was seldom, she would tease them out of their anger with a lie, and they would end up laughing with her.

Gabriel once asked Lee, "Why do you let Francie hang around you? You never know when she's going to get mad."

Lee fidgeted. "I dunno," he said. "You never choose her; you always choose Diana. Francie is fun, so what's the difference?"

"Diana plays fair."

"Francie plays fair if you watch her."

"Be nice to her, boys," Pierre advised. "She doesn't get much upbringing at home. She's to be pitied more than anything."

"Do you pity Diana because she has to stay at home and work?" Gabriel asked. "At least Francie gets out of the house, even if she has to sneak out. And she's never missed a party, if she was invited."

"Certainly I feel sorry for Diana," Pierre said. "And for her relatives, too, so old and crippled. They did a wonderful thing, taking Diana in at their age—they're eighty now, mind you! They need her help. She doesn't complain, does she?"

"Nope!" declared Gabriel. "She just says they're sick and need her."

At the age of fourteen, Diana was doing all the housework for the frail old couple and nursing them when they required it. They had a small income, enough to pay taxes, provide food and electricity, and buy an occasional dress for Diana. Sometimes they had to buy medicine, but they used even that sparingly.

"We should be doing for you, child, not you for us!" they said worriedly.

"Please don't worry," Diana pleaded. "Soon as I finish school, they'll hire me at the tobacco and magazine store, they've promised! And the first thing I'll buy is a second-hand radio so you can listen all you want!"

At school, she confided her plan to Gabriel.

"You'll get married," he predicted. He didn't like the idea, for this sweet blond girl had wound herself into his very being. And he had to get older and get the education Pa was set on.

She smiled. "I'll not marry. I'm staying with Richard and Tessie as long as they live. They took me in when I was little; I'll never let them down."

Diana made the mistake of telling Francie the same thing.

Francie sneered and scoffed. "Honestly! What a ninny you are! Planning to spend your money on those old harpies!"

"They're not harpies, and they've spent their money on me," Diana said coolly.

Lee flushed at her words. Maybe this was one reason Ma didn't want Francie to play at L'Acadie but did want Diana. He looked at Francie's pixie features and still couldn't dislike her. Maybe Francie was right. Diana should live her own life.

Francie looked sidewise at Gabriel. His handsome face showed he didn't like what he'd heard. She bit her lip and regretted her hasty words. She had set her cap for Gabriel, heir to L'Acadie, and marry up, way up. She'd get Pa to send crazy Phrony to New Orleans to live, and people here'd forget she had a crazy grandmother.

Her quick glance touched Lee's face. Perhaps she'd marry him. She'd still be marrying up; she'd still be a Leblanc. Even now she could get Lee to do almost anything she wanted, except cheat. She could hardly wait for school to end, for time to pass, for a chance to make her dreams come true.

*   *   *

In 1938, much to Francie's disappointment, Gabriel married Diana. Her old relatives had died within a month of each other. Gabriel and Diana moved into Old House to live.

Lee, crazy about Francie, courted her despite his family's reservations. Unable to get a job, Francie had stayed at home, fighting with her grandmother, listening to the new radio she'd begged from her and reading movie magazines. When she could get money from her pa, she went to the movies, sitting through the same picture two or three times. The talkies had come to St. Martinville, and she was entranced.

Lee also took her to the movies, but they would watch the movie one time, then get into his Ford car with a rumble seat that Maebelle had encouraged him to buy on time. They would drive around, then park and neck.

It was the necking that did it. Francie would let him go just so far, then make him stop. Finally he got to the point where he asked her to marry him; she instantly said yes, then set about getting her pa to send crazy Phrony clear away from the bayous. When that was accomplished, Francie and Lee eloped because she said it was the only way.

"Then your folks can't say a thing," she told him. "Or do a thing. I'll be a Leblanc they'll be proud of, wait and see," she promised. And he, beside himself with passion, gave in.

It was still 1938. And Francie had married up.

XXII

Guy Mercer, son of Silas junior, had been educated in New Orleans and had put on the airs of a gentleman. He'd also been trained by his father in how to trade on the stock market. He displayed a talent for it and garnered thousands and thousands more for the clan.

Of medium height, Guy tended toward his mother's stoutness. His hair and eyes were Mercer brown. He also had the Mercer selfishness and ambition, despite his gentlemanly airs.

Guy had decided it was time to buy more of L'Acadie, and his elders agreed. One morning, he put on a new white suit and drove to L'Acadie, parked his jaunty new car, and knocked at the front door of the main house.

He was shown to the library where Pierre and his sons, Gabriel and Lee, followed by an obviously excited Maebelle and her lovely daughter, Elizabeth, joined them. Maebelle had come to her maturity, Guy noted, and was obviously prettier now than years ago when she was a bride. Her hair was even more gloriously red.

"Sit down," Pierre said stiffly to Guy, who made himself comfortable in one of the big leather chairs.

"I'll come right to the point," Guy said, deliberately making his voice sound smooth and trustworthy. "As you know, we've grown outstanding crops of sugar cane on the land you sold us twenty years ago. You recall, of course, that we've tried since then to purchase more land from you."

"Then you recall," Pierre replied, "that we've consistently rejected your offers."

"Regardless, we're offering again. We're interested in the two thousand acres adjoining the original land we bought. At the same price of twenty thousand dollars."

"No sale," Pierre said flatly. He glanced at Gabriel, his heir. His strongly cut features were set in displeasure. Meeting Guy's eyes fiercely, Gabriel repeated his father's words. "No sale."

Pierre looked next at Lee, his younger son, who resembled Gabriel except that his hair was brown, and his eyes a paler blue and features a bit heavy. His expression was less certain although he, too, repeated, "No sale."

"Pierre, darling," Maebelle suggested, "why not? We'd still have eight thousand acres, and twenty thousand dollars is a lot of money, and we could use it!"

"This is L'Acadie, dear, and will remain so."

"But the houses—they've all grown shabby again! They haven't been refurbished since I was a bride! Please, Pierre, pretty please!"

Elizabeth murmured, "I'm with the boys, Mama. I like having lots of land."

Gabriel listened to his mother intently, then glanced at Lee, who shifted in his chair and looked troubled. Lee's mind roiled with the scene he'd just had with his bride Francie down at Honeymoon House.

"Don't you dare come back and tell me your pa says no if Guy's message is right and he wants to buy land!" she had screamed. She grew angrier, and her few freckles stood out on her white skin, and her piquant features sparkled. Lee thought he'd never seen her lovelier—or less lovable.

"Be reasonable, sweetheart," he said. "I can only try. Pa owns the land. And Gabriel . . . I know he's against selling. Elizabeth, too. She says L'Acadie's a kingdom."

"And Gabriel's the heir and his word carries law!" Francie spat. "Well, you have a tongue! Use it! Make them sell!"

"Pa's the one, Francie. He hasn't deeded L'Acadie over to Gabriel yet."

"But he listens to Gabriel! Make him listen to you! You'll be heir if anything happens to Gabriel before he has a son."

"I don't think we should sell either, Francie."

"And why not? What's a few acres? And we'll have some

money for a change! I declare, I never knew I'd be downright poor when I married a Leblanc!"

"We'll not stay poor, not if we keep our land. Our profit is growing steadily. Each year we make more."

"You'll be poor unless I keep after you! When money comes, you get our full share, hear? I don't want your ma lording it over me, or that ninny Diana, who thinks she's so important, married to the heir! She pretends to like that horrible, bittersweet Grape House wine just to impress everybody! Give me money . . . today! That's an order if you want me in bed! Or you can just suffer until I see fit to tend to your wants!"

Lee looked around the library again and saw the implacable looks on Gabriel's and his father's faces. He sighed. It would be useless to argue with them, even if he were so inclined.

Maebelle put her arm around Gabriel. "Please, son. Reason with your father. I've told you how that first twenty thousand helped, the marvelous things it accomplished. It even helped us plant scads more sugar cane. He'll listen to you, I know he will!"

"No, Mama. I'm sorry, but no."

"Isn't it important to you what your mama wants?" pleaded Maebelle, now on the verge of tears.

"It's very important, Mama. But there's Diana and the sons we're going to have. Not just one, but six. We need every inch of land."

Mercer spoke up. "I'll raise the offer—thirty thousand dollars."

Silence.

"Think of the machinery you could buy," Mercer said, looking at the men in turn. "The fields now unplanted you could get back under cultivation. Think of how you'd prosper."

The faces of the Leblanc men were expressionless.

Maebelle quivered visibly, then crossed to Pierre, her hands out.

"Yes, Pierre, my love . . . Gabriel!" breathed Maebelle. "Even I can see it, and I don't know much about planting. It could even get L'Acadie back to what it was in the beginning!"

"Less four thousand acres," Pierre said sternly.

"Right," Gabriel agreed.

"The answer, Mercer," Pierre said, "is still no."

"Well," Mercer said, "we're patient in our own way. We have already waited twenty years, and we aim to own all of L'Acadie in the end. We're willing to buy it piecemeal, two thousand acres at a time. Day'll come when we make you an offer you couldn't be in your right mind to turn down."

Now all three Leblanc men were on their feet, their faces set in anger. "The faster you can get out of here, Mercer," Pierre said, "the better we'll like it."

Mercer picked up his white panama. "Whatever you say. You want me to go now, I'll go. But I'll be back. Or my son will be."

The three Mercer men sat on the front gallery, drinking. Guy reported the outcome of his visit and grinned. Silas junior guffawed and so did Silas senior. Guy joined them, and they laughed on, sure of themselves.

"When we do get L'Acadie," Silas junior boasted, "we can get back to work on the Rivard scum. We get their five hundred acres and the twelve thousand at L'Acadie plus what we got now in our two plantations and what land our kin's got, we'll rule the roost! Us three Mercers'll be the biggest guns of the bayou country, all of it, not just the Teche!"

"That Maebelle, she can easy make the men change their mind," Guy said, laughing. "And if she doesn't, there's other ways."

They sat and talked and drank, anticipating their eventual victory. All they had to do was wait until the iron was hot and then strike.

"They'll have to give in. We'll just keep offering. We'll give them a good hard shove if needed. Our day'll come!"

XXIII

A week after Mercer's visit, Pierre handed Gabriel the deed to L'Acadie. Gabriel thanked his father profusely, then went directly to Old House with the deed. Diana was in their bedroom.

She took the deed into both her lovely hands as if it were a treasure. "How generous!" she exclaimed. "And how lucky I am to have your parents for my very own! Sometimes I feel my very blood is theirs, that they are my natural parents."

She unfolded the deed and read carefully. He gazed at her in utter content. She was so beautiful, so serene and kind he could hardly believe his good fortune to have married her.

She looked like a portrait in her short new dress, and he took new joy in her golden hair, brown eyes and delicate features, in hearing her soft murmurs as she read aloud. That voice never uttered an unkind word, not even in response to Francie's spitfire tongue. Diana's health was excellent, and in this Gabriel rejoiced also, for she could easily bear many sons and daughters.

When she finished reading, she gave the deed back to him with a glowing smile. "Darling," she murmured, "are you too busy now, this minute?"

"Too busy for what?"

She lowered her golden lashes coyly and lifted them.

"Hell, no," he said. "I'm never too busy to make a son!"

Hurriedly he undressed, then disrobed her slowly, garment by garment, revealing her slim, sweet form. At last, bursting with love and passion, he entered, and they moved together gloriously.

It fell to Lee's lot to tell Francie about the deed. She was looking unusually pretty and bright when he came in for supper. She was wearing his favorite dress, and the table was set as for a party. She flew into his arms and kissed him fiercely. Her anger at him and the family for not selling to the Mercers was in abeyance, and Lee stole an extra kiss before she escaped his arms.

"What's the occasion?" he asked. "Are we having a party?"

"We are—just you and me! And after that, we're going to try for a baby. I just know I can beat Diana!"

Suddenly nervous, forcing a smile, he sought the right words. "Even if we have a son before Gabriel does, Francie, it's still their son who will inherit."

"Oh, I know it's been that way! But maybe they'll never have a son. In that case, our son will be next in line! Think of that!"

"It'll be a miracle if it works out that way. You mustn't count on it. Then, if it does happen, you will get what you want, but if it doesn't, you won't be so disappointed."

She glared, her uncanny intuition flashing. "Something's happened, I know it! Diana's pregnant!"

"Nothing like that."

"What, then?"

He told her.

Her face hardened in anger. She no longer looked pretty. "So! Your pa's in an awful hurry, isn't he? But that

deed won't be worth anything at all if la-de-da Diana
doesn't have a son and I do!"

"How do you figure that? L'Acadie always goes to the
descendant of the eldest son."

"We'll change it! We'll say, 'Here's the first son born to
the Leblancs.' We'll force them to see that's only right."

"That would be cheating, Francie!"

"So, what's a little cheating, if we get our way? Let's eat
now, then go straight to bed. We'll do it every single night
until I'm pregnant! I'll never give up, Lee Leblanc, never!"

Bank failures and the depression had torn the country.
Money was scarce; all the Leblancs had had to chip in for
the payments on Lee's Ford, which was now the family's
main means of transportation. Money was handled with
extreme care; no one in the bayou country spent an
unnecessary penny. It seemed that everybody was poor.

Through it all, Francie and Lee strove to produce a son.
Gabriel and Diana had already started their family. Diana
glowed in pregnancy while Francie, barren as yet, simmered
and seethed with impatience, willing Diana's baby to be a
girl. And she was secretly delighted when Diana's child, a
boy, perfectly formed, was delivered stillborn in 1939.

Diana was grieved and wept without end. Gabriel longed
to bellow his own grief, to curse it out, tear his hair, to cry
like Diana and Maebelle and Elizabeth. But he could not.
He had to be tearless and strong for Diana, and he wanted
to comfort her tenderly, for she had borne the pain of
birth. And now her maternal agony was her bereaved
mother's right, and he gave his stalwart sympathy to her
unbegrudgingly with love.

Diana recovered quickly and wanted to try again for a
son. In 1940 she was delivered of a yet another stillborn
male child. The doctor said it was a malfunction of the
infant's heart. Once again, Gabriel crushed back his own

grief to comfort the desolate Diana, and thanked God he could be her mainstay and comfort.

She insisted immediately on trying again, and Gabriel could not sway her. She could bear a child; it simply didn't make sense that they'd lose any more babies. Even the doctor said that future infants stood a good chance of surviving.

Francie triumphantly bore a healthy, squalling son, William, in 1941 when Diana was carrying her third child. Diana sincerely rejoiced for William's arrival, and Francie privately crowed to Lee. "I told you we'd change things. William is the first son born in this generation. He'll be the next heir!"

XXIV

It was while the twins were still three and Babette Rivard was trying to walk, that the killer hurricane hit the bayou country. The Teche got only a sideswipe, with torrents of rain and little wind, but the storm hit squarely on the bayou where Pearl's ma and brothers lived, and dozens and dozens of people were killed.

Pearl, who still longed to see her ma and her brothers, was frantic. She hadn't even dared write Ma lest Pa find out where she was and make trouble. Trembling, she searched the papers from New Orleans, going down the list of those known killed, searching for the names of her loved ones, not finding them. It brought back memories of the war.

When the papers stopped printing the lists, Pearl wept even more. She almost wrote to former neighbors, but the ones she knew best had been listed among the dead. She appealed to Ben.

"You should think of them as alive," he told her sympathetically, "since their names aren't listed among the dead."

But she wept for them as if they were dead. She'd always think of them, always love them.

The Rivard twins were a happy pair so long as they didn't have to share anything. Ben learned that lesson when he came home one day with a red ball. He took the three-year-old twins outside and showed them how to play catch.

They learned fast, and the game progressed. But when Ben gave the ball to Floyd and told Floyd to throw the ball to his twin, the child's face lowered and he shook his head violently.

"Floyd's ball!" he screamed.

Fred instantly charged Floyd and wrested the ball away and hugged it to himself and fled to Pearl. "Fred's ball!" he shrieked.

Ben took the ball away from both of them and put it away, leaving them screaming and weeping. He tried again and again to get them to play together with the ball, but it wasn't until the second ball was purchased that they played. And so it went through their childhood. Pearl and Ben were helpless; the boys could not be taught to share.

It was when they became interested in girls that the situation between Fred and Floyd got worse. Invariably they were attracted to the same girl, and invariably the girl kept them both dangling because she couldn't make up her mind between them, they were so exactly alike.

This situation peaked over Andrea Douglas during the war. Andrea, an octoroon, had come to live with Granny and help look after the toddlers whose mothers worked in the fields.

Andrea was on Granny's porch crocheting when the twins crossed the Quarters. They saw her at the same time, stopped, stared. They saw that she was comely and delectably filled out. They gazed at her light brown, wavy hair, her light brown eyes, and her delicately slanted eyebrows.

She let them grin and make eyes and step around in the dust and stare, because she was so busy staring at them. She was entranced by their six-foot height, their husky build, their hair which curled in small black ringlets, their handsome features, and their bright skin. And, best of all, they were identical.

The way they consumed her with their eyes was arousing, and she liked the excitement. She began flirting back.

"You must be Andrea," one of them said.

"Our pa seen you?" demanded the other.

"N-not yet. You'd all gone to bed when I got here."

"Then that's why Pa didn't tell us you're a knockout," said the first twin. "He always warns us not to flirt with a looker and get in a fight over her, but it don't help. We do, just the same."

"We beat each other up regular," said the other one. "Pa warns, but we scrap when we need to."

"Who is your pa?"

"Ben Rivard."

"And he knows that we'll fight over you," said the first one.

She went suddenly wary. "Why should you fight about me? I'm my own person, and no one has ever fought over me. I wouldn't like that, not a bit."

"Because you're such a knockout," said the first twin. "Prettiest girl ever came to Rivard. If one of us wants you, then the other one'll want you, for certain, and we'll fight.

You've got no say in it. We'll flirt with you till we get tired of you or want more, then we'll fight."

Andrea looked frightened. "You scare me," she said. "Go away."

"Okay, but you'll see me tomorrow," said one. "I'm Fred. I'm the heir."

"I'm Floyd," snarled the other. "Got a right to be co-heir."

Suddenly Andrea laughed. They asked in unison what was so funny.

"You two are!" she giggled. "You're so different! Oh, not different from each other, but you're not like other men. You're cocky—act like you're used to having things your own way, both of you!"

From that day on, the twins flirted with her. They were always together when they saw her, always flirting and cutting up, but with moments of seriousness that frightened her.

After three months they came to her. She smiled at them, but the smile soon faded. They looked solemn, even fierce.

"Fred talking," said the first twin quietly. "Will you marry me?"

Before Andrea could answer, Floyd said, "I'm nuts about you. Will you marry me?"

Now that the moment she had feared was upon her, she could scarcely breathe. "I'll marry one of you," she said, her voice trembling, "but which one is the question. When you talk, Fred, you being heir and all, I think you're the one. But when you talk, Floyd, I think you're the one. I simply cannot make up my mind whether I love you best or Fred! You've got to give me more time. I can't be hurried."

For once the twins heeded what was said, but each was wildly determined to win Andrea, and though they treated each other in a surly manner, they did refrain from fighting. And they agreed that maybe a big dance in the Quarters would put Andrea into a gay mood, and she would make her choice. So they persuaded Pearl to give a dance, and each twin set about winning Andrea's promise before the evening was over.

Babette, now old enough to dance, teased them, saying she knew what they were plotting and she bet Andrea wouldn't have either one of them. They scowled.

Andrea's chum, Angelique, from a plantation down the bayou, arrived in a bright yellow dress. She was shapely, light-skinned, as pretty as Andrea, and had dimples.

"Wish I could snag that Floyd," she confided to Andrea before the dance. "I've wanted one of them twins since I was thirteen, but they never noticed me. They were always after some other girl, the same girl. Like now, with you!"

"We'll work it tonight!" cried Andrea. "We'll fix everything! Get one of them stuck on you, and I'll take the one that's left! Can't either one of us lose!"

"How'll we work it?" asked Angelique doubtfully.

"I won't dance with either twin unless the other one dances with you! And then we change partners! Back and forth, and you show your dimples and talk sweet and sassy to them! One of them's bound to fall, and then I'll promise to marry the other. The one that's stuck on you is bound to be yours, and then you and I'll be sisters, married to the twins that way!"

The Quarters filled with merrymakers from far and wide. Ben played piano and one of the men fiddled, and the dancers went to town. Andrea's plot seemed to be working. Both twins danced and flirted with Angelique, until at the end of one number, Fred refused to change partners and held onto Andrea.

"I'm going to marry her!" he yelled for all to hear.

Floyd gave Angelique a shove and went for Fred, landing a fist on his windpipe. Everybody closed in as Fred got
his balance and ran at Floyd, ramming his head into
Floyd's belly, and Floyd hit the dirt. Fred jumped on top
of him, and they rolled and pummeled and punched.

When several men moved to yank them apart, Ben
angrily motioned them back. "Let them fight it out!" he
roared. "It's been coming on all their lives! Let's get it
settled!"

When Pearl laid her hand pleadingly on Ben's arm, he
held her to his side. "They've got to have it out sometime,
honey," he hold her. She nodded sadly, and he realized
again how close he and Pearl had grown over the years.

"Nobody else," he went on, "can settle this but Andrea,
and it seems like she can't bring herself to do it."

Thus, the parents stood with all the party-goers and
watched the fight. Hating each other, the brothers bit,
kicked, slugged and tried to choke each other. At last they
lay exhausted, their bodies touching. Suddenly Floyd's
fingers found a sharp, fist-sized rock and he closed his
hand on it. Floyd gathered strength, struggled to his
knees, brought the sharp edge down on the forehead of his
twin, then dropped again, half-conscious.

Andrea went flying to the one with the injury. "This
one!" she cried. "He's bleeding, and for me! He took
punishment for me! He'll have a scar for life! This is the
one I'll marry!"

Pearl knew that Andrea was unaware which twin she
cradled in her arms, but Pearl knew. She'd always been
able to tell her sons apart from the peculiar jut of Fred's
chin.

Pearl knelt between her sons. Andrea was wiping blood
off Fred's forehead with her handkerchief. Floyd was
beginning to stir.

"You're going to marry Fred?" Pearl asked Andrea.

Andrea nodded vigorously. "And from now on, every-body will know who he is, the one with the scar—Andrea's man!"

XXV

After Andrea made her public choice of husband, Floyd at first grew sullen but managed, with great effort, to deport himself acceptably. This was interspersed with fist fights between the brothers, all instigated by Floyd who resented the loss of the girl he wanted and brooded about Fred's being the main heir.

Inside, he was torn by jealousy and envy. Finally he decided to court Andrea so ardently she'd change her mind and he stopped provoking fights with his twin. At last, seeing Andrea's happy tenderness toward his brother and her courteous but reserved attitude toward himself, he dropped his plans. Andrea was going to marry Fred, and he couldn't stop it.

At the wedding, Floyd kissed the bride on the cheek and called her sister. Then he gripped Fred's hand, but let it drop as fast as he could decently do so.

Fred, overcome by the wonder of having Andrea for wife and this friendliness from his twin, threw his arms around Floyd, and they embraced. In that hard clasp, they came together again as an entity. It seemed to Floyd that the eating at his heart had vanished. What mattered was that his twin was happy.

Floyd touched Andrea on the arm. "I was a fool," he murmured. "What can I do to make up for it?"

Andrea, quivering with joy, smiled at him. "I can't stay mad at you, Floyd. It'd be like being mad at Fred. Get your mind on Angelique . . . marry her. She's gold, and one of the prettiest girls on all the bayous."

"Look at you, match-making!" grinned Floyd. But his heart gave a twist because she was so anxious to hand him over to another girl. He knew then that he'd never marry.

As the months passed, Floyd did dance with Angelique at parties, but he danced with other girls as much, even with the smiling, reserved Andrea. For despite the fact that his sister-in-law treated him in a friendly manner, it was plain that it was Fred she adored. And each time he saw Andrea in Fred's arms he'd feel his face settle into hard lines.

"Floyd's still crazy about you," Fred said.

Andrea treated it lightly. "He's my brother-in-law now. I hope he does like me, so he'll be real close to you again."

"I mean he's crazy in love with you."

"If he is, he keeps it to himself."

"It's in his eyes. Remember, I can read him like a book."

A year passed. Both Floyd and Fred were granted deferments as farm workers and somehow the war didn't seem to touch the plantation. A few of the young men went off to war, but the horror stories coming out of Europe had little effect on their day-to-day life. Although they all had ration coupons, there was always enough to eat. They grew their own fruits and vegetables, and when meat was hard to come by, the men went out hunting.

One night, when the twins and the other men were again hunting, Andrea was taken by a desire for making love early in the evening. She waited impatiently for Fred to get home, bathed, put on a clean gown and got into bed. To her joy she heard Fred come in early, quietly, so as not to disturb her.

"Don't turn the light on, honey," she called. "Just undress fast. Or are you too tired?"

He chuckled, and she thrilled. Fred was never too tired. Now he was on the bed, entering her, and they moved as to music. He seemed as hungry for her as he'd been on their wedding night, and she responded with more fervor than she'd known how to show at that time. When it ended, she held him. He moved to leave the bed, and she sought to kiss the scar on his forehead, but it wasn't there.

She shot up in bed.

"Floyd!" she gasped, stricken.

"See?" he exulted. "I'm as good as Fred . . . better! What you going to do now? Far as I'm concerned, you got two husbands for your whole life!"

She began to tremble violently. "Where's Fred? What did you do to him?"

"I didn't lay a finger on him. He's huntin'."

"He'll kill you!"

"Not if you don't tell him. He won't ever know. All our lives you'll have two husbands. And you'll love them both."

"You mean," she whispered, horrified, "you want to share me with Fred, that for the first time in your life you'll share with him?"

"Only way around it. All you got to do is—"

"All she's got to do is what?" asked Fred's voice from the darkness.

At first they froze. Then Fred turned on the light. He saw the mussed bed, saw Floyd naked and Andrea naked, smelled the recent lovemaking. His flesh crawled.

He stood, his rage a great fire in his belly, a fire which spread and spread. Floyd had raped Andrea. His head pounded with the rage.

Suddenly he lunged at Floyd; it was all but impossible

to get a hold on that naked, sweaty, slick body. Fred dug his fingers in at the collarbone, at the neck, at the same time driving his knee into Floyd's groin. Floyd dropped, doubled over, and Fred stood over him, ignoring Andrea's screams, waiting for his twin to stir.

"Get up!" he spat out. "Get up so I can kill you!"

Floyd pushed to his knees; Fred kicked him in the groin again. The downed man rolled in agony.

Andrea screamed, and as Floyd staggered up, fists ready, she ran between them, still screaming, and the impact of their bodies crushed her breath away. She fell back a step, gasping for breath.

The house was filling with half-dressed Rivard folk; in seconds they crowded the four-room cabin. Ben and Pearl and Babette were there, and the girl rushed to her slugging brothers, screaming for them to stop fighting and behave. Rivard people moved to separate the fighting twins.

Like a flash, Ben lifted a hand to warn them off, then himself leapt forward, pushed Babette away, and flung Andrea toward the onlookers, who caught and steadied her, holding her back from the fray.

Andrea wept, screamed. "They went hunting . . . Floyd sneaked in . . . I thought he was Fred . . ."

The Rivard men again jumped in, trying to pull the twins apart. But Ben roared, "Leave them be! It's Fred's right! Stand back! Keep out of their way!"

The people backed away, shocked and silent as they realized what had happened.

When Fred got his hands on Floyd's neck and began to squeeze his twin's windpipe, Pearl ran to separate them. But she couldn't force herself between them, and the Rivard men took hold of her and pulled her away. She cried out, "They've got to be stopped! You stop them!" but they only held her the tighter.

"Fred's got to battle it out!" Ben shouted. "Floyd violated his wife."

The twins were hugging each other now, staggering about, neither able to get in a blow. Their heavy breathing filled the room. Pearl, heart-stricken, let Ben hold her. A sick realization that Fred was entitled to revenge filled her, but she prayed, "Please, God, let them both come out of it whole!"

A moment later, Floyd, his eyes bugging from the pressure of Fred's hands on his windpipe, his loins aching, managed a mighty twist of his body and at the same time punched Fred in the kidney. He was free; he moved away to keep distance between them.

They both danced about. Suddenly in a lightning move, Floyd dived for Fred, ramming his head into Fred's belly. But a mighty blow from Fred glanced off Floyd's neck, and Floyd fell back against the solid wall of onlookers.

They came together again with such force they both hit the floor, where they rolled and gouged and bit, and each sought the other's vulnerable windpipe. Fred got his teeth into Floyd's throat, and Floyd dug his thumbs into Fred's eyes.

They tore free from each other and staggered up, exchanged blows, staggered through the doorway, through the opening the people made for them, and into the kitchen. They traded rocking blows, their panting ripping the silence. Finally they grabbed knives, polished and razor sharp, from where Andrea kept them on a shelf. They circled, unsteady and fatigued, knives up.

Fred lunged first, his blade just missing Floyd's shoulder. He drew back, dancing and ready, but Floyd, quicker, darted in and drove his knife into his brother's heart. Fred plummeted to the floor, breathed once, and died.

With a roar of anguish, Floyd threw himself upon his knees beside Fred's body. "I didn't mean this, oh, God, I didn't mean it!" he bellowed, tears streaming. "I want you back, Fred. I want my twin back! I want to undo everything!"

XXVI

Someone had put a robe on the shaking, stricken Andrea. Ben went to Floyd, lifted him to his feet, and they stood together. Pearl and Babette knelt beside Fred. Babette wept; Pearl's face was blank. They could hear Floyd's gulping sobs. The people were sobbing, too.

Slowly Andrea knelt beside Fred and kissed the scar she would never kiss again.

Babette sobbed in Pearl's arms, and Pearl, dry-eyed, knew that the world had opened under her own feet and dropped away. Her firstborn, her adored Fred, lay lifeless, lost forever, while her other son, the one who had killed, lived and breathed and needed her.

Ben, gripping Floyd, felt him quiver even as he himself was quivering.

"Floyd," he said, for all to hear. "The law must come."

"No!" Pearl cried, leaving Babette and flying to her naked, living son. "No law! He must get away!"

Hands thrust some of Fred's clothes at Floyd, and he began to put them on. "You're to run, Floyd!" Pearl cried. "No, Ben, I won't do it your way, not this time! He's got to have his chance! I can't have two dead sons!"

Ben paused. "He'll have his chance. I'll wait an hour. Somebody fill the gas tank and crank up; Floyd can leave the car in New Orleans."

In minutes Floyd was ready. He packed a roll of extra clothes and a good supply of food, took what money those

present could dig up. He had the old car and his mother's
kiss on his lips.

"Go straight to New Orleans!" Pearl urged. "Get a berth
on a ship . . . working! Spend your life on the other side of
the world from here, and never risk sending us a letter!"

Floyd was near New Orleans when the right rear tire
blew out. There was nothing to do but leave the car and
take to his heels, but not along the road; he'd have to use
the bayous. He took his bundles and entered that bayou
world that he knew so well.

He was running, slogging, walking, running again, when
he heard the dogs. They were far off, their barks and cries
a fearful threat. They'd be in a car, let out at intervals to
hunt for scent. He began to run for longer periods.

Grady Miller and his men, Bullwhip and Nastor, set
out right after Ben Rivard had phoned the law. He
grinned wickedly at the eagerness of his hounds; their
moment would come. Their noses would catch that killer
nigger, and Grady would be paid cash for bringing him
in.

In no time, it seemed, they found the Ford. "Look at
that blowed-out tire. The nigger's scent's on this Ford for
sure." Grady let the hounds out of his pickup, and they
went crazy. He let the dogs smell and snuffle, and then
straining at the leashes, they headed for the swamps.

"Bad luck he took to the swamps," Grady said. "He's
been raised in 'em, knows all the tricks. If we ain't keerful,
some real old trick'll fool us, and we'll have to chase him
clear to New Orleens."

The hounds found where the trail went into the water,
and the posse, leaving their cars, followed the bayou as it
wound toward New Orleans. The dogs pulled them hither
and yon, sniffing both sides of the bayou, hunting nigger

spoor, not finding it. And the men slapped at mosquitoes and sweated and cursed every nigger ever born.

By dawn, they were sure that the nigger was still in the water. "He'll set on the bayou bed and breathe through a reed that looks like all the other reeds," grumbled Grady. "Oldest trick in the world! But we ain't goin' to let him git away with it!"

Behind them, Floyd surfaced very slowly, without sound. He had to leave the water before they backtracked. He dug into the mud, buried his sodden bundles, covering them with mud and rocks.

Dripping, he climbed ashore and began to run toward New Orleans. When he came to a side road which would take him into a city street, he ran faster.

By the time his pursuers reached the outskirts of the city, Floyd was at the waterfront. While they were picking up his scent, he was signing on as crewman for a not-too-particular captain in need of another deckhand. By the time Grady and his men had hit the docks, Floyd's ship was sailing briskly down the pass toward the ocean, bound for China.

XXVII

In St. Martinville, townsmen who met on the street and Teche elite entertaining callers spoke of the murder at Rivard. "Cain and Abel all over again," one man said, summing it up, and all agreed. "Floyd Rivard deserves death," they added, "but they'll never catch him. He's on the other side of the world by now, got clean away."

At Rivard, Angelique was the only one that Andrea, the

widow, would let stay with her. Andrea just sat and stared, empty-eyed.

"Cry, honey," Angelique urged. "Ease yourself."

"I can't cry, can't take in what's happened. One day, I'm so happy with Fred, and he goes hunting. But when he comes back, he isn't Fred at all." She threw her hands apart. "Just like that, just that quick. One minute a bride, the next a widow. It can't be real."

"It is real, honey. Think how Fred will never hold you again. That ought to help you cry."

"He'll never come in from the fields again either, asking, 'What's for supper?'" She'd never wash his clothes again, never laugh when he teased, never kiss that scar again. The tears finally burst forth at that and flowed for days, bitterly, steadily, helplessly, and they cleansed her of the first awful grief.

At the funeral Ben stood with his arm around Pearl as the pine box was set on its cypress base and the cypress casket was fitted over it. As tears slipped endlessly down his cheeks, he held Pearl more closely, seeking to ease her terrible rigidity.

She stared at the tomb, heard the chanting singers, listened to the preacher, sensed all Rivard gathered close. Grief ripped her inwardly. She gazed at the weeping Andrea and yearned for tears of her own. She looked into herself, seeking tears, but found instead a great, consuming, festering wound—ugly, repulsive, rooted in to stay. She dared not look at her agony again; it was the only way. Both her sons were lost and could never be restored to her.

Andrea returned to her regular work in the gardens. Daytimes she held back the tears. At night they ripped and tore, weakening her.

"You can't keep cryin' ev'ry night, honey pie," Angelique

begged her. "Life goes on. Please, let's go see Lola tonight, find out what boy she likes best now—her so fickle."

"It'd only remind me."

"It'll remind you, sure, but also show you that other people court and marry. Now—hold in—let me say it. Young as you are, you're bound to marry again, even have babies!"

"Fred was so young. It isn't fair."

"Nothing's fair, honey. You'll find another good man, that's a promise."

"Angelique! How could you think such a thing . . . and twice?"

"Because it's the truth, girl, and you've got to face it. Your crying was good, but it needs to end now. Don't forget, I was crazy about both those twins, and I've done some crying myself, but it's over for me, and it's got to end for you."

Andrea recognized the painful truth of what her friend had said. They did spend the evening with Lola, who was so excited about a new man that Andrea not only kept from tears, but even smiled once. And that night she wouldn't permit herself to weep, and she was strangely comforted.

In the morning she threw up her breakfast. And the next morning and the next. It was Angelique who put this condition into words.

"You're pregnant, honey!"

Andrea's heart skipped a beat. Fred was in his tomb, and she was going to bear his child! Suddenly, the awful possibility struck—would it be Fred's child? Floyd had bedded her long and vigorously; his seed had flooded her.

She could barely put her fear into words.

"Oh, piffle!" Angelique sniffed. "You slept with Fred ev'ry single night, didn't you?"

"Yes."

"So! The one time with Floyd doesn't count!"

"It fits the time . . . six weeks."

"Get that out of your head, Andrea Rivard! You're going to have Fred's baby, and he's going to be the heir to Rivard! Hold your head high."

Andrea came to feel that Angelique was probably right. She smiled when she accepted congratulations from the women of Rivard and from Pearl and Ben. And she smiled when Angelique married the new man, Ches Jones.

When Andrea's time came, she gave birth to Camille, a beautiful baby who looked as though she'd been dipped in honey. Camille resembled neither Fred nor Floyd, but bore a likeness to her loving, wondering mother.

XXVIII

Pearl was ironing in the kitchen of the big house, and Babette sat with her, carefully polishing her fingernails a shade of light rose. Each was deep in her own thoughts. Pearl was thinking about Floyd. Where was he? What was he doing? She both longed for a letter from him, yet feared the law might somehow catch him if he wrote. Her thoughts moved sadly to Fred, sleeping in the ground. And she longed to know whether her ma and brothers lived or not.

She sighed, glanced at Babette, and her heart lifted. Babette had become a healthy, glowing beauty. Pearl loved the girl with her eyes, was grateful to have her alive and well, was content that her daughter didn't have her own white skin. Because Babette was perfect.

Only two inches over five feet, she was slim and shapely, her hair grew in big, loose black curls, and her eyes were so dark they were almost black. Her features were even and lovely with a delicate nose like Pearl's own, and her lips were curved and dark red.

Pearl sensed the return of an uneasiness she'd felt lately between herself and Babette. "Babette . . ." she said, turning down the radio.

The girl stared down at her fingernails, looking confused. "Yes, Mama?" she responded in a half-whisper.

"I . . . you've always come to me with any problem, however small, dear. You wouldn't just . . . stop . . . would you? Because no problem is so big you can't share it with your mother."

Babette's great eyes filled with tears. "I've just been getting up my courage, Mama," she said in her rich voice. "How did you know there was . . . something?"

"I know you, my Babette, know every sweep of those long lashes. When there's hesitation and not much smiling, there's something troubling you. It's always been that way, and you've always talked, but this time it's been a while. Aren't you ready to talk, sweetheart? I'm here for you; I'm on your side, no matter what."

Tears suddenly covered Babette's cheeks, and she got up and came straight to Pearl, who set the hot electric iron on its end and held out her arms.

Babette sobbed out her story, words spilling from her, tumbling over one another.

"It started three months ago," she said. "I was going to take some sweet corn to the Mabry plantation, and when I came through that grove of oak, I saw this red-haired man—a white man, Mama—and he was so handsome I held my breath. He walked toward me and I nodded. I would have gone on, but he stopped me."

Pearl stiffened. "He didn't lay hands on you?"

"N-not then. He stopped me with his voice, told me to

stand so he could look at me, and I . . . did. We were both
surprised, meeting unexpectedly that way, and he just
stood and stared at me and me at him. He's so tall and
slim, and his skin, with that red hair, is very white and
freckled a little, though not enough to take from his looks,
because he's so awfully handsome.

"While we were still staring, he said, 'Well, hello there.
I do hope I'm not trespassing. I've been in these parts
only a few days and thought I'd explore, it being a
Saturday and my not having to work.'

"I told him he wasn't trespassing, and then I smiled at
him. I couldn't help it, Mama. He looked so worried that
he'd done something wrong. He smiled back, and I asked
what Saturday had to do with his working.

" 'No school,' he said. 'I'm the new schoolteacher in St.
Martinville. My name's Paul Baxter.' He held out both his
hands to me, and I let him take my hands, sweet corn and
all. His hands were warm and I could feel a pulse in them,
I really could."

"Go on, sweetheart, get it all out." Pearl said. Her heart
set up a tremendous ache that wouldn't stop.

"I told him my name was Babette Rivard, and he
squeezed my hands, and that sent prickles up my arms
and down my back. Prickles inside, too, all through me.
Then for some reason I told him about you, Mama. 'My
mother,' I said, 'is white as you are. They talk about it in
town, because my father is black as coal.'

"Paul said he'd already heard the story. But he hadn't
heard about the real you—how beautiful you are, or how
well-spoken and filled with love."

"What then?" Pearl asked on indrawn breath. Babette
was nearing the important part, the dangerous part, and
Pearl wasn't ready to hear it, to cope with the knowledge
of what it was to be.

"Paul's eyes . . . they turned bold, and that scared me,

but I liked it, too. He asked me if I had a beau. I shook my head no. 'Well, you have one now.' He whispered to me, Mama, and all the strength went out of me, and he pulled me into his arms and put his lips on mine. And there were prickles everywhere, all inside even, and I couldn't get rid of them. He kept kissing me, and I couldn't stop kissing back, and when he begged me . . . I let him. And I promised to meet him there the next Saturday."

"But you didn't meet him," Pearl pleaded, "not after what he did, after—"

"I met him, Mama. I couldn't help myself. He's so . . . no girl could refuse. 'I love you,' that's what he told me that next time. 'I've found you, and you're never going to get away from me!' And I let him . . . like before . . . and it was better, Mama, truly it was!"

"What kind of plans did he have for you?" Pearl asked, trying to keep her voice calm.

"He was working on them, Mama, he really was! He said so, and I believed him. I still do! He said if worse came to worst, we'd go to Havana, and he'd marry me and teach English to the Cubans. We'd have a little house with a tiled patio, and I'd have a girl to scrub the place down every day because the floors and the walls are tile and they sparkle when they're washed!"

"You believed that, darling? You kept meeting him?"

"Yes, Mama."

"And you let him make love to you?"

"Yes, Mama."

"How . . . many times?"

"Every week for three months." She spoke in a whisper. "Oh, Mama, I knew it was wrong, but he was going to marry me, and I was so happy!"

"He wanted it kept secret from Ben and me?"

"Y-yes, Mama. And I was ashamed of that part, but it seemed I couldn't help myself!"

"And now?" Pearl asked, heartsick, as she held her sobbing daughter.

"A b-baby." The words were wrenched and almost indistinguishable. "And Paul doesn't have the money to take me to Havana and can't get it. He can't do anything about it, can't help me. He can't even see me again because he's white and he's the schoolmaster and has his reputation. He loves me, he really does, but he's helpless to do anything about the baby. Or me. Oh, Mama, what can I do?"

Pearl held her daughter even closer, ran her fingers through the big curls, kissed the forehead. "You can stay right here with your mama and papa, darling. Your baby can stay. We'll be proud of him, love him because he's a part of us. And one day, after your heartbreak is over—"

"I love him, Mama, love Paul! I'll never love another man, ever!"

"I know, sweetheart. But one day there'll be a young man for you, and you'll marry, and all this unhappiness will be forogtten. I promise you that, promise for me and for Papa—after he realizes he can't do anything about this, not to a white man, after he calms down."

"He won't kill Paul?"

"Of course not. Ben's not a killer. He'll help build your life, as I will. Trust me, darling, no matter how you hurt. In the end, things will be all right."

Babette took on new beauty in pregnancy though it was a solemn beauty, for she rarely smiled. She clung to her parents, especially Pearl, who managed to get her interested in making baby clothes. The people at Rivard helped.

"He'll be a Rivard and one of the rest of us, too!"

declared Christa, Pearl's dear friend, long since married
and the mother of three.

Gradually, because she was surrounded and cushioned
with love, Babette drew out of her first despair, smiled
more often, and helped Ben polish the cradle he'd built
for his first grandchild. "If he's a boy," he told her one day,
"he'll be heir to Rivard. He'll be a very important little
guy."

One day a stocky, muscular octoroon man of twenty-
seven appeared at Rivard and asked to speak to the
master. He had rough, curly black hair and an arrogant tilt
to his head.

He and Ben sat and talked on the edge of the back
gallery, legs dangling. "I'm Clarence Rogers," the young
man said. "I heard in town you're in need of a blacksmith
who can also repair cars and machinery."

"That I am," Ben admitted, slightly annoyed at the
man's cocky manner.

"I want that job," Clarence said boldly.

"What experience do you have?"

"Two years smithing, one fixing automobile motors, one
fixing farm machinery. Before that I was a dockhand. I've
got the strength—you can see for yourself." He jumped to
the ground and stripped off his shirt.

Ben approved of the iron muscles so blatantly displayed.
"You'll get a cabin and garden produce, and a ration of
milk," he said. "And you can keep chickens and hunt and
fish within reason. When we sell the sugar cane, you will
share equally in the profit with all the rest of us."

"But no steady cash?"

"Steady once a year, after harvest."

"I'd get an equal share, not working the fields?"

"Naturally. You'll earn it smithing and repairing."

Clarence scowled, pulling his shirt back on. Finally he

accepted the terms. "But I'll expect more in time to come," he warned. "I'll prove myself to you, make tools you can sell, bring in more cash. You need such a man, and I'm the one."

Ben nodded. All he hoped was that the new man do well what he was hired for.

The second day he spent at the forge, Clarence saw Babette walk past, noted how her slender, provocative body was rounding out with child, and wished he could have seen her before the other guy did. When she was no longer in sight, he said to his helper, "That's a damn pretty girl."

"She the mastah's daughtah," said the helper. "She was done dirty by a white man, a schoolmastah in town. Evahbody at Rivard treats her like a lady 'cause she is a lady, jes like her white mothah."

"Her mother's white, her father's black?"

"That's right. They bin same as married for yeahs. Lost two growed sons. Babette's all they got left, her and the suckah she's carryin'."

Already Clarence's mind was abuzz with this startling information. The girl needed a father for her baby. She was a beauty, and the road to court her was wide open. Married to her, Clarence would be son-in-law of the owner. Overnight, he'd become a man of substance. He hammered at the hoe he was shaping, determined that it be perfect, as would his courtship.

He started courting her the next day. He spied the girl on the back gallery of the big house, shelling peas. Holding his swagger down a bit, he strode directly toward her, stopped at the steps, and identified himself.

She nodded, murmured that she already knew about him from her father. He grinned suddenly, came up the steps uninvited and sat on the floor at her feet.

"You," he told her, "are the most beautiful girl I ever saw."

She smiled sadly. "You say that to all the girls."

"To some, sure. But I don't say they're the sweetest looking I ever saw. And you are."

She indicated her stomach. "You've heard of this."

"So? What's the difference?"

"Maybe it's changed me."

"Nope. A lot of folks here have told me you're sweet, always have been."

She smiled again. "Why have you been discussing me?"

"Because I like your looks." Boldly he reached up and touched her stomach, barely touched it. "Even with this. And maybe partly because of it."

"You don't think I'm . . . bad?"

"I think you're wonderful. I like a girl with spirit. Why, I'd be struttin' all over the place if you'd let me kiss your hand."

Smiling more easily now, Babette declined and he left, warning her that she hadn't seen the last of him. Which, indeed, she had not. He pursued her daily, showered her with compliments which were surprisingly sincere. He found himself wanting her for his own, inheritance or no inheritance. On her part, she admired his strength, enjoyed his lavish talk, and took pride in his outspoken desire for her company.

Within a month he was kissing her, and she was kissing him back. Paul Baxter was forgotten. After a week of kissing, he begged her to marry him.

Babette was happy in Clarence's arms. She appreciated the fact that he never tried to bed her, and yet she grew anxious to take this opportunity to marry before her baby was born.

"You'd be taking a white man's child to raise," she warned. "I won't give it up."

"Of course not," Clarence assured her. "It'll be our child, not just yours. And we'll have other children to keep it company."

And other children to inherit Rivard, he thought. An illegitimate baby would never be made heir; he'd see to that.

Ben and Pearl weren't enthusiastic about the proposed marriage. "Wait, sweetheart," Pearl begged Babette, "until the baby's born. Clarence may feel now that he's willing to be father, but when he actually sees the baby, his feelings may change, and your marriage would be unhappy."

"Even ruined," Ben agreed. "Because your baby, if it's a boy, will be heir to Rivard. My hunch is that in time Clarence will be of the opinion that a son of his should inherit."

Babette, disturbed, asked Clarence. Alarmed for his own future, he replied that the baby she now carried would be heir, but secretly he determined to get around that when the time came.

Eventually Ben and Pearl gave in. Clarence had proved to be an excellent worker, and they had heard him profess and swear to full cooperation about the baby. So, prodded by Babette's almost hysterical pleas, the two were married in the plantation church.

Thus the child was born legally. Benjy Rivard Rogers was almost white, liberally freckled, his hair straight and nearly red. And mentally retarded. When he realized that part, Clarence deemed his problem solved; no backward kid could learn to run Rivard, ever. The inheritance was in the bag for his own future son.

Ben and Pearl adored Benjy, loved him doubly because of his dull, sweet mind. Pearl held him tenderly, for Benjy was the white, or almost white, member of her new family for whom she had yearned so many years. She felt close to him and adored every move he made.

*   *   *

In 1942, when Benjy was a year old, Babette bore
Clarence a dark son whom she named Curtis. Curtis had
big black eyes, loose curls like Babette; he was squarely
built and promised to be muscular like Clarence. Curtis
had pleasant, good features, resembling Pearl somewhat,
and Pearl loved him almost as tenderly as she did Benjy.

Curtis was very bright; he talked at nine months and
enchanted everyone. But even so, Benjy remained Pearl's
favorite, and it maddened her to see Clarence's fierce
devotion to Curtis and the way he now neglected Benjy.

Clarence did indeed love Curtis fiercely. He was strutting proud of him. He thought the baby boy should
eventually own all of Rivard. In fact, Clarence was certain
the only thing Ben could possibly do was let Curtis take
the name Rivard and be heir since Benjy was incapable of
ever running the plantation.

"I been thinking," he told Ben one day. "With Fred and
Floyd out of the picture, you ain't got a son to leave Rivard
to. Fred's baby's a girl, so she can't take over."

"She can if I want. Babette can, for that matter. She's
my daughter; Camille's just my granddaughter."

"But you have been giving the problem some thinking?"

"And talked it over with Pearl."

"There's another way, 'case you ain't thought of it."

"What's that?"

"I could take the name Rivard. Run things for Curtis."

"You mean, make Curtis heir?"

"It's the natural thing."

"Maybe. But with you in the picture—you might be
tempted to sell to the Mercers. Influence Curtis."

"Why'd I do that?"

"Money . . . profit. They'd up the price to where you'd

figure it could be divided to give every Rivard a good sum."

"What's wrong with that?"

"Rivard stays Rivard."

Exasperated, Clarence demanded, "What do you figure on?"

"I will remain master of Rivard until age changes things. When Curtis is twenty, I plan for Rivard to go to him. He'll be fully trained. He already likes the soil, digs in it when he plays."

"The other one digs, too."

"Benjy." Ben paused. "It's tragic that he's retarded. But he'll grow into a good worker under supervision and get his share of the profit like everybody else."

Temporarily defeated, Clarence turned away. His only consolation was that he was father of the heir. And he, too, would do some intensive training; Curtis would think as his father wanted him to think. Let Ben Rivard cope with that.

Soon Clarence began his training. "Why you playing with that dummy Benjy?" he asked Curtis.

"He can dig a bigger hole than I can. Why is that?"

"His hands are bigger is all. He's only a dummy. And you're the heir."

"What's that mean?"

"Rivard is yours. All of it."

Far too young to comprehend, Curtis asked, "Can I dig holes?"

"You can do anything you want, son. I'll learn you that."

The next morning Clarence drove the Rivard's old Ford to Guy Mercer's plantation. Guy wasn't cordial.

"What do you want?" he demanded. "We invite only whites here."

"I got information," Clarence said cockily. He wasn't

going to let this white trash scare him. "You'll be interested in it."

"Spit it out, then."

Clarence looked at the plantation house set on a grassy
rise, looked out over tidy fields. "You folks bought L'Acadie
land," he remarked.

"So what?"

"So, my boy Curtis ain't but a baby now, see. But I'm
trainin' him to do what I say. He's heir to Rivard. And I
understand you tried to buy Rivard, but Ben wouldn't
sell."

A grunt, a sharp look. "Go on."

"You folks being neighbors to Rivard, your L'Acadie land
touching ours, it's best nothing gets stirred up right now.
Let both places build, raise good crops. I know you folks
are patient, see, so when my boy gets Rivard, him and
me'll talk price with you."

Another grunt. Guy and Clarence had come to an
understanding. Rivard would eventually be on the market,
and the Mercers would buy.

Clarence drove homeward, a new idea developing in his
mind. "Benjy ain't to eat at the table with us any more,"
he announced to Babette that night.

She was stunned. "Why not?"

"He's a bastard, he's too light-skinned, and he ain't got a
brain. I ain't having his dullness rub off on Curtis."

"But you said . . . before we were married . . . !"

"Things are different now. Curtis is the heir."

"But Curtis loves Benjy! He seems to know that Benjy
is . . . different! He tries to take care of Benjy and both of
them babies yet! And they are brothers!"

"I won't be mean to him Babette. The boys can play
together. He just ain't to eat with us. He drools. Curtis has
got to be treated like the heir, treated better than anybody

else on the place. Looks like you could see that for
yourself."

Babette flared. "By rights, Benjy—"

"No, he ain't the rightful heir, so don't say it. He's too
slow-witted to do more than run a garden patch. Ever."

And so it went Clarence's way. Benjy who loved everybody, including Clarence, had to eat alone in the kitchen.
As a result, Babette felt less affection for her husband and
loved Benjy more than ever, more than any other human
being, even her bright, sunny Curtis, who was forever
disobeying Clarence and doing what Babette or Ben or
Pearl told him to do.

Pearl accepted Clarence's attitude toward Benjy—often
Benjy did drool—and got Babette to permit her to give
the child his evening meal in the big house. The meals
went smoothly, Benjy drooled less, soon not at all, and in
time, he was able to carry on a simple conversation. And
Pearl loved him so she sometimes thought her heart would
burst. He was her white family, all she'd ever have again—
she'd never know if her ma and her brothers were still
alive—and she rejoiced in him.

Andrea, widow of the murdered Fred, after a time of
widowhood and mourning, looked with favor upon John
Hall, a field worker. John, too, was recently widowed and
very lonely.

It was a marriage of convenience on both their parts.
Andrea accepted him into her cabin and her bed willingly,
and they found a quiet delight together.

John was tall, not handsome, but strong and kind. He
was tender with Andrea, and he and baby Camille were
captivated by one another within a week.

Camille was only a year old. She was a lovely child,
constantly singing in her baby voice as she crept, then
walked. The moment John came in from the fields, she

was in his arms, patting his cheeks and trying to kiss him,
and Andrea glowed to find herself momentarily neglected
by her bridegroom.

As for John, he loved the entrancing, honey-colored,
singing little girl as his own. And he knew he loved her all
the more because he could never father a child.

XXIX

Elizabeth LeBlanc was in a swivet. She flounced out of
bed at nine—she'd been up late at Richard Hebert's
party—but instead of feeling happy, she was cross as two
sticks.

Men! She wished she'd never seen a man! She surely
did! They were all so silly, so demanding!

She flipped off her lace-trimmed nightgown and glared
at herself in the long floor mirror, then scowled ferociously.
She was sure enough a young version of Mama—everybody
said so. But Mama had Papa, so handsome and sensible;
other men didn't pester Mama at all the way they did
Elizabeth.

She frowned at her tiny, white-skinned, slender, yet
voluptuous figure, accented by that nest of red between
her curving thighs, a red which narrowly escaped being
flaming, like the short, vibrant curls of her bobbed hair.
She made a face at her fine-drawn features and glared into
the blue, blue eyes about which men raved and tried to
write poems. The silly, ridiculous creatures!

"I am like Mama," she whispered, though she'd never
seen her mother naked. "And she admits that she had lots
of men after her, too, living on the *Maebelle* with her

daddy and with all sorts of men riding the steamboat! And it took Papa to coax her to L'Acadie."

However, Mama had been lucky. There'd been only Papa she was sweet on. But Elizabeth had two men drooling over her and had to make up her mind which man to marry. How was a girl to know which man she loved best, anyway?

Men had always chased her, begged her to marry them, and she'd had to fret herself since she was sixteen. And now she was absolutely sick of it and absolutely torn between the two who simply would not give up. She couldn't marry both of them, for crying out loud!

Slipping into a rose-sprigged below-the-knee dress, she put her mind on Robert Hebert, heir to Double Oaks, the plantation up-bayou from L'Acadie. He'd been after her even when they were children and going to school in St. Martinville. He was two years older, but that didn't stop him from hanging around. 'Course it wasn't too bad, because she'd known him all her life and really liked him.

When she was sixteen, ready to go to New Orleans to school, Robert came formally calling on her. He carried a bouquet of red roses, which he gave her with a small bow.

"I've come to say good-bye," he said, his strong-featured, tanned Hebert face solemn. "If you press one of these roses in a book, it'll remind you of me while I'm gone."

She giggled. "Such a notion! I'd never forget you, Robert. How could I?"

"Just promise about the rose."

She giggled again. "Okay. I promise."

"There's more—take a good look at me."

Still giggling at first, she looked. But the giggles faded when she saw how like a man he suddenly was with that stocky, strong Hebert build, those jutting Hebert features. She felt a tingle—why, he was a man grown, and she was only sixteen! But he'd brought her red roses for love.

"I know how young you are," he said. "But we've got sort of woven together since you were born. I can't remember a time when there wasn't you; I don't want such a time ever to come. I . . . I'm trying to say that I want you to marry me when I'm twenty-one."

"But why?"

"Because . . . I love you. Because we fit. Oh, you're a bit flighty, but I'm steady enough to offset that. We'll make a perfect match, see if we don't."

She stood stiffly, surprised, and before she knew it, he had her in his arms—roses, thorns, and all. He kissed her lips for the first time, and she liked it and kissed back. They both got stuck by thorns and bled together, laughing shakily.

"See," he said unevenly, "we like to kiss."

"Nobody ever kissed me before," she whispered.

He drew her and the roses closer, and she, filled with his tenderness and his flowers and his hurting thorns, let him kiss her again. After that, he picked which rose she was to press, and they promised to write to each other once a week.

Later, she knew the kisses had done it. The memory of the tingles made him her special boyfriend. And she was absolutely certain when he slid the big Hebert family diamond onto her finger that she wanted to be engaged to him.

Except now there was José Herrera, a black-haired, black-eyed, Creole god who'd come to visit an aunt in town. José, invited to the party given to announce Robert's engagement to Elizabeth, took one look at her, and from that moment, the mischief started.

Elizabeth was in the receiving line with Robert and her family; she caught her breath when she saw José enter. Her very blue eyes met his very black eyes. The eyes

clung as he neared, and they carried on a startled yet
intimate conversation.

Robert saw it and went rigid. Then he relaxed; there
was no cause for alarm. It was only Elizabeth's flightiness.
Actually, it made him proud to see her effect on men. She
was engaged to him, and in a few weeks they would be
married. He took the hand of the next arriving guest and
smiled.

José, his pulse racing, bowed over Elizabeth's hand, not
quite kissing it. When he lifted his head and let go her
fingers, he saw the pulse fluttering in her throat. He
glanced at Robert. An upstanding chap, but not light-
hearted enough for this girl. José saw nothing to hold him
back; this was different from other times, other girls.

Before the formal announcement could be made, he got
Elizabeth alone in the library. He took her left hand into
his, and she was helpless to do anything but let it lie
there. Her insides were trembling; she'd never been so
inflamed by a man.

"Why do you wear this ring?" he asked boldly.

"Why . . . you know. It's my engagement ring. It's to be
announced tonight. That's what the party's for."

"The ring . . . it's an heirloom?"

"Yes."

"You're engaged to marry him."

"Yes." A whisper.

"This will not be. I have seen you. You are mine."

"No," she said, still in a whisper. "It'll be announced in
just a few minutes."

She tried to leave the room, but he caught her in his
arms and kissed her boldly, passionately, and she responded
as never with Robert and trembled in José's arms. It
seemed her whole self was quivering, afire. Her lips felt
naked when he lifted his.

"You'll tell him now, before the announcement," he said sternly. "You'll return his ring."

Numb, she shook her head. A few sane thoughts remained in her despite the agonizing excitement of this man's behavior. She'd known Robert all her life. She would not let herself be swept off her feet. She'd refuse José. Besides, she'd promised Robert to press a rose, to write letters, to marry him, and she'd never broken a promise to him yet. Exciting or not, José's handsome allure was not to be surrendered to. Robert was not to be jilted, not her own dear Robert.

She told José this. "I've promised Robert. You can't . . . mustn't . . ."

He drew her closer, and they kissed again, and she forgot Robert. There was only José. She didn't remember how things were until he spoke.

"You made Robert a promise," he said. "Now I make you one. You will marry me. You'll be my wife, not his."

"Y-you've only seen me once!" she cried, suddenly outraged. "You have no right!"

"Herrera men always choose their women at first sight. It's a tradition. And they always get their women, no matter what. I'm staying in the bayou country until I win you, Elizabeth. You may as well accept that."

This time he let her march out of the library. She went straight to Robert's side and stood with him, shaking inwardly. His ring felt heavy on her finger.

He took her hand and announced their engagement, his voice ringing out. Elizabeth, standing so close she touched him, submitted to embraces and kisses and wishes for happiness from everybody. She began to feel safe with Robert, until José's kiss touched her cheek, barely touched. He looked at her, one eyebrow lifted, and it was then that she slipped her arm through Robert's and clung to him.

Francie's knock at her door interrupted Elizabeth's

tormented thoughts. Her sister-in-law entered with an unpleasant, sharp expression on her face. This didn't bother Elizabeth; Francie was sharp all the time.

"I want to carry your beaded bag at the dance tonight," she announced.

"The one Robert gave me yesterday?" asked Elizabeth, flabbergasted at Francie's bold request.

"What other one do you have, Miss Priss?"

Her mind occupied by the problem with Robert and José, Elizabeth gave her the bag.

"You look sour as clabbered milk," Francie remarked. "If you want to use the bag yourself, say so! Goodness knows, everybody else in this family doesn't bother to consider my feelings!"

Upset about the two men in her own life, Elizabeth began to cry and blurted out her problem. "It's not the bag! It's José—he wants to marry me! And there's Robert— he's loved me forever! And I—I don't know which to take, Francie! I love them both!"

Francie's face took on a keen expression. "José's an importer; he's rich. Take him."

"I d-don't know! He . . . when he kisses . . . but Robert's so sweet! And he'd be so hurt!"

"You're fickle, that's your trouble!"

"I am not! Just because I can't decide—"

"You're fickle, and you're spoiled! You don't know how lucky you are!"

"You're lucky, too, Francie! You're married to the sweetest—"

"Lee may be a sweet brother, but as a husband. . . ! Take my advice. Marry the importer, be rich!"

On that note, swinging the silver beaded bag, Francie left. Elizabeth returned to her brooding.

That evening she went to the dance with Robert. On the way he warned, "Herrera's nuts about you, darling."

"Are you jealous?"

"Only if you stop loving me," he said, and kissed her.

"I'll never stop loving you, Robert," she murmured.

And she never would, not even if she married José, because Robert was a part of her very life, like L'Acadie, like the bayous. She'd love Robert that earth-deep way always, no matter what.

She divided her dances between them, miserably wishing that she could divide her life the same way. She felt so safe, so at home, so at peace with Robert. With José, she was in a constant, though delicious turmoil, a ceaseless quiver dancing through her. She was elated, excited, and happy, waiting for the next thrilling kiss.

José put his cheek against her bobbed hair as they danced. "I feel your response," he whispered. "And you're trembling! There's not but one way out of this, you enchanting minx!"

"W-what way?"

"It's simple and will avoid all argument. We'll elope, get married in town tonight, board the *River Queen*. She's to sail for New Orleans at midnight."

"I can't, José! It would be fairer to give you both up!"

He drew her closer, danced more slowly. She could feel his heart thunder, feel her own heart.

"I c-can't elope with Robert's ring on my finger!"

"This is the way we'll do it," he murmured and the lure of him filled her. Caught by his fervor, she slipped away from the dance with José, leaving the ring with an astonished and pleased Francie to return to Robert.

She married José in the parlor of a Justice, and José hustled her aboard the old, white sternwheeler which still plied the bayous. She had only the clothes she wore and moaned about this.

In their cabin, José stripped her clothes off eagerly.

"We'll buy more," he promised. "And a wedding ring and a diamond twice as big as the one you left behind."

In their bunk, he made a woman of her, a fiery, blazing, eager, hungry female, and she knew that she had chosen right. She came to him for more, and again more.

And, even though he was destined to keep her happy and she was to bear a tiny, red-haired girl baby, she was always to love Robert even as she would love the bayous.

She sent him a note: "I couldn't resist José, Robert dear. If it's any comfort, I still love you the way I always have and know that love will never change. I shan't come back home to visit often until after you are happily married and settled in life. Forgive me the hurt, Robert, and try to think of me kindly. Elizabeth."

XXX

While Diana carried her third baby, Gabriel refrained from lovemaking lest he harm the baby. He hungered for sex, hungered wildly as did all Leblanc men, but pushed it out of mind and tried to endure.

Francie, having already produced a son in 1941, wasn't upset over the coming baby. "My plan's going to work!" she gloated happily to Lee. "Diana's baby will either be stillborn or be a girl. We've got a head start—William will one day be master of L'Acadie. It's simply got to happen!"

Gabriel, driven by that Leblanc sex urge, drifted into an affair with Madge Bellamy, daughter of the owner of a plantation so small it was little more than a farm.

Madge was squarely built, strong, and plain-featured. But there was invitation in her gray eyes when she and Gabriel met by chance at the small bayou at the back of

L'Acadie. Sun and shadow mixed into her straight, blond hair, her breasts jutted under her thin voile dress, and he was instantly bursting with need.

"I haven't seen you around in a while, Madge," he said.

"I been busy since Ma died, keeping house for Pa. Today he chased me off, told me to forget chores. He does that when Randy comes over, too."

"Randy?"

"Randy Gross. He clerks in the hardware store."

"Is he your boyfriend?"

"He'd like to be. And Pa'd like it."

"And you?"

"Oh, Randy's all right, I guess. Nice looking, too."

But her slow look at Gabriel belied her words, and before he realized what he was about to do, he had her in his arms. Boldly, she pressed her mouth to his.

She was virgin, and he found that exciting, and he took his fill of her. He asked to see her again, and she nodded between smiles and tears. Then she went running for home.

They continued to meet even after she was pregnant, even when her stomach was enormous. She bore a premature boy three days after Diana produced her third still-born son. Torn between the two births, once again denying himself the luxury of tears as he comforted Diana, Gabriel was convinced that she could never bear a living child. With this in mind, he acted swiftly.

He went to Madge. "Have you thought of a way to handle this yet?" she asked sitting in bed, swathed in a white gown. "Pa's fighting mad, and wants to know who done this to me. I've asked you over and over, and you always put me off. Are you going to get rid of your wife and marry me?"

"I've thought of a way," Gabriel told her. "I'll take the baby, adopt him. He'll be a true Leblanc."

"Never!" Madge refused. "I'm going to keep my baby!"

"Nonsense! He'll be my heir, don't you understand? I can give him everything. You can give him only shame. This way you can let him have a father, his real father...and a mother."

"Your wife? She'd take him?"

"Of course she will."

"No. I'm the mother."

They argued quietly, then hotly. In the end, Gabriel lifted his tiny son and strode out of the house to his Chevy. He laid the sleeping infant beside him on the seat of the car and headed for home.

He carried the baby into Old House and took him directly to Diana, lying sad and pale in their wide bed. He deposited the small bundle beside her. "He's ours," he said without preamble, "to adopt and rear."

She lifted the small blanket, stared at the tiny red face. The baby woke, screwed up his face, and began to cry.

Diana breathed, "Where did you get him?"

Steeling himself, he told her the truth and watched her turn white. Even her lips were colorless.

"You...betrayed me!" she whispered, and it took all her strength. The agony of the betrayal was greater than the pain of labor. "How could you?"

"My damned Leblanc passion!" he blurted. "It ate at me."

"So you got a son from another woman! You wanted her!"

"No, not that! I swear it, my darling! It's you I love, only you! It simply happened. I didn't plan it. Then, when the baby was born and he was a boy—we can adopt him, don't you see, sweetheart? And we'll have a son. He's got the Leblanc blood, you see. And we can still try for others!"

"This baby's mother—does she want to give him up?"

"No. But she will. She has no other choice. With us,

he'll have a name, a home, a heritage. Just look at him,
darling, really look! Take him in your arms! He needs you
to be his mother!"

She turned her head away. Tears wet her cheeks. The
baby stopped crying and fell asleep, and Diana turned her
back to it, sobbing.

Pierre burst into the room accompanied by a sturdy,
square-set man dressed in work clothes. One glance told
Gabriel that this was Madge's father and he was boiling
mad.

He advanced on Gabriel. He looked at the baby, at the
weeping Diana.

"What's my grandson doing here?" he demanded.

"I brought him," replied Gabriel unashamedly. "I'm his
father. I mean to adopt him, give him my name and
L'Acadie, everything he has right to as a Leblanc."

Pierre started to speak, but Gabriel motioned sharply
and his father remained quiet.

"My Madge don't want him adopted by you," growled
Bellamy. "She just told me 'bout you and how you seduced
her. She begged me not to fight, and like a fool, I
promised. But it's her baby, and she aims to keep him."

"I'll not give the boy up, sir," Gabriel said firmly. "I'm
the father, and I'll permit no son of mine to grow up
nameless. As for Madge, she'll be better off without a
fatherless child. Stop and think about this rationally."

Diana turned onto her back, looking up at the men.
"Let him take the baby, Gabriel," she said. "The mother
has first right. I refuse to help you adopt the baby, and
that is final."

"Thank you, ma'am," Bellamy said. Then, to Gabriel,
"Madge had her boyfriends, believe it or not. Her childhood sweetheart—on his part, he was her sweetheart—
was at my place when Madge told what you'd done. He's

got plans of his own, and he come here with me to make 'em clear to you."

The room fell silent. Bellamy called out, and a determined young man strode in. When he looked at Gabriel, he went even harder of jaw and clenched his fists.

"This is Randy Gross," said Bellamy. "He's got a thing to say, and all of you are to know I'm behind him and so is Madge. Randy, you speak right out."

Randy's voice was courteous but icy. "Madge has just promised to marry me because she wants to keep her baby," he said. "I'm takin' her and the boy—I'm going to adopt him—to the Delta to live. There'll be no scandal there." He shot a challenging look at Gabriel. "There's not a thing you can do to stop it. Where there's been no marriage, the baby is legally the mother's. You, sir, have no legal voice in this matter."

"You know he's right, son," Pierre said quietly.

Gross scooped the baby into the crook of his arm, and without another word, he and Bellamy left the room and closed the door. When they heard the front door close with a quiet slam, Pierre pressed Gabriel's arm sympathetically and left him alone with Diana.

Thus Gabriel lost his only living son. Diana began to sob again, and he, fully clothed, lay in the bed and held her. He wished he dared shed tears of his own for his last stillborn son, for all three of them, and for the son to whom he had no right, but Diana needed him as she never had before. She sobbed as though she'd never stop. Her face pressed into the side of his neck, and her tears ran down inside his collar.

"I dare not ask you to forgive me," he murmured. "Yet I beg and plead for it, my love."

"Forgiveness . . . of course!" She wept still more. "You tried. I understand, think I do! But there's only one way you can get an heir, darling! Divorce me, marry again, have your sons. I mean it, darling."

"Not that, not ever!" he whispered, cradling her, kissing her cheeks, tasting the salt of her tears.

"This much I can do for you, darling!" she insisted.

He held her closer. "What you can do is forgive me."

"I d-do."

"And get well again. We'll have our sons, I promise you!"

The bayous had been alive with talk of war ever since a German named Adolph Hitler had marched into and subdued Poland. Gradually, Europe was drawn into this war and, as predicted in the bayous, so was the United States, which declared war on Japan after that country attacked Pearl Harbor. Within days, Germany and Italy declared war on the United States. The bayous seethed, and dozens of men, both black and white, enlisted to fight this new war, World War II.

Gabriel, twenty-three at the time and Lee, twenty-two, opted to stay at home and raise food for the troops along with Pierre, who was then forty-six. Both younger men were drafted but were soon deferred because of the foodstuffs they could produce if left at home.

Now the war seemed to color their lives more and more. The women knitted for soldiers, wrapped bandages, prepared boxes of home preserved food to be sent overseas to American soldiers.

Gabriel, robbed of his son, brooded and pondered to somehow get another. He would try again with Diana, of course he would, but he had lost faith in her ability to produce a living child. Slowly a plan came to him, and he determined to carry it through. That he must this time persuade Diana to accept the child was a problem he would solve when the time came.

One evening when Diana had gone to bed early, he drove to St. Martinville and parked in front of Cowan's Tobacco Shop, where he always bought tobacco for his pipe and the *Ladies' Home Journal* for Diana. The neighborhood was going downhill and he feared the shop's business was going with it. He'd known Hiram and Eloise Cowan when they were all in school together, knew they had a solid marriage, and had often noticed their bright little son, now about three. Hiram had a slight limp from a boyhood hunting accident so he hadn't been drafted.

The shop was dark, but he'd expected that. He went around to the back, where the Cowans lived in two rooms attached to the shop, and tapped the knocker.

Eloise opened the door and smiled when she saw who it was. Not for the first time, he noted that her smile was like Diana's, slow and soft and warm.

"Why, Gabriel!" she exclaimed, her voice like music. "Come in! Or should we open the shop? Do you need tobacco?"

"Give the guy credit, honey," put in Hiram, a tall, thin, gentle man. "It's seldom enough that he comes to visit. He doesn't have to spend money every time!" He, too, was smiling, clapping Gabriel on the shoulder.

Gabriel laughed, trying to sound normal, nervous about his mission. He had to tread with care. What he came to ask would come as a shock to these friends.

"I did come to talk," he said, "serious talk, no offense intended. If you're willing to listen to my . . . er . . . unorthodox wants."

"Sit down," said Eloise. "Johnny's asleep in the other room, but we can talk. I can heat up the coffee. It's real good tonight."

"Fine," agreed Gabriel, and sat in a rocker. Hiram sat, too, and looked at him in a welcoming, friendly manner.

Eloise got cups and spoons, set them on the table. She moved to the refrigerator for cream, which she set beside the sugar bowl.

Her every movement was as graceful as the music of her voice. She was slim, her waist so tiny her breasts stood out, seeming larger than they actually were, and there was a provocative tilt to her hips. He watched her grace; it was like Diana's. But her dress was faded and several years out of date.

She was brown-haired, with very white skin, blue eyes, and patrician features. Her little boy had inherited those features. Her lips were curved and rosy and sweet. It was remarkable how much she reminded him of Diana.

They sat, the three of them, drinking the savory coffee. Hiram seemed tense, and Gabriel knew he was curious about the reason for this visit. Gabriel smiled at him, sobered, heart pounding.

"Hiram," he said, "I'm going to ask you a personal question, but I have a reason."

"Go ahead," Hiram replied easily. "You know practically everything about us anyhow; you know the shop has been failing for months."

"That was the question. Has business improved?"

"Not a whit. We barely clear enough to eat."

"Do both of you still want to go north and open one of those hamburger stands?"

"Don't we though!" exclaimed Hiram. "A drive-in. But that'd take thousands that we haven't got. It's just a pipe dream."

"Maybe not," Gabriel said quietly.

"You see a way?" retorted Hiram.

"I know a way," Gabriel told him, "if you'll listen without taking offense."

They both stared at him, puzzled.

"Within a year you could go," he said.

"Tell us how," breathed Eloise.

"Understand, both of you, I mean no offense or disrespect. Hold in mind that I've always had the highest regard for you both and still do. Or I'd never make this proposition. Can you accept that fully?"

Scarcely breathing, they nodded.

Gabriel continued. "Elizabeth and I have lost three stillborn sons. You can understand that we long for a child, an heir."

They nodded again and listened on.

Gabriel spoke more slowly. "We want a child such as your Johnny, bright and handsome, and above all, intelligent. You, Eloise, are beautiful and kind and in splendid health. I ask that you bear me a child, let me have it, adopt it, make it my heir. In return, I'll give you and Hiram ten thousand dollars in cash and you can go north and make your fortune instead of starving in this little shop."

Hiram fell stone-silent. He swallowed, stared at Gabriel, at Eloise. The room seemed to throb.

"It would mean being untrue to my husband," said Eloise. "And I'd be selling my baby."

"You'd hold my wife in your arms," Hiram said. "You'd enter her body." He was white with shock.

"Only because it would be necessary, Hiram. A few times only. Those things would have to happen for me to get a baby of my own blood. There'd be nothing . . . dirty . . . about it."

"And Diana? What would she say?" asked Hiram.

"She'd know nothing about it until the baby was born. I can persuade her after she sees the baby, touches it, realizes that half his blood is mine and that you both were willing partners in his conception. She'd be a good mother, Eloise, a true mother."

Hiram and Eloise looked long at each other. Gabriel felt the heavy thud of his heartbeat. Somewhere a clock was ticking.

"If it was anybody but you," Hiram said, "I'd... but I know you."

"You'll want time to think," Gabriel said. "To decide. Eloise needs time."

"She's to have it," Hiram said, as in a daze. "She's the one...."

They all sat silently for several seconds. Finally Eloise laid her hand on Hiram's arm, pressed it lovingly. "No, we'll not take time and maybe talk ourselves out of our only chance, Johnny's only chance. This is a way, the only way, to get out of this bind we're in. While I carry it, I can think of this baby as Gabriel's heir I'm merely taking care of, not my baby in any way. I can do it, and I will."

The next morning Gabriel went to see his parents. His pulse stepped up when he saw them, sitting together so content.

He held his voice steady when he spoke. "I have news... shocking news," he said, watching their faces.

"Well," Pierre said, "let's have it."

"I'm going to sell two thousand acres of L'Acadie."

"You're—" Pierre broke off, bone white. "No, it can't be! You're joking!"

"I'm dead serious, Pa."

"What's come over you? I know we need more machinery, but surely not badly enough to sell more land!"

"We need the money, Pa. I'm selling the parcel adjoining the one the Mercers bought years ago."

"Surely you don't mean to sell to that tribe again!"

"None other. It hasn't been a month since Guy Mercer cornered me in town and offered twenty thousand."

"You can't do it!"

"And why not?" Maebelle asked. "It's been years since I decorated! Everything's so shabby! And we'd still have eight thousand acres—think of what we could do with that much money!"

"Count on ten thousand only, Ma. Half is for me, half for L'Acadie."

"What're you going to do with ten thousand dollars?" demanded Pierre, angry now. "Fling it around? Travel? Buy diamonds Diana doesn't even want?"

"It's vital and it's my private affair, Pa. Half the money will be for L'Acadie; that's fair enough."

"And you won't tell me what you'll do with the rest?"

"No, Pa."

Maebelle was excited over the prospect of money. Pierre grew increasingly furious.

"The others aren't to know of my private half," Gabriel said. "Diana would worry, and Francie would try to force Lee to get his hands on part. She'll be bad enough, knowing there's ten thousand. I pity Lee."

"Are you," Pierre demanded, his mind racing with terrible possibilities, "ashamed of what you want ten thousand for?"

"Not ashamed, Pa. Proud."

When they rose from the table, the quarrel between father and son broke off, but it wasn't over. Gabriel submitted to pats and kisses from Maebelle, then went home to Old House and Diana. He would, in time, tell her of the sale, and let her believe all the money was to be spent on L'Acadie.

That afternoon he deeded two thousand acres to Guy Mercer and Silas Mercer, Jr., then opened two bank accounts. One was in his own name, one in the name of

his father. There was ten thousand dollars in each. L'Acadie
was now comprised of eight thousand acres.

XXXI

Gabriel thought almost constantly of the two women
pregnant by him. Both Eloise and Diana were in blooming
health. He considered the possibility that this time Diana's
baby would live. What, then, would he do about the child
Eloise would bear? Twins, he decided. I'll raise them as
twins, as full brothers. If Diana has her own baby, her
warm and loving heart will open to the other.

The women went into labor within two days of each
other, Eloise first. Hiram telephoned the news to Gabriel,
saying, "It's a boy! Eight pounds! Perfect!"

"Diana's in labor now," Gabriel said in a low voice. "As
soon as she delivers, I'll be there." Hiram knew of Gabriel's
plan to raise the babies as twins if both lived. They hung
up.

Alert, hovering over Diana, Gabriel waited. At last she
gave birth and again the child was a boy, perfectly formed,
but stillborn. Gabriel took Granny aside and spoke to her
seriously, and she nodded, surprised. When the doctor
had left and Diana had fallen asleep, Granny put the
blanketed child into Gabriel's arms. He left the house and
got into his car, undetected.

Able at last to weep for a lost son, he stopped outside
the Leblanc cemetery and laid his dead son in a little
grave under a spreading magnolia tree. There could be no
tomb for this Leblanc; it must be as though the child had
never existed.

The tiny grave covered, he drove to the bank, then to Hiram's shop.

Hiram was behind the tobacco counter. "Thank God!" he exclaimed. "You can take him away before she becomes attached to him! That baby looks like you, Gabriel," he added softly.

Gabriel pushed the envelope with ten thousand dollars into Hiram's hand. "What about Eloise? Is she strong enough to leave tomorrow?"

Hiram frowned, then agreed. "The sooner we leave, the better—before folks realize there isn't any baby, and ask questions. We can trust the midwife, but beyond that. . . ."

"What about the shop?"

"We managed to sell it at cost," Hiram said. "It'll rouse no suspicions."

Gabriel, after pressing Eloise gratefully on the shoulder, looked at his lusty son. The infant was shrieking and flailing naked arms and legs. The cord had been cut and tied. He wore only a diaper.

Eloise began to cry. "Take him away," she sobbed, "before I dress him . . . while I can still part with him . . . what about the other one?"

"Stillborn," Gabriel said, wrapping his son in the small blanket Hiram produced.

With that, Gabriel rushed for his car, laid his wailing son on the front seat, got behind the wheel. The baby quieted as he drove.

At home, Gabriel rushed into Old House, carrying the baby. His breath cut into his lungs like a blade. He was terrified at the thought of being discovered just as his plan was working so well. Suddenly his heart leapt as he realized fully that this was his son he carried, his living, breathing, flesh and blood.

Pierre and Maebelle came face to face with him in the

hallway on their way out. They saw the bundle, heard the sounds which began to come from it.

"Whose baby is that?" Maebelle gasped. "I saw Granny hurry out with that poor stillborn. Surely you're not—you've got to let him be buried, son!"

Gabriel was caught. He had to tell them.

"You mean to adopt this baby, I suppose," said Pierre. Suddenly he turned pale. He said nothing for a moment, turned paler still. "Do you plan to pass him off as yours and Diana's?" he asked softly.

"If Diana will, yes!"

Shakily, the grandparents looked at the infant.

"I expect you to accept him fully," Gabriel said.

They nodded, said nothing.

Then, though Maebelle tried to get him to wait, he took the baby to Diana. He laid the small, shrieking bundle in the curve of Diana's arm.

Instinctively, before she woke, she drew the little form close, then she gazed at the tiny face, and up at Gabriel in pale wonder. "But it can't be! Is it really our baby?" she whispered, and tears stood in her golden eyes.

"Ours, my darling. René Leblanc—named for my grandfather."

She looked hungrily at the infant, touched his brow, caught his waving fist, held it quietly, and he slept. Tears wet her cheeks.

Knowing that at this moment she believed this to be her son, now miraculously alive, Gabriel sat on the edge of the bed and stroked her golden hair. It was like silk under his fingers.

He touched his son's dark hair. Perhaps he could deceive Diana forever; perhaps she would rear René in the belief that she had borne him. But that would be living a lie. And she might discover the truth later and be more brokenhearted than if she learned it now, her defenses down and a living, beautiful, breathing baby lying on her arm.

Steeling himself, he told her.

Diana lay unbreathing, too weak to move. His words, the awful things he had said, throbbed in her with painful, agonizing truth. Somehow, in spite of the pain, she understood it all—his motive, the way he'd crushed back his own grief over his stillborn sons until he was frantic, his need for a son a rage. She felt his love for herself as well. But despite all, she felt as if she were dying.

He told her where he'd buried their fourth son. Tears flowed down her cheeks once again. "I wish you hadn't done it, Gabriel, oh, I wish you hadn't! And I wish you hadn't—with Madge Bellamy! These are painful things you have done to me!"

"I had to, my darling. You'll come to understand that L'Acadie must have an heir, and we've tried four times."

"Why Eloise Cowan, Gabriel? Did you . . . feel drawn to her?"

"I chose her because she is like you in many ways, and because I knew they needed money badly. Because they agreed—both of them—to give us a child."

Through sheer exhaustion, her tears ceased. She was so weak she could scarcely breathe.

"Nurse him; he's awake," Gabriel whispered. "Give him of your milk. He's in need of it."

Weeping again, she nursed the infant, his alien lips pulling at her nipple. She held him tenderly, as she would have held her own baby, oh, as she would!

Gabriel, watching, saw no dawning of love on her. But gently he coaxed her, explaining that René was in need of a mother, that Diana was in painful want of a baby, and because of this, they belonged together.

At last, in her weakness, she promised she would mother René and keep his secret. Gabriel, in turn, vowed

to try, if she wished, to father future sons by her in love
and in hope.

XXXII

As Diana continued to nurse René, Gabriel relaxed. He
observed with joy her tenderness toward the infant and
above all, her refusal to turn him over to a wetnurse.

"If I'm to be his mother, I'll go all the way," she said.
"I'll treat him as I'd treat my own." She didn't mention
love, however. Not once did she say she might sometime
grow to love him.

Nightly she turned to Gabriel in her bed. "You should
be at your strongest before you have another baby," he
would caution.

Always, when he spoke so, she would curl up next to
him with trust, with forgiveness, with love. "It isn't just for
a baby, my dearest," she would murmur. "It's so I can
know you love me and only me."

This was the nearest she ever came to hinting that he
might harbor affection for Eloise, mother of his child.

"What I did was for the purpose of siring René," he
assured her unfailingly. "Never for an instant have I felt
affection for any woman but you."

Weeks slid by. Diana took exquisite care of René,
lavishing on him the attention she would have given her
own child. But not the love, never the love. She was
drawn to the baby, she rejoiced in René's handsome looks,
his resemblance to his father, the quickness of his baby
mind, but she could not forget that the blood of another
woman flowed in him.

She felt a stir of affection as he gurgled at her, as he

grew and held out his little arms to her, accepting her as his mother, as the font of all good things. And because he was an enchanting baby, she held him often in her arms, smiling as he nursed at her breast. And her heart wrenched that she could not give him the boundless love of a real mother.

Her milk dried up, and she put him on the bottle. Immediately, she conceived. Gabriel, instead of being delighted, was concerned.

"It's too soon, darling. The doctor said—"

"Piffle on the doctor! Also, I had full cooperation from you, so don't be so pontifical! Oh, I know you didn't approve, that you gave in to me only because I want my own baby so much!"

"René's your own baby, dear. He turns to you, he trusts you, he gives you more attention than he ever gives me. You've got his little heart in your hand. Please, Diana, you really are his mother!"

René walked at eight months. One day, clinging to Diana's hand as they strolled toward the stable, René was staggering and laughing and drooling, for he was also cutting teeth. Francie and her son, William, now two and being carried by his nursemaid, walked with them to get the fresh morning air before it grew unbearably hot.

Francie, true to form, was making unpleasant remarks. "You'll be sorry," she said to Diana, "if you don't let a wench carry René. Walking so young, he'll be bowlegged. Wait and see if he isn't!"

She glowered at the baby, whom she and almost everyone believed to be Gabriel's and Diana's own. Francie was still determined to have William made heir because he was born first.

"The doctor says it's all right for René to walk," Diana replied after a moment. She made it a rule never to let Francie irritate her.

"Well, you carry him part of the time, that's true," Francie persisted. "But it's just as bad now that you're pregnant again." She spat the final word.

"I'm only six months along," smiled Diana. "The doctor says I'm fully strong enough to lift René."

"Why always head for the stables?" demanded Francie. "Why not the rose gardens? That's where we should walk or down the driveways under the trees and moss behind the garages."

"René loves the horses," Diana reminded her sister-in-law. "Gabriel thinks René's going to be a horseman."

"That a fact!" ventured William's nursemaid, out of breath from the heavy child. "Mastah René, he crazy for horses!" Catching Francie's scowl, she added hastily, "Mastah William, he like horses, too!"

They continued on toward the stables where half a dozen horses were corralled and peacefully drinking from the water troughs except for the big black stallion, Demon. He was trotting restlessly from one end of the corral to the other, whinnying. Diana decided to tell Gabriel he'd better take the animal out for a run to wear off the edge of Demon's fretful, high spirits. His ears were pulled back, and he had a mean look that Diana didn't like.

Suddenly Demon raced to the far end of the lot, whirled to face the opposite direction, then galloped toward the fence at full speed. He jumped the fence, his hind feet kicking off the top rails, and headed toward Diana and the children. The other horses, now excited, came streaming through the fence going full gallop.

Francie and her wench, dragging William, escaped to one side as the horses raced madly past. Diana snatched René up, and having no time to run, threw him toward Francie for safety, and he landed on the ground, howling. Francie grabbed him and ran for the back gallery, where her wench stood screaming, clutching a crying William in her arms.

Diana knew she must run. She heard the growing thunder of hoofs behind her, but her movements were slowed by her swelling body. As she was struck down, she saw it was Demon who had crashed into her.

She had fallen on her back, and as she struggled to get to her feet, the stallion's sharp hoofs ground into her stomach. She felt the pain and screamed, "My baby!" When she tried to get up again, the other horses swept over her, hoofs cutting, and she lay helplessly beneath them.

She felt the pain upon pain. Pain blotted out time, blotted out the feel of hands lifting her, carrying her to a grassy spot, lowering her.

"Diana!" she heard Gabriel cry, over and over.

Her lips stirred to answer, but they couldn't speak. At the end, in the midst of agony, she knew she loved René, her baby, her son. She gasped it to Gabriel, whispered it, but only God could hear, and then she drifted into blackness, and there was nothing more.

XXXIII

Six months later Gabriel courted a young woman, Dorcas Smith, whose husband had been killed in the Pacific. She lived in St. Martinville, worked in the dry goods store, and he'd been on speaking terms with her for several years.

Her appearance pleased him. She had ash-blond hair, blue eyes, features balanced on that fine line between comely and plain. She was kindly in manner, lively, intelligent, and a pleasure to talk to. She'd make a splendid mother for René.

He was quick to let her know his intentions were serious. "You may not think I'm showing Diana proper respect," he said, "asking you to church so soon after her death."

"Not at all," she replied. "You have a small son in need of a mother. You're a man of action and not accustomed to wasting time."

"Then you don't mind if I . . . ?"

"Look me over? Not at all. I can look you over too, you know."

He laughed, pleased by her open mind, her honesty. "And what do you see when you look at Gabriel Leblanc?" he asked, smiling.

"A very fine man. One I'm honored to go to church or anyplace else with. A man whose company I enjoy."

"That's the way I see you as a woman," he said quietly. "No sudden love, nothing like that. However, to be honest, if we hit it off, I'm going to propose to you."

"And I'm going to accept. Without romantic love."

"The love I had for Diana—I can't replace that. But there'll be feeling which will grow into affection, and that has been known to go into love."

"Mature love," she agreed. "I couldn't say it better if I tried."

Pierre and Maebelle liked Dorcas at once. Elizabeth, home for a visit, welcomed her as a sister. Francie looked down her nose at her new sister-in-law because she had worked behind the counter of a store.

Dorcas fell swiftly in love with little René. He lost the bewildered look he'd had at times and cuddled into Dorcas's arms as if she were the only mother he'd ever known.

"William's going to be handsomer than René when he's a man," Francie said often. "Much handsomer."

Dorcas smiled. "Perhaps," she agreed. "He's handsome now; he has inherited his good looks from both you and Lee. You must be very proud of him."

Gabriel, overhearing once, asked Dorcas, "How do you put up with her? What difference does it make which boy grows up to be handsomer than the other?"

"She can't help it," Dorcas replied. "Not really. She was born the way she is. And she's eaten up with frustration that René, not William, will eventually inherit L'Acadie."

"Must be one reason she is forever trying to get more money out of the L'Acadie bank account through Lee," mused Gabriel. "And why she's always ready to pick a fight with anyone, Lee included. William's the only one she treats halfway decently."

Gabriel, pondering, decided it was only fair to tell Dorcas of René's true origin. They were in bed, the night-light on, and she listened quietly as he spoke slowly and in detail, beginning with Madge Bellamy and the son he begat with her and ending with the truth about René's real mother.

"I'm happy it worked out for you, Gabriel," Dorcas said, when he had finished.

"One thing, never let Francie get wind of it. If she knew about René, she might start trouble about who's to inherit L'Acadie."

Dorcas shuddered. "You're so right!"

Francie, when she wasn't feuding with someone, spent her time plotting how Lee could become master of L'Acadie instead of Gabriel. She perfected a scheme, and one night when the whole family was invited to the big house, they sat in the library after dinner, chatting and drinking the traditional bittersweet Grape House wine.

Francie, as usual, complained. "I can't see why everybody is so crazy about this wine! So dry, so dark, and it's bitter as gall!"

"It does, however," Dorcas said, "have an edge of sweetness, don't you think, Francie? I've grown to quite enjoy it."

"Well, I haven't," snorted Francie. She glanced scornfully around. "If you could see yourselves, smacking your lips over this gall!"

"If you don't like it after all this time, Francie," Gabriel said mildly, "don't drink it."

"Oh, I'll drink it! I'm as much a Leblanc as any of you!" She took a sip, swallowed. Her lips twisted.

Lee's face was red, and he shifted uncomfortably, obviously at a loss for any comment. Then the three men—Pierre and Gabriel and Lee—began to discuss the war. Francie had never paid much attention to war talk, all those confusing battles, until she had perfected her plan, but now she listened.

"Gabriel," she interrupted, "I've been wondering."

"About what, Francie?"

"You hate this Hitler so. Why don't you enlist and help get rid of him? Lee could run L'Acadie for you. Couldn't you, Lee?"

Silence grabbed the room.

At last Gabriel spoke. "I got a deferment because I thought I should stay here, putting in more sugar cane, raising extra foodstuffs for the soldiers. That's what L'Acadie men did during the Civil War; they did the job they knew best."

"Just the same—"

Lee had had enough. "Francie!" he thundered. "Enough!"

She was stunned, but equally determined not to let the family hear herself and Lee quarrel. She dropped the subject until the two of them were at home in Honeymoon House.

"What came over you tonight?" Lee demanded. "You outdid yourself!"

"I don't know what you're talking about, stupid!"

"Needling Gabriel about the army!"

"If he's so patriotic, he should go!"

"He's needed here."

"I don't see why! You can run the place!"

"And inherit if Gabriel doesn't come back? Is that it?" he shouted angrily. Then, seeing he had hit the mark, he whispered, "I knew you were petty and back-biting, but to connive and scheme. . . !"

"It wouldn't happen! He'd be back—trust him! Somebody should represent the Leblancs, should represent L'Acadie, and it should be Gabriel, the master!"

Lee was bone white. He stared at Francie as if he'd never seen her before. "You're so right," he gritted. "L'Acadie must be represented, but I'm the one to do it! I'll enlist first thing tomorrow!"

"If you do," she screamed, "it'll be pure spite! It'll be just to get away from me!"

"How right you are!" he snarled.

When she cuddled near him in bed, he turned his back. When he was in uniform and ready for war, he submitted to her good-bye kiss because the family was present, then pushed her away even though she was weeping wildly.

And she, choking on sobs and rage, knew she had to stay behind and tend her son. She knew also that she must provoke petty quarrels among the family members. It was the only way she could hold her head up and be a Leblanc.

XXXIV

Francie, in her obsession to make sure that Lee, and after him, William, inherited L'Acadie, schemed without ceasing. She discarded plan after plan until gradually one method made itself beautifully clear to her, and she concentrated on how to bring it to pass.

"May I sit with you?" she humbly asked Maebelle one morning, gazing big-eyed at her mother-in-law, cozy with her knitting, alone in the back parlor. "It's so lonely with Lee gone off to war."

"Of course. Sit," said Maebelle warmly. "Where's Will? I haven't seen him today."

"With Cindy and them, playing at the Quarters. I felt he needed to be with children his own age. And I know that Dorcas doesn't allow René to romp down there early."

Dorcas, carrying her knitting, entered in time to hear this. She smiled at Francie, and Francie managed a brief, answering smile. Oh, these senseless, grinning bitches, Francie thought. I don't want to do any of this, but I have to, simply have to! Well, I'll not put up with their sugary sweet airs long. We'll see how fast they melt away!

"René," Dorcas explained, settling herself and starting to knit a scarlet square, "doesn't play at the Quarters early because he's still taking a morning nap, which he needs because he's so active. When he misses the nap, he's cross all day."

"Of course," agreed Francie, then continued. "I have an apology to make," she said, furthering her plan. "It's for the whole family. It's Lee being in the army that's opened

214

my eyes. He always said I was too snippy toward everybody at L'Acadie, and now I realize he was right. From now on, I'm going to be gracious like the rest of you, be a true Leblanc."

Maebelle dropped her work went to Francie, kissed her cheek. "Then you'll really be a daughter to me!" she exclaimed. "Lee will be so pleased when he comes home and finds how pleasant things are!" Tears came to her eyes for which she apologized. "Forgive me! I just want him back home safely!"

Dorcas embraced Francie and kissed her cheek, and Francie kissed Dorcas. Then they sat knitting, talking of Lee, and Maebelle began to make plans for a huge party to be given in his honor when he got home. Francie, delighted at how smoothly her scheme was going, sat in pure happiness. She had no fears about Lee; he would come home. He would be master of L'Acadie. She would be mistress. All she had to do now was carry on with her plan.

Francie started spending long hours in the library, reading the old books. When this new passion was commented on, she said that she wanted to improve her mind, to keep up intellectually with Lee. She read one book over and over, concentrating on a particular chapter.

As time passed, she was increasingly gentle in her attitude, and all the family members, even Gabriel, warmed to her. She invited them to Honeymoon House for supper, and they came willingly. She made a point of admiring René aloud, while silently wishing she could find some way of discrediting him. She said he was getting handsomer every day, kissed him, saw to it that William shared his toys with his cousin.

"They're growing up together like brothers." Francie smiled.

The others agreed, pleased. They're fools, she thought.

Maebelle said that when Lee did come home, William might soon have a real brother. With a loving look at Dorcas, she added that René, too, might have a little brother. Francie watched the color rise in Dorcas's cheeks and ached to slap her.

Instead, Francie led them to the dinner table, playing the smiling, gracious hostess, enjoying the power she held to make them so friendly, scorning them for being so easily deceived. She served Grape House wine after dinner, and Pierre and Gabriel drank two glasses each. Francie sipped her one glass of wine, hating it, but made no comment and kept a smile on her lips.

On the spur of the moment Maebelle decided to give a family dinner party. "To celebrate our new closeness with you, Francie," she explained. "To honor you because, in your love for Lee, you have truly become a Leblanc."

Francie embraced her mother-in-law and pecked at her cheek. Her pulse was jumping. This was it! This was the time she must act, must implement her plan, no matter how risky it was.

She dressed carefully for the evening, choosing a blue lace dress which enhanced her beauty and shapely shoes with Cuban heels. The dress had been Lee's favorite before he had enlisted. Her mouth set. That was another problem. She'd won over the rest of the Leblancs; when Lee returned, she would have to keep up the act and win him again. In fact, she'd have to be an actress the rest of her life if she was to be mistress of L'Acadie.

Gabriel called for her and, after a peek at his sleeping nephew, escorted her to the big house. All three women were in their loveliest dresses and looked as beautiful as Francie herself. Pierre and Gabriel were handsome, perfectly groomed in white.

They only spoke briefly of the war. Francie read them

portions of a letter from Lee, pretending to withhold
tender passages, although, in fact, such passages weren't
there. She made up the end out of whole cloth. "So, with
a tender kiss for you, my darling, and one for William, I'll
close for this time. Your devoted husband, Lee." Actually
the letter read, "Hoping all at L'Acadie are in good health,
and with a big hug and kiss for William I am, Lee."

Maebelle read aloud the letter she and Pierre had
received. It was tender and loving, and Lee said he would
write to Gabriel and Dorcas soon. Francie burned at the
warmth in their letters, but continued her show of complete happiness.

Later, in the library, when Gabriel suggested a glass of
wine, Francie stiffened. The time was here. There could
be no hesitation. She would do it and get it over with.

She spoke. "I'll pour the wine, Gabriel. You usually take
turns pouring, and now . . . well, I'd like to."

"Of course," agreed Gabriel. "What better time? So
pour, my dear."

Heart in her throat, she moved to the small table where
decanter and glasses stood. Her back was to the others,
and they continued to chat and laugh.

Cautiously, her hand deliberately steady, she poured the
wine. Not breathing, she drew the folded bit of paper out
of the pocket of her dress, spilled the crystals it held into
one of the glasses and slipped the paper back into her
pocket.

She watched that one glass. The crystals dissolved rap-
idly, as they had done when she practiced at home. She
lifted the tray, went directly to Gabriel. "You first," she
said gaily. "The master of L'Acadie should be first!"

She held the tray so that the doctored glass of wine was
nearest to his hand. Would he take it . . . would he? She
ached with the need to hand it to him, yet dared not. He
must take it—all her efforts had led to this moment.

"Why, thank you Francie," Gabriel said. He smiled, then picked up the glass.

Inwardly trembling, it was almost impossible to serve the others, but she did. She returned the tray to its place, took her own wine, sat down, and managed a sip.

Slyly she watched Gabriel take a good swallow. Would the bitterness of the arsenic be masked by the wine like the book said? By that sharp, bittersweet edge of Grape House wine? She sipped again from her own glass, holding it steady by sheer will. Everything depended on whether Gabriel detected anything amiss with the wine.

He took another sip, as did the others. Francie sipped again. Gabriel looked at her, and for an instant she was terrified, frozen, but then he smiled. She sat, hardly breathing, fighting not to tremble.

"Has your palate adjusted to Grape House wine?" he asked her.

"Yes, it has. To an extent," she managed to reply.

"Do you detect that far edge of bittersweetness?"

"Yes, I really do, Gabriel."

He drained his glass, looked into it thoughtfully. Francie's insides twisted. She jumped up, reached for his glass. "You're ready for seconds now," she said, and even managed a smile to go with the words.

She brought him the second glass, resumed her seat. Without seeming to, she watched him. He sipped his wine very slowly, enjoying it. He joined in the conversation and didn't look into the glass this time when it was empty.

What if it doesn't work? thought Francie. Maybe I should have put arsenic into the second glass, too? But the book said one. Of course it would work; the book had told exactly how. And then she had burned the book.

Francie didn't sleep all night long. Had Gabriel begun to suffer? Had Maebelle called the doctor? Would the doctor suspect poison? What would he diagnose as the cause of death?

And if the doctor did suspect poison, would the wine be suspected? Her heart stopped again at the very thought, then leapt and raced. How could they blame the wine? Everyone had drunk two glasses. Would they, heaven forbid, pin importance on the fact that she, Francie, had poured the wine? But even if they did, how could they prove anything? The glasses had long since been washed and she had burned the arsenic paper and flushed the tiny ashes down the drain.

She'd taken only a spoonful from the box in the stable, the very box that Gabriel himself kept to kill rats. At first light, she'd have the blue lace dress washed. She'd already turned the pocket inside out to see if any crystals had spilled, and they hadn't.

There was no possible way they could pin murder on her. It was almost certain that murder would never even enter their minds. And so, she reasoned and pondered and worried through the endless night. She thought of excuses to go to the big house, rejected them. Her only course was not to call attention to herself.

It had to go as planned, simply had to. René would be next in line to inherit if this plan with Gabriel worked. If only she could be sure, as René grew up, that he'd do some terrible thing or some secret about him would spoil his chances of being master. That was useless thinking. Well, he could be disposed of in childhood—a snake bite, maybe. She could manage it. She'd let it be an accident, like with Diana and the horses. Not right away, but say in a year, maybe a bit more. By then Lee would be home and would inherit.

Her throat was dry. There was so much at stake. And all of it was on her shoulders—the planning, the doing, the waiting—and then acting as a loving, shocked, and grieved

Leblanc through it all. She could never let the least thing
show the way crazy Phrony used to do, for she would then
lose what she was trying to accomplish.

Dorcas sent for Francie, and she hurried to the big
house, ready for anything. She tried to question the black
girl who had come for her, but the wench only bawled and
shook her head. At least Francie knew that Gabriel had, at
least, fallen ill. Her plan was working! She ran all the way.

It was happening. If she was lucky, it had already
happened. Now was the time she had to keep her head,
be shocked, sympathetic, worried, helpful, even weep a
bit.

Gabriel was in the master bedroom, lying on his back in
the great bed. Dorcas and Maebelle, wife and mother,
were in each other's arms. Pierre stood at the foot of the
bed and watched the old doctor who was working over
Gabriel.

Maebelle put out a hand to Francie, and their trembling
fingers clung. It's all right, it's good that I tremble,
Francie thought. It's natural. "What's happened? What's
wrong?" she whispered.

"Gabriel," Maebelle whispered back. "He must have
been in great pain before Dorcas knew."

"Pain? . . . What pain? . . . Why?" Francie gasped, careful
to sound bewildered.

"His stomach, his chest, his entire body—he's in terrible pain," Dorcas agonized. "I sent for Doctor Murray as
soon as I found out."

"Why Doctor Murray?" demanded Francie. "Why not
Doctor Gilbert? He's the best—"

"Doctor Gilbert's in New Orleans taking a special course,"
Maebelle explained.

What luck! exulted Francie. What wonderful luck! Dr.
Murray was an old-fashioned doctor! Then fear grabbed

her, terror. Suppose, being old, he'd read that same book?

The doctor came to them. He was white-haired, faded of eye, of body. "It's his heart," he told them.

"How bad?" asked Pierre.

"Very bad indeed. I recall, Pierre, that your father died of a heart attack."

"Yes, he did."

Francie's elation grew.

"Die?" gasped Maebelle. "You mean that my son's going to die?"

The old doctor looked at her sadly.

"How . . . long?" asked Pierre.

"Hours, perhaps. I've given him morphine so he feels no pain now. I'll come back later to give him more if he . . . needs it."

As he spoke, Maebelle came to Pierre. She stood erect, weeping quietly, her head up. Even in his sorrow, Pierre realized how beautifully she had mellowed since those long-ago days when she was a bride. He mused that she had become a loving, considerate wife and mother, and he loved her for it.

And then he gazed at Gabriel and wept quietly with Maebelle, holding her tenderly.

Francie spent the day and evening on sick watch. She comforted the other women. She herself wept. Why was it taking so long? Why couldn't he die and the suspense be over? She felt no remorse, only anxiety that the end took so long to come.

The doctor returned, gave more morphine.

That evening, twenty-four hours after he drank wine laced with poison, Gabriel Leblanc gave one great moan and moved, then fell still. Francie, watching the doctor write "Cause of death—massive heart attack," was filled with victory.

She'd gotten away with it. She was safe. The first step of her plan had been accomplished. Crazy Phrony could never have done it so well.

XXXV

In 1943, Lee had been sent overseas to fight the Germans. He was both frightened and elated. He feared being killed in battle, yet he had enjoyed the ocean voyage. Before reporting for duty, he was given a few days' leave in Paris, where he spent every hour sight-seeing.

He strolled the boulevards, visited the Louvre, admired the sculptures. He wished he could take home a couple of marble figurines for the lawns of L'Acadie and a painting by an old master, but that was out of the question.

It was a happy, free time, empty of Francie's nagging, empty of her complaining letters. He spent some time with other soldiers but kept mostly to himself, not wanting to go to the houses they patronized, no matter how comely and experienced the girls there might be. He did, however, wish for the company of some decent, pretty girl, but there seemed to be no way to find one in so short a time.

Reporting to field headquarters, he was singled out for special duty. "Private Leblanc, for-ward!" barked the sergeant.

Lee stepped out of line, saluted, stood at attention.

"You will serve as assistant on ambulance detail," the sergeant ordered. "Corporal Hawthorne will be your superior officer. Hawthorne—for-ward!"

Out of the corner of his eye, Lee glimpsed a neat uniform coat and skirt which didn't hide the curves they covered. The corporal—to Lee's surprise, a woman—

looked exceedingly trim. Lee saluted her, and she returned the salute. He judged her to be about thirty years old.

"Proceed to your post!" the sergeant barked and they complied, the woman leading the way to a battered, dusty ambulance. Following her, Lee noted again how the uniform failed to tone down her womanliness.

Nothing could tone down her quick smile. It was as dazzling as her blond hair, which curled from under her field cap, as dazzling as the whiteness of her skin. When she leaned, twisting, to reach a canteen, her sleeve rode up, baring her arm.

"We can't sit here all day and not talk, Leblanc," she said, and even her voice sparkled. "We've nothing to do until there's fighting. Leblanc—that's French, isn't it?"

"Yes. I'm from the bayous of Louisiana, Cajun country. My ancestors were driven from Nova Scotia by the English when they took over the country."

"I'm from the show-me state—Missouri."

"My father went up the Missouri River years ago."

"Did he get tired of the bayous? Do the Cajuns still have trouble? I've read how the English treated them so despicably!"

"No trouble like that, no. It's just hard to make a living on the land now."

"Isn't it hard everywhere?"

"Not for those in factories making airplanes and such."

Her deep blue eyes sparkled. "You're a farmer?"

"Yes. The place has been too much for us to handle since the slaves were freed. But we work at it, hoping to get the whole eight thousand acres under cultivation."

Her eyes widened. "Goodness, what a job! I hope you have machinery and plenty of hands."

"We have both, but not enough. Each year we do a little better, but it's a slow process."

She looked at him in frank admiration. "Handsomeness must run in your family," she said.

He blushed. "Nobody ever called me that before."

"Well, you are handsome! Your body is wiry but strong. And the delicate blue of your eyes is most unusual. And lovely."

"You should see my parents and my brother, before he died. They all have smooth features, not rough like mine."

"Yours aren't rough! A trifle rugged, but most intriguing! I won't have you running yourself down, Leblanc, and this last name business is plain silly! What's your first name?"

"Lee."

"Lee. I like that. Mine's Danielle, and you're to call me by it."

"But you're my superior officer."

"Shucks. I'm just an ordinary Missouri woman—a thirty-year old widow. My husband died of Spanish influenza, and I enlisted the day after his funeral. Phil was four-F—his eyes. So he couldn't join up. He had a shoe repair shop that kept him busy, but he brooded. He asked me how I'd feel about enlisting. I caught right onto the idea, and when he died, well, it seemed the thing to do, so here I am, one year later. What about you—why did you enlist?"

"For all you know, I was drafted."

"Uh-uh. Not you. You enlisted."

"I was deferred to farm. Then I enlisted."

"See?"

"It seemed that L'Acadie—that's the name of our plantation—should be represented in the armed forces. My brother, who has since died of heart attack, my father, and all our hired help, are working double-time to produce food for the army."

Carefully, he had avoided mentioning Francie. But Danielle asked about a wife right out.

"You married?"

"Yes."

"Kids?"

"One. A boy."

"I bet you miss your wife."

"I miss William."

"Your son?"

"Yes. He looks like his mother. He's very handsome."

"But your marriage went sour," she murmured, putting the sunlight of her interest on everything about him.

"I guess you'd call it that," he admitted.

"Did you enlist to get away from her?"

"Partly. No, almost wholly."

"What did she do that was wrong?"

"She quarrels, even with William. She finds fault. She was angry with me because I'm the second son and won't inherit L'Acadie."

"But surely she knew that before she married you."

"First, she wanted to be a Leblanc. Then she wanted more. She even tried to get my older brother to enlist before I did."

Danielle's eyes filled with shock. She whispered, "And you came instead? Because she hoped he'd be killed. Then he died anyway. Does that make you heir?"

"No. Gabriel left a son, René. René's only a child now, but when he's grown, he'll be master."

"What does she say about that?"

"She wants me to get released from the army and run L'Acadie. God knows what else she has in mind."

"But you're not going to do it."

Their eyes locked, hers so very blue, his a delicate blue. It was in that moment, he later believed, that he started to fall in love with her. How she felt, he couldn't tell. And it was too soon for him to hint at such a thing.

As time passed and she drove their ambulance through enemy fire so they could pick up the wounded, admiration for her bravery entered into and strengthened Lee's love for her. Working with her, he found he could handle mangled, screaming, wounded soldiers, unload them at the hospital tent, race back into the field for others. He grew used to gunfire and not knowing if or when they themselves would be hit, used to other men's blood on his uniform, used to dirt and filth.

And Danielle, ever conscious of Lee at her side, strong and ready and dependable, came to have a fondness for him that deepened steadily into love. That he returned her feeling, she knew without being told. She wanted to tell him about her love and could not, for their ambulance was always on the run, always filled with blood and moans and throaty screams.

Lee knew, as they sped through the line of fire, that he and Danielle had developed a wonderful closeness. They'd worked together only two months, yet it seemed to him that he'd known her forever, loved her forever.

They labored on.

One day, a battle ended, the enemy routed, they cruised the battlefield, working through the night to collect the wounded and even the dead. Afterwards, white with fatigue, streaked with dirt and blood, they went to the canteen.

It was still dark outside; dawn wouldn't break for another hour. Every defense suddenly down, Lee wanted Danielle with the Leblanc hunger, wanted her now.

They were sitting apart from other soldiers in the canteen, talking quietly. "You know, of course," he said, "that I love you."

"And I love you," she replied quietly.

They gazed starkly at each other. They had so little time, such heartbreakingly little time amid constant danger.

"Listen to the lovebirds," she said, with a ghost of her

smile. "Another night like this, and there'll be a couple of dead ambulance drivers who'll never think of love."

"I want you to marry me."

"There's Francie."

"I'll divorce her."

"You're twenty-four: I'm thirty, too old for you."

"The war matured me. If that hasn't done the job, you will. Besides, six years' difference is very little."

"We need to think about it, Lee. All of this—the war, our working together, our falling in love—may be just an interlude, a space of time that's different, and when it ends, we'll simply go back to our old lives."

"You can't. Phil's dead."

"I can go back to Kansas City."

"I'll get my divorce, come straight to you. Will you call this an interlude then?"

Tears flashed in her eyes. "How can I know, Lee?"

"Let me make love to you now, tired as we are. It may be our only chance. If you need a test, Danielle, please try. In each other's arms, we'll know whether it's right or wrong."

Because she was too exhausted to argue, she went with him to a secluded place amongst the trees. She wanted him fiercely, needed the comfort of his body, knew it would soothe and heal her more than bathing, more than sleep.

They didn't speak as they entered the grove. She knew that Leblanc hunger was raging in him, for he had told her how every male in his family was beset by it. And now here she was, torn by the same kind of hunger.

He found a soft green spot beneath a spreading tree. Clouds had moved away from the moon, and there was faint light. A small breeze sprang up and rippled the leaves of the tree.

"Undress," he whispered. "Hurry, my darling!"

Stripping himself, he watched her. Her body emerged, clad only in moonlight, so beautiful, more beautiful than he had ever imagined it. Together they sank to the dewy grass. He felt her wetness along his body as they lay in each other's arms.

He caressed her face, her neck, her lovely breasts. She caressed him the same way, kissed the light down of hair on his chest, delighted in the feel of it against her lips and face. Sweetly, passionately, tenderly, they kissed.

He lifted himself and hovered over her. But when he would have taken her, he could not. And she lay helplessly back, legs like lead, unable to receive him.

They rested, tried again, failed, lay exhausted. "We're too weak!" he exclaimed, and she chuckled and agreed. They laughed together, laughed until they cried, and promised to make love at the first opportunity. At dawn, they dressed and returned to bathe and put on clean uniforms, then met for breakfast.

It was noon when the enemy attacked again. Before one o'clock, Lee and Danielle were blood-smeared and filthy. As they sped and jolted onto the battlefield still another time in the dirty ambulance, firing started again. Danielle stomped on the gas pedal, and the vehicle leaped forward. It was then that the piece of shell plowed into Lee's chest, and Danielle knew by instinct what had happened, though he did not so much as moan.

She braked, almost standing the ambulance on its nose. It surged to a halt, then surged back, and then she had him in her arms. Blood was pumping out of his chest and she could not stop it.

He died in her arms, her tears in his mouth. "Mistake..." he managed. "Francie...mistake...love you..." And then there was more of the salt of Danielle's tears in his mouth, and he hazily wished that he could swallow them, to take that much of her with him, but he did not have the time and the tears lay still on his lips.

XXXVI

Francie wouldn't let Pierre or Maebelle make any suggestions about the funeral; Lee's body, in a sealed casket, had been flown back to L'Acadie. Ever since word of his death had come, she had reverted to her natural, razor-tongued self with bitterness added for good measure. Now, she raged inwardly, Lee would never inherit. She'd have to wait until William was grown, and she had as well the chore of eliminating René.

She'd already tried—once, planting a rattlesnake nearby, then again, leaving a loose board at the edge of the hay loft—but both times, René had a narrow escape, and the episodes were accepted by the family as accidents. Any more childhood accidents would rouse Pierre's suspicions, for he'd begun to keep a close watch on both his grandsons.

On the morning she had set for the funeral, Francie went to Maebelle's rooms, fire in her eyes. Her black taffeta skirt rustled cheerfully, but her face was stern and determined. She found Maebelle dressed in soft black silk, tears in her eyes. Francie, herself tearless, angry over Lee's death, gave her mother-in-law a bitter glance.

"I see you're wearing the jet brooch and earrings!" she snapped.

"Why...yes," Maebelle responded, puzzled. "I put them on because Lee loved them so when he was a toddler. He'd grab at them and try to get them into his mouth."

"Everybody knows they were his favorites! You've told it

often enough! I'd have thought, for that very reason, I should be the one to wear them. I'm the widow, not you!"

"It's only that Lee. . . . Here, wear them, Francie." Maebelle stripped the earrings and brooch off, fingers trembling. "He loved them so, the dark glitter. Wear them, and take comfort."

When Francie had left with the jewels, Maebelle didn't cry. Lee had enjoyed smiles and laughter when he was alive; it would hurt him to know that his mother had sobbed throughout his funeral. She fastened the collar of her dress with a black onyx pin, drew on black gloves, adjusted her small black hat and the seams of her last pair of silk stockings. She was ready in time to give Pierre a quick, sad smile when he came to escort her downstairs.

It was a singularly tearless funeral. Elizabeth, who had come alone from New Orleans, had been the only one to sob heartbrokenly. She was still sobbing when she and Francie, dry-eyed, sat alone in the library. Francie was looking at her keenly without a trace of sympathy.

"You haven't got so much to cry about," Francie snapped. "With Gabriel and Lee gone, if you want to press it, there's no reason you can't inherit L'Acadie. You're Pierre's own daughter; René and my William are only his grandsons. Actually, you're next in line." Francie waited, unable to breathe at her own daring, panicked by the idea she may have planted in Elizabeth's mind. But she had to know—had to find out what she must cope with next.

Elizabeth hiccuped, her sobs abating. "L'Acadie always goes to the oldest male in line," she said. "I l-love the place, but even if I asked for it and got it, I couldn't take over. José lives for his jewelry business; he'd never give it up to manage a plantation. And my baby, my Kiki—she's a girl, so she's not in line. And the doctors say I can never have another baby, so there'll be no male heir through me.

Besides, there's René coming up... and William. L'Acadie's well provided with heirs!"

Francie sniffed, her wariness eased. So. There'd be no trouble from Elizabeth. Francie could proceed as she chose. With a toss of her head, she left the room. Elizabeth was alone, drying the last of her tears. She had just tucked a damp handkerchief into her small handbag when a tap came at the door. It opened, and Robert Hebert stood there in black. His strong Hebert features were composed, yet showed signs of grief and sympathy.

"Elizabeth," he said quietly. "It's good to see you, though the occasion is sad."

She nibbled at her lips, nodding her head. This was the first time she'd been alone with him since she had eloped with José. She murmured, "I haven't been home often."

"I knew when you were here. I didn't so much as phone, didn't want to make you uncomfortable," he said gently. "But now... with Lee... I hoped you wouldn't mind speaking with me."

Heart aching for her dead brother, for this man she had jilted, she forced herself to agree. "It's good to see you," she whispered.

"You're... happy, Elizabeth?"

"Very happy, Robert. I'm not sorry I married José," she rushed on, "only sorry that I treated you the way I did."

"It was for the best," he told her slowly. "If you'd married me, you might never have gotten him out of your heart."

"That's right," she whispered, her eyes clinging to his. She dared not tell him she'd been unable to get him out of her heart, either. And knew that she would come to L'Acadie rarely because it hurt to see him, hurt to remember their young, lost love. "And you," she whispered, wanting to know, having to know, "is there a girl?"

"No special one, Elizabeth. She must meet a very high

standard, you understand. But there will be a mother for my children one day, and she'll have my devotion, but only my devotion."

Devotion, not love, Elizabeth's wild heart rejoiced. She couldn't help it, any more than she could deny Robert a chaste farewell kiss on her cheek. When he left, she was both comforted and torn. Hurrying to her room, she packed swiftly. She was eager to get away, to be in José's arms, to let him make her happy.

After Elizabeth had left for New Orleans, Francie accosted Maebelle in the library. In her hand she carried the jet jewelry.

"I'm returning your jet promptly," she said sharply. "I suppose Elizabeth will inherit it, being the only girl."

"Perhaps," said Maebelle, bewildered.

"I suppose you want me to leave L'Acadie now," Francie continued, nose twitching.

Maebelle, even more bewildered, held herself calm. This was grief speaking, she thought. Poor Francie, a widow and so young!

"Why should we want you to leave, dear?" she asked gently. "Any more than we wanted Dorcas to leave when Gabriel—"

"Dorcas has René to raise! The heir, if you remember!" Francie spat. "But, of course, you remember. You treat him like a little prince!"

"We treat William the same, dear. L'Acadie is big enough for all of us. If you feel that you and William will be lonely in Honeymoon House, you can move into the big house with the rest of us."

"Too many people!"

"There are enough rooms and suites."

"Just the same—"

"Or you could move into Old House."

"Move here, move there!" wailed Francie, crying angrily now, that twitch to her nose, an 'her to her lips. "The only word you can use is move! Which means one thing! Now that Lee is dead you want to get rid of me. You never have liked me, and now you hate me! You want to kick me out of L'Acadie, you know in your heart you do. I'm your own son's widow, mother of his child, and I've no doubt you'd try to take William away from me out of sheer spite! You'd keep him from me, let him forget he ever had a mother!"

Pierre, coming into the room, hearing most of what Francie said, settled the matter firmly. "You don't know what you're saying, Francie," he told her. "We'll accept it for what it is, natural grief. But your place is at L'Acadie, unless you marry again."

Now she turned on him. "Ha! You want to marry me off!"

Suddenly Pierre was angry, and the cold look on his face made Francie take a step back. "You were our son's wife," Pierre said evenly. "He chose you, and we accepted you. You're the mother of his son, and William has every right to grow up at L'Acadie. It's settled. Honeymoon House is yours for your lifetime."

Maebelle stroked away her own tears and sighed. Maybe Francie would change again after the edge of her angry grief had dulled. Francie was obviously very angry at Lee for getting killed. Maebelle's tears started again, and now she let them come. She wept in Pierre's arms, wept for the two sons she had lost, and as she wept, a balm settled into her.

Francie watched her sharply. "You do feel bad, even if Lee was only a second son, don't you?" she asked the entwined pair, for there were tears on Pierre's face, too.

Maebelle nodded, tried to smile, nodded again.

Francie left them abruptly. Let them blubber. She had

to somehow dispose of René. If only she could discover something so wrong with him the family would do it for her.

But no such luck. She'd have to do it herself.

XXXVII

Gradually, deliberately, Francie acted sweetly toward the family once again, even toward Dorcas whom she despised. Dorcas was proud to be mother to René, heir to L'Acadie, and admitted it honestly. She sought advice about rearing the child from Pierre, on whom she relied.

Francie gave a dinner party in honor of René's twelfth birthday. The family gathered, dressed in their best. Francie treated the boys as equals.

Before René cut his cake, Francie set a filled wine glass at every place. "The boys are to have their first taste of Grape House wine tonight," she said, glancing at the other grown-ups. "If no one objects?"

Everyone smiled their approval.

"Why tonight?" demanded William.

"Because René is twelve and will soon be a man."

"I'm fourteen. I didn't have wine when I was twelve. How come?"

"It wouldn't be proper for you to taste it before René, dear. He's the heir."

"Oh, that stuff!"

"Watch your manners, William!" she snapped. Then she smiled at the others. "You truly don't mind?"

"They'll not be Leblancs if they don't drink Grape House wine," Pierre responded. "Lift your glasses, boys, for a toast: May René become a fine master of L'Acadie and

William remain his companion and right hand all their lives!"

They drank. The boys drained their glasses, set them down, faces wry. "I don't like it," René said. "It's bitter!"

"It sure is," agreed William. "I hate it!"

"Manners, manners," chided Francie. "You'll have a glass of it on special occasions like true Leblancs. In time, you'll appreciate its bittersweet bouquet. It's happened to every Leblanc, even me."

Francie was sweating. She was disappointed but not discouraged. René would come to tolerate the wine. Later when he was a young and active man, a candidate for heart attack such as ran in the family, she could use the poison again. Before he married, definitely before that.

Reluctantly, in the late fifties when he was sixty-three, Pierre sent for Guy Mercer to call at L'Acadie. Mercer climbed out of his powder blue and white Cadillac and strutted in at the appointed time, full of swagger. This was his first invitation to L'Acadie, and he had a gut feeling that great things would come as a result.

"You wanted to see me?" he demanded.

"Yes," Pierre said. "I do. Come in; we'll use the library."

Guy sat, looked about the room at the leather bound books, noted the quiet, restrained, and somewhat shabby decor. It had the makings of a fine room; he remembered that from the last time he was here.

"When I own L'Acadie lock, stock, and barrel," he said boldly, "I'm going to get rid of all those books. Put up paintings of women in the raw. Get a big television set in place of that little one. Do all the houses on the place over so's they'll knock your eye out."

"You seem certain you'll own L'Acadie one day."

"Got four thousand acres of it now, ain't I? Figure you're ready to sell two thousand more at least, seeing you sent for me. I know you ain't done well enough to buy any back."

Pierre's mouth clamped. Maebelle, who had come into the room, looked unhappy, not as she'd looked the other times, eager and tense. Then she'd been wild to buy jewels, to redecorate. Now she wanted only security.

"I'm offering you the two thousand acres at the extreme north end of L'Acadie," Pierre said. "At the same price as the other. The acreage doesn't include Honeymoon House, though it begins within five hundred yards of its grounds."

"At what price did you say?"

"Twenty thousand."

"It's robbery, you know that. I could offer less, since you're the one asking this time."

"My price is firm."

Guy studied Pierre boldly. Eventually he spoke. "If I agree to your price, I'd like to know why you're selling this time. What do you want so much Mercer money for?"

"More machinery. And to send my two grandsons to school in New Orleans, see them educated."

"That leaves you with six thousand acres and us with six thousand. We'll own half your place. It ain't but a question of time, and we'll have all of it."

"That day will never come," Pierre replied. "This sale puts us in good shape. With two young, educated Leblancs, they'll take over and bring L'Acadie back to its old glory, smaller, but as fine. Even finer."

Eventually the deal was closed. Five days later, Guy had a deed to two thousand acres of L'Acadie land and Pierre had his check for twenty thousand dollars. And Maebelle wept.

During the fifties, bayou men who had gone to fight in the Korean War began to trickle home. Some men returned with shy, dark-skinned wives who were pretty in their own way, but most could speak only a few words of English and none of French. Other bayou men had died in action. Pierre and Maebelle had been relieved that René and William were too young to be drafted.

The two boys, only dimly aware of the war which had been fought while they grew up, were quick in their studies in New Orleans. William took history courses and read whatever he could find about the growing of sugar cane. René studied only music and literature. They were schoolmates as well as cousins and were considered the most handsome young men in all their classes.

"You run after too many girls," René warned William when they were older. "You'll get one of them in trouble."

"Not a chance!" scoffed William. "I'm careful and the girls are careful, too."

"Well anyway, I don't want to be forced to marry or let my son be a bastard!" René said determinedly.

"Look, you haven't turned into . . . I know there are guys who don't like women."

René laughed heartily. "I guess I'd better confess," he said. "I do have a girl, a perfectly safe one. She's older and divorced: the setup's perfect. We get along fine, fit like this!" He held two fingers up, pressed together.

"She isn't trying to hook you because of L'Acadie?"

"Not Betty. She hates the country. She's studying to be a registered nurse. She means to snag a doctor, a specialist. Where she's working, she meets lots of them. They're the ones who make the money, she says."

William clapped him on the back, and after that they double-dated. Betty was broad-minded and accepted the fact that William rarely showed up with the same girl twice.

Francie, her plan for René unshaken, remained on fairly good terms with the family. She all but ignored Dorcas and treated both her and Maebelle as if they were senile, but always with enough courtesy not to rile them unduly. She was warmest toward Pierre. After all, he too would insist that René and William develop a palate for Grape House wine.

She became a proficient baker and often brought a chocolate cake or a cherry pie. She had slipped into the parlor one evening with a cake when she heard William's name mentioned. She stopped just inside the door and listened.

"I wish William could take over L'Acadie," Pierre was saying. "He's devoted to farming. It seems to be his life's blood, while René thinks only of his music."

"Is that the whole reason, dear?" Maebelle asked. "Or is it partly because René isn't a true Leblanc, because Gabriel paid that Cowan woman to bear René for him so he'd have an heir of his own blood?"

Francie burst through the door. "I heard that!" she cried. "René's a bastard! William's the true heir, not him!"

Shocked, Pierre and Maebelle stared at Francie. "I know what you said, I heard it!" Francie continued. "René's a bastard, only half Leblanc! He's got no rights!"

"He has every right," Pierre said through gritted teeth. "Gabriel's blood flows in his veins, and Gabriel and Diana adopted him. Those two things give him every right!"

"But he's still a bastard! His mother was a whore! L'Acadie can't have a bastard mother!"

"I see you're ignorant of a fact much worse than René's origin," Pierre told her. "Either Lee didn't believe the truth or he chose not to tell you. Every Leblanc from the first René on has carried Negro blood in him. Even your own son, yes, William, too. There's a trace in him!"

Francie's brain stopped. "Unless William can be heir," she screamed, "I'll tell! Tell that René's nigra—bastard and nigra!"

"It would be news, Francie, but you'll not tell. You'll think of your own son, see to it that he lives white, is known as white. You'll not stir up old gossip, which most people never believed at the time or have forgotten. You won't shame William—or yourself, widow of a man with Negro blood in him!"

Francie slammed the cake onto a table and stormed out, flushed and weeping. She would say nothing. But there was one thing that she would not give up. William simply had to be heir.

XXXVIII

William gradually became enamored of a girl who wouldn't go to bed with him. She wouldn't even neck and consented only to movie or dinner dates when René and his nurse were with them. At the end of the evening, all William would get was a chaste kiss on the lips. This was five foot nine inch Josleen Laird. He saw her first on the dance floor at Armando's Restaurant and contrived to meet her.

The next day, having gotten her phone number, he called and asked her to dinner at Armando's. She coolly accepted, as if it were her right. This intrigued him. She wasn't like any of his other girls. He had to promise that René and his date would go, too; otherwise she wouldn't accept, saying she was no man's pickup.

René's little nurse looked scrubbed and healthy and pretty. Josleen, who carried herself like a tall princess, chatted coolly with Betty. She asked about Betty's nursing courses, but didn't listen to the answers. Her attention was on René, for William had told her that René was heir to L'Acadie.

William watched as Josleen turned her charms on René, smiling at him regally, yet with cool seductive quality. William gazed at the thick, sandy hair which she wore short, the ends barely touching her jawline. He tried to catch her dark blue eyes to assess them, but they were on his cousin. He studied her lovely, patrician features and wondered how much effort it would take to get her into bed.

Josleen was aware of William and turned a smile on him at intervals. Persistent by nature, she wanted René. It would be a fine thing to marry him and be mistress of a plantation. Much better than marrying a bank clerk, the only solid proposal she'd had. Still, she wanted to keep William on the string. It wouldn't be too bad to be second lady at L'Acadie.

As time passed, she realized in frustration that she had no chance with René and concentrated on William. He, thinking to bed her, responded. She allowed some necking, and let him French kiss her once. Other than that, she held him off. "Any man gets me in a bed puts a wedding ring on me first," she told William bluntly, and he, consumed by desire now, proposed and she accepted instantly. He even bought her a nice diamond. She decided it was not as big as she'd get out of him later, but nothing to be ashamed of either, and she flaunted it before René and Betty, neither of whom could have cared less.

William took Josleen home to L'Acadie one summer evening, driving the old Chevy he'd managed to buy from his allowance. He had planned their arrival as a complete surprise. None of the home folks knew Josleen existed, much less that she'd been his wife for two weeks.

The family was sitting in the library after dinner, watching television. They looked up, startled, when William escorted the regal Josleen into the room. Slowly they rose to their feet.

Francie took a step toward them, stopped. She had gone very pale. Dorcas murmured William's name in surprise.

"Folks," William said with a throb in his voice, "this is Mrs. William Leblanc—Josleen. We've been married two weeks. It was my idea to surprise you."

Pierre moved first. With a stunned expression, he offered Josleen his hand, and she extended her fingers coolly. "My dear," he said with a searching look, "this is indeed a surprise."

Pierre presented the others. A dazed Maebelle offered her cheek, but Josleen proffered those regal fingers instead, repeated the action with the equally dazed Dorcas.

Francie, before Pierre could introduce her, regained her voice. "William! How could you without telling me, your own mother? Where's René? Why didn't he warn us?"

"He's at school, sworn to secrecy. He likes Josleen, Ma. She's never had a mother, needs one. She's my wife, your daughter. Aren't you going to kiss her?"

Dorcas watched the cool, motionless Josleen and the quivering Francie. If they do move, she thought wryly, it'll be like two strange cats ready to fight. William shouldn't have done this, shouldn't have brought this snobbish woman to L'Acadie, but it's done now, whatever comes.

"I take it," Josleen said stiffly to Francie, "that you didn't want your son to marry."

"Not like this! We don't know your age, your background, nothing!"

"I'm twenty. My father is a butcher. My mother died."

Francie whirled on William. "Why didn't you warn me?"

"I guess I knew you'd take it like this, Ma. Come on, now. You two have got to be friends because you both love me."

Silence hit the room. Pierre, at a loss to do anything else, poured glasses of wine for everyone. "We must drink to the happiness of the newlyweds," he said, "and to the hope that we'll love our new family member and that she'll love us."

William downed his wine at a gulp, set the glass aside, made a face. Josleen sipped hers, set the glass on a table and shuddered.

When Josleen drew William to a divan, Francie sat down between them on the seat. "Where do you intend to live, William?" she asked sharply. "Have you given that a thought? Honeymoon House isn't big enough now that you have a wife."

"We'll live wherever Grandpa says, Ma."

"Old House," Pierre decided.

Josleen glanced around. "This house is big enough, isn't it?"

"Old House is big," Pierre told her. "It'll hold any family you have, no matter how large."

Time crept. William, sitting with his bride and his mother, was torn between them. Every question Josleen asked about Old House brought a comment from Francie, repeatedly demanding to know whether he'd finished his studies before he'd married. At last he told her that he had not, that he preferred to go to work on the land, and Francie, though indignant that he had quit school, was pleased that he'd be working the land because she meant for him to own it someday.

This initial situation never changed. The two women hated each other, and when both were with William, vied for his entire attention. William, dejected over how things were going, tried fruitlessly to please both of them.

A few days later William finally managed to talk privately with his mother. He asked and pleaded that she invite himself and Josleen to dinner. "It's only right, Ma," he argued. "She's your daughter now. Give her a chance."

"I notice nobody else has entertained her!"

"That's because it was so embarrassing, you and Josleen snarling at each other. Please, Ma, do it for me!"

Francie, honestly and deeply hurt in addition to being jealous, gave in because of her love for William. She told him to take the invitation to Josleen that they were invited to dinner that same night.

Josleen refused to go. "She hates me!" she stormed. "And I'm as good as anybody! Better! She'd hate any girl you married! You can go alone, you're so crazy about her!"

He made love to her. That was the only way he could ever soothe her, persuade her to listen to reason. Wrapped in his arms, legs entwined, she sullenly consented to go. The evening was miserable, for the two women exchanged catty remarks, some of which were openly insulting.

Josleen remained cool toward the other members of the family, her manner growing more regal by the day. She was polite to Pierre, treating him with cool respect, which he forced himself to return. She treated Maebelle and Dorcas as if she herself were queen and they were her ladies-in-waiting. Secretly she considered them useless bores.

Ever unhappier, William assured Josleen that Francie would mellow when they had a baby. The others would be more friendly, too. "They're all crazy about kids," he added.

"I couldn't care less," Josleen sniffed when he mentioned their reaction to a baby. "But I do fancy myself as a mother. I have the looks of a Madonna and the ability to carry it off. Actually, I'll not mind having a family. It'll give me something to do, rearing them properly."

William, grateful for what he took as blessed cooperation, made love to Josleen every night. She waited for the first signs of pregnancy. During the days, he spent as many hours as possible working the land with the new tractor. They'd planted still another hundred acres to cane, more than they'd been able to plant since slave time. L'Acadie began to prosper.

Time passed, but Josleen didn't become pregnant. Impatient, she went to a doctor in New Orleans to find out the reason. The doctor, an expert in his field, said she would never conceive. Her condition was so complex there was now no known surgery to correct it.

William, much to Josleen's rage, let the family know the situation. Icily, she acknowledged their sympathy and rejected any suggestion of adopting a baby. Francie tried, but failed to keep secret her own mixed emotions—elation that the aloof Josleen was less than a woman and disappointment that William couldn't have a son. Then she saw the solution. William would tire of Josleen and divorce her. He'd marry again, the right kind of girl, and she would give him sons. She clung to this idea; it almost made her happy.

As for William, his one pleasure now was working the land. He corresponded with René, still in college. He made love to Josleen, because she couldn't conceive. He tried doubly hard to make her happy, could not.

Sometimes, riding the tractor, he wondered how many other men were in his same situation.

XXXIX

Pearl, after giving Benjy dinner at her table for a month, asked Babette and Clarence to let the boy live with her and Ben in the big house. "It's hard for us to understand your not letting Benjy eat at your table, Clarence," she finished, and looked at Babette.

Babette's eyes fell. "I've got to do what Clarence wants, Mama," she said. "He's my husband. I promised to obey."

Pearl then looked steadily at Clarence. "Why? That's what I want to know. What's so wrong with Benjy being a part of your family?"

Clarence was sullen. "Things have changed. Ben told me for certain that Curtis'll be the heir. Benjy ain't . . . well, he don't fit. It's enough that I let him use my name."

"Then," Pearl said quietly, "there's no reason he can't live with Ben and me. We love him because he's sweet and retarded, because he needs us."

Clarence shrugged. "He can go for all I care."

Babette sobbed her consent. "It's best, I know it is. And it's not like I wouldn't see him every day!"

The arrangement worked out well. Benjy's table habits improved and soon were faultless. He and Curtis played together, later worked together, and always loved each other. As he grew, all Rivard accepted Benjy for what he was—a hard-working, retarded, young man, a friend to all.

Now, in 1959, Lora Gordon, as light-skinned as Benjy and as retarded, came to live with her granny. She was a sweet, quiet girl with straight brown hair, light eyes, a slatlike body, and reddish lips which curled often into a smile, making her neat, plain features beautiful for an instant.

She first saw Benjy in the choir where he sang tenor. She was pleased by his light color, his blue eyes, his pleasing build. She kept looking at him that Sunday and all the Sundays.

Eventually, his eyes met hers across the church one Sunday. He felt a surge of passion when she smiled, didn't

know exactly what it was, but found it exciting. Some
Sundays later, they talked shyly, and he felt her friendliness when she smiled.

"I'm Benjy Rogers," he told her that day. "But I live with
my grandma and grandpa Rivard. Clarence—he's married to
my ma—don't want me around because I'm not smart."

"I live with my grandma, too," Lora said. "That makes
us alike, because I'm not smart either."

Slowly the weeks passed, and as they talked longer, they
realized that they were alike in the head, just slower than
other folks. It was Benjy who put it into words as they walked.

"Clarence says I'm dull, and when I asked Grandma and
Grandpa, they said I'm just not as quick as I could be. But
they said I'm smart enough to work at Rivard all my life."

"Me, too," said Lora. "Granny says I'm slow, but it don't
matter. She says long's my brain's like now, I can get along
fine. I can read and add," she finished proudly.

"Lora—" Benjy stopped, not knowing how to go on. She
looked so pretty smiling that way, her head with such nice
straight hair, so different. "Lora," he stumbled on, "I'm
crazy about you. Are you crazy about me?"

She nodded, still smiling. "Real crazy, Benjy."

"Then we got to get married."

"Why?"

"Because that's what folks do when they're crazy about
each other."

"But will they let us? Your grandma and grandpa? And
your mama and her husband? And my granny?"

"We'll make them let us," Benjy promised. "Right after
supper. We'll have them all at the big house; I'll say it's
very important. We'll have the meeting tonight, then get
married tomorrow."

"Get married?" hissed Clarence when Benjy blurted out
his desire to those assembled. Clarence threw a horrified

look around. "These two? Married? Raising a crop of halfwits named Rogers?"

"Now, don't be hasty," Ben said. "Benjy isn't a dummy. I took him to New Orleans, remember, had him tested. He's got a sound enough mind. And Lora's fully as bright."

"We're crazy about each other, Grandpa," Benjy said bravely. "We need to marry each other because we're alike."

"Pah!" Clarence spat.

Babette objected. "This is Benjy's whole life we're talking about, and Lora's, too. No mistakes must be made."

"They're suited to each other," said Pearl.

Granny agreed. "My Lora, she keep a clean cabin, and she cook as good as me. She ready for a man, and he need to be one like Benjy. They made fo' each othah."

Clarence started to speak heatedly, but Ben quelled him with a look. "These two should marry," Ben said, "but they must have no children."

"They's ways," said Granny.

"But why?" Benjy asked. "Everybody else has babies."

"You do understand that you and Lora are different from other people, don't you, darling?" Babette asked.

Benjy considered, frowned, and so did Lora.

"We're not smart like other folks," said Benjy. "But we work good. Grandpa says so. So why can't we have babies?"

"Do you want babies who maybe aren't smart enough to even sit up?" Babette pressed, heart wrenching.

Both youngsters considered, stared at each other, then painfully nodded. Benjy spoke slowly. "If we do what Granny says, then we can get married and have our own cabin?"

"That's right, dear heart," Pearl half-whispered. "Yes, if you promise, you can get married."

The others began to nod and murmur. Clarence remained

quiet, scowling and outvoted. The retarded sweethearts agreed eagerly.

But they weren't married next day, for Pearl insisted they have a wedding in the big house. She got out her supply of dress goods and sewing materials to select a length for a wedding dress. Lora watched, hardly breathing.

When everything was unfolded and on display, Pearl insisted that Lora pick out the material she liked best. Lora didn't speak, but put one shaking finger out and touched the gleaming white satin and then the cobweb lace beside it.

"These," she murmured. "One of them. They're so beautiful and soft! Could I have one of them?"

"You'll have both, dear," Pearl told her. "The satin for the dress, the lace for the veil. You have good taste."

There were tears in Pearl's eyes over the goodness of this girl, and the way it matched the goodness in Benjy. Watching, as Lora stroked the lace, Pearl knew Ben would understand. He'd bought this material years ago for Pearl to use if ever the Louisiana laws changed so blacks and whites could marry.

Benjy and Lora, both dressed in white and with utter purity on their young faces, stood before a bower of white roses in the big parlor for the ceremony. Benjy, solemn and handsome, and Lora, smiling and beautiful, took their vows earnestly as all Rivard watched.

Pearl gazed through the mist in her eyes, as did Babette and Granny. Ben had explained birth control to Benjy, as had Granny to Lora, and they understood fully.

After cake and wine, all the Rivard people made a circle from the back gallery to the cabin which had been prepared for the newlyweds. They started to walk, smiling, toward their new home. Babette followed, carrying a purring tabby cat.

Benjy and Lora stopped on their porch, and Babette put the cat into Lora's arms. "She's to have kittens any day," she explained. "And you'll have her babies to take care of."

"For always?" breathed Lora. "We can have all the baby kittens we want?"

"For always," Babette agreed, tears on her face.

When Guy Mercer and his son Simon heard about the marriage, they stormed onto Rivard, straight to Ben. Guy did most of the storming. Simon had recently graduated from college and was becoming famous locally for his fantastic luck in the stock market and his polished airs.

"This is my oldest boy, Simon." Guy introduced him needlessly. "This is Ben Rivard, Si, the one that's got a white woman."

"Indeed!" said Simon in a silvery voice. He didn't offer his hand.

"What we're here about," Guy said hotly, "is those dummies. Is it true that you let them get married?"

"Benjy and Lora are married, that's quite true."

"What are you up to, letting dummies marry? Aim to fill Rivard with halfwit niggers? Ain't things bad enough a'ready? Think the Teche'll stand for it?"

"Now, Pa," Simon interrupted, all silvery, "what can people actually do? The marriage is legal."

"They can't do anything, I reckon, without somebody to show 'em the way!"

"That someone being yourself?" asked Ben tightly.

"You hit it, right off! There is a way out. I'll buy Rivard, pay you ten thousand dollars cash, and you can take all your people and move lock, stock and barrel!"

"My answer to that is the same as before," Ben said. "We'll never sell Rivard. As to my grandson and his little bride, rest assured there'll be no more like them. Set your mind at ease. This is Rivard business, this wedding, and I'd appreciate it if you'd leave."

They did leave, driving away in their new Oldsmobile, but with ill grace. Guy was scowling and Simon was frowning, the perfect picture of displeasure. Their only hope now, Simon knew, was Clarence and that proposition he'd made to Guy years before.

XL

During World War II, many bayou folk had gone north to work in factories for high wages, and it was difficult for plantation owners to keep enough help. The Mercers were among those who prospered. They'd bought enough machinery to work their land and needed fewer men to run it. They'd built up a whole clan of Mercers in the bayous and boasted among themselves that Mercer blood would eventually dominate Bayou Teche. This Guy repeated to Simon still again, and the son promised in his polished manner to revive the old story about black blood in the Leblancs and to precipitate more of the old gossip about Rivard, as well.

"I know," he told his father, "that Clarence Rogers made a deal with you, and we'll carry it out if circumstances warrant. But I don't trust that fellow. He's looking out strictly for Number One. He couldn't care less about his in-laws."

René had finished college and was working back at L'Acadie when Francie decided to put her scheme into action. She started by trying, very cleverly, to encourage both René and William in the first few days to develop a palate for Grape House wine.

"It's good to have you home again, René," she coaxed, one evening after dinner in the big house. "We must drink a toast to that."

René made a slight grimace, as did William, but neither objected. Both drank a bit of wine, but didn't finish it. Next time, Francie decided, she'd tease René into draining his glass.

She studied him. He had matured. He was six feet tall and splendidly built. His dark hair seemed to be more auburn than before, his eyes looked darker, his features were even more handsome.

Still, to her eyes William was better looking. He, too, was six feet, had sandy-red hair which glinted in the sun, blue eyes, and good features. He was big-boned and husky, a powerful as well as handsome man. He'd be the perfect L'Acadie master, especially if she could get him to divorce Josleen.

She was delighted when René made no effort to evade the draft for the war in Vietnam, wherever that was. She pulled a long face, added her plea that he remain on the land and grow food, but secretly she hoped that he would go and be killed in battle, so she wouldn't have to take action.

She was mortally stricken when William enlisted and went to training camp with René. She didn't speak to Josleen for days, blaming her. It brought back all the horrid memories of Lee's enlistment.

As for William, it was a great relief to escape the bickering of his wife and his mother. In a day he'd forgotten their bitter farewells and had begun to look forward to what was to come.

He and René ended up in the same company and spent their off-duty hours together. They saw what sights were to be seen in Saigon, visited the local bars and clubs. William found himself a girl whenever he wanted one; René, though he was attracted to some of the local lovelies, refrained from sex with them. When William challenged him about this, René grinned and said, "I don't aim to leave a little half-breed or two running these dirty streets. I can wait until I find a girl to marry."

They threw themselves into the jungle warfare. They donned the camouflage gear, smeared dirt on their faces, blended themselves into the wild, deep growth through which they moved, ever on the lookout for the enemy.

On the first mission, they were sent into a dangerous area known as Charley's Playground. They fired not one shot, saw no palm frond stir, encountered none of the enemy. Only the jungle birds screeched and the monkeys chattered in the trees.

It wasn't until their second foray into the area that they saw action. Silently, the members of the company split, spreading out, creeping across the jungle floor. René and William stayed within sight of each other. As René slithered along on his belly, rifle ready, the whisper of each sound he made seemed to him like a crashing, tearing, ripping thunder. He couldn't hear William's passage, just his own.

He sweated profusely. Any instant a bullet might take him and he'd never know. A falling frond rustled and fell in his path. He cringed.

Instantly all the birds went quiet. All the animal life in the trees and bushes fell silent. René and William stopped their crawl and lay without breathing, listening, staring into tropic growth. The utter quiet of the jungle hurt René's ears. Then, as if reassured their world was again safe, birds called and flew again, monkeys swung from branch to branch chattering, and René, soaked through with sweat, began to breathe.

This meant that no enemy soldiers were on the move nearby. If they were near, they were lying hidden and motionless, waiting.

Finally René dared to belly-slide through the lushness. His attention was focused on a thickly fronded palm tree where a sniper might be lurking. He moved, wary of death which might be anywhere.

He came up slowly, looked for William, who signaled him to flatten, then pressed himself downward into long grass. He listened. He heard the shriek of a monkey, caught the shrill of birds.

The hackles rose on the back of his neck. He began to sweat more heavily. There were Vietcong here; he could sense it. Maybe one, maybe a hundred, hidden as only Vietcong could hide, deadly, ready to drop from any tree and stab an American in the back, ready to snipe from tree or ground growth.

He ached with the need to climb the nearest palm and conceal himself in it, to stand guard over William. Wait the bastards out. Force them to make the first move.

He crept toward the palm. His throat was dry. His knees quivering from strain, he rose halfway, bent over and advanced to the tree. He climbed its rough trunk quickly, as he'd climbed many a tree at L'Acadie, scrambled into the midst of its fronds, and was hidden.

He peered down at William, a hundred yards away. Suddenly a shot came from a nearby palm. The blast shattered William's leg, and he lay motionless. The second shot struck him in the abdomen; he screamed, then lay still again, his middle covered with gushing blood.

René pumped shot after shot into the sniper's palm tree, and a Vietcong crashed to the ground, his face blown away. René, swallowing vomit, dropped to the ground, crouched, ran through rifle fire to get to William.

The jungle was now a wilderness of rifle fire. The

members of René's company rose up from tree and bush and fired at the enemy, and the enemy poked their rifles through leafy growth and returned the fire. And René's company now responded with an unceasing wall of fire, pressing closer and closer to the Vietcong.

The Vietcong retreated through the jungle. The Americans, aware of the strategy, followed, splitting again, spreading out again, belly-crawling, taking to trees, pursuing the enemy, weapons ready. The once fragrant air was now laced with the stench of gunpowder and blood; the jungle was a bedlam of shots and screaming, terrified wildlife.

René had just reached William when two Vietcong appeared from nowhere, and René found himself in hand-to-hand battle with them. Somehow he got his big hands around the little neck of one, and he choked the life out of the enemy soldier, letting him drop when he was dead. The other soldier stabbed William in the heart, then crashed through undergrowth toward René, gripping his knife, ready. Burning with hatred and with the need to reach William, René grabbed the Vietcong by the wrist which held the knife and twisted it mightily and forever to the right. René's hatred gave him strength, and the enemy's wrist snapped. René caught hold of the soldier's knife and drove it into the Vietcong's cursed heart.

He'd almost made it to William when a third Vietcong appeared, aimed his rifle, fired. René heard the shot, and then he felt a thump on his right ankle and fell, unconscious.

He came to while being dragged along by one of the Americans, but by the time he reached medical aid, he had fainted again.

The next day he was told the bad news by the medic. "I had to amputate your foot, soldier." The medic had gray in his hair and kindness in his eyes. "It was shattered. Gangrene would have set in."

René went very still, then asked about William, but the medic couldn't tell him anything.

A field officer came to see René several days later. "William is reported missing in action," said the field officer, who had kind eyes like the medic. "Or the Vietcong have him in prison camp. Or he may be dead. Undoubtedly he is, after you saw what happened. The Cong kill the badly wounded."

After René recovered, they fitted him with an artificial foot, and the army discharged him and sent him home.

When he got home, René found Josleen established in the big house with the others. "I have a right to be here," she told him haughtily. "I'm staying until I find out what happened to my husband, to my William."

Francie, crazed, wept and wailed agrily. "I'm bitter . . . bitter!" she cried repeatedly. René, the bastard, was back safe and her son was missing. And she had yet to clear the inheritance for William, for when he came back. "No woman has as much to bear as I do," she moaned, "my husband killed in war and now my only son . . . . But he'll be back, I know he will. I'll never give up expecting him, getting things ready for him!"

René said nothing. Maebelle and Dorcas sometimes smiled ruefully at each other over things Francie and Josleen said.

Dorcas would put her arm around her mother-in-law. "We'll get through it," she'd say. "Time does heal. Francie and Josleen have no blood tie to L'Acadie unless William does get back. And if he doesn't, they have nothing to gain by spending all their lives mourning and drifting about L'Acadie without husbands. Just wait, it'll all work out."

And Maebelle would smile a bit and agree and hope for the best, accepting in her heart that her youngest grandson was dead.

XLI

Worried that only René now remained to carry on L'Acadie and he wasn't even married, so there was no prospect of heirs in the near future, Pierre made a decision. He discussed it with Maebelle, and she supported him.

Soon after, Pierre took René and Maebelle into the library where he told his grandson the true Leblanc story, how the English drove the Acadians out of Nova Scotia, how the first Gabriel established L'Acadie, how he fell in love with a mulatto slave girl and begot a quadroon son by her. Then he revealed the secret of the present generation, how René's own father, Gabriel, had paid a white woman to bear him an heir, paying her and her husband ten thousand dollars for the service.

"So now you know," Pierre finished. "You have dark blood, as I do and all other Leblancs."

René considered. "All I can say to that, sir," he responded at last, "is that I'm the same person now that I was before you told me. I feel no different."

"There's more. The Rivard family is connected to the Leblancs by blood—through an illicit relationship many years ago. The Rivards are good, honorable people."

"That I know, sir. They attend to their own affairs and are excellent conscientious farmers."

"I'm relieved that you feel this way," Pierre said. "For your grandmother and I have agreed—the Vietnam War alerted us—to what is best for L'Acadie should you die without an heir and should William never return. I've devised a will to be put into effect should L'Acadie be left without a direct heir. Here it is. Read it and speak your mind."

René took the long sheets of paper and read first that every Leblanc living at L'Acadie at the possible time of René's death was to be allowed to remain his or her lifetime if he or she so desired. This privilege extended to in-laws.

"In the event that I, René Leblanc, die without issue," the will read, "it is my personal wish that L'Acadie, its remaining six thousand acres, its houses, stables, cabins and their contents are to come under the management of Curtis Rogers, grandson of Ben Rivard of Rivard Plantation.

"My aunt, Elizabeth Herrera, will also have the privilege, which is her legal right, if she so desires, of living at L'Acadie with her husband and child and to share in the ownership of L'Acadie, which the law demands. Curtis Rogers is related to me and other Leblancs by blood and will, under my wishes, be the man to run L'Acadie in the event of my grandson's death. Said grandson, René Leblanc, will also sign this document, the purpose of which is to keep L'Acadie in the possession of male Leblanc blood, however thin the strain.

"This paper is to be read to those on Rivard who are touched by it. This is so that Curtis Rogers, direct descendant of Ben Rivard, will know and can prepare for possible added responsibility. It is my desire, that should these possibilities come to pass, that he reside at L'Acadie and that he sees to it that L'Acadie never vanishes from Bayou Teche."

René took the papers to the desk, reached for a pen and asked, "Where do I sign, Grandpa?"

PART III

1960–1967

XLII

Curtis Rogers, now twenty-one, was full of the sap of youth. He was of powerful size, with big, black, loose curls like his mother. Despite his good looks, he usually avoided girls. Yet he desperately wanted a steady, even wanted a wife to take comfort in. To say nothing of the mighty urge he had to bed a girl, an urge which both Babette and Clarence had schooled him never to give in to.

"You get a girl in trouble, Ben Rivard'll ride your ass until you marry her, grandson or no grandson," Clarence warned. "I know, I know. He ain't married to your grandma, but that's because the law won't stand for a white and a Negro to marry. Not in this state. They've lived for years, same as married. But it won't work for you, not for one minute."

"Besides," Babette added, "Pa and Ma love each other. You look at them together, and you can feel it. I wish" —she glanced at Clarence—"that all legal marriages were as sound."

Babette sighed, remembered fondly that Clarence had married her, a pregnant girl, pregnant by a white man. She was still fond of him, and he had never looked at another woman. And he hadn't meant to be mean to Benjy, she assured herself. She felt satisfied with her marriage, despite his attitude toward her retarded son.

Curtis had been quietly looking over the girls at Rivard and other plantations, and he finally decided to pick one and go after her. He sang in the choir, which gave him a good view of the girls every Sunday.

The girl he picked to go after was Marie Duval, about eighteen. She wasn't much over five feet and had a come-hither figure that moved so gracefully it was hard to believe. He'd watched her from time to time as she grew, and was pretty shook up when he realized what a stunner she now was. A couple of times he caught her looking at him, then turning away real fast, and that made up his mind.

Curtis edged over to where she was laughing with some girls after church. "Marie," he said, "want to walk some before dinner?"

She turned; the girls giggled. Her blue eyes were very wide, very innocent. She didn't know he'd like to have sex with her this minute. Dark blond, softly curling hair framed her chiseled features, making her almost white skin appear even whiter in the brilliant sunlight.

Marie was upset over the invitation—Curtis was the master's grandson—and she hesitated, turning to the other girls. "Go on," they urged. "The man wants to walk—so walk."

"You'll tell my mother that I'll be back for dinner at three?" she asked a girl friend.

"You might tell my grandmother the same thing," Curtis said, suddenly bold. "Tell her I'm with Marie," he added.

The girls giggled, then fled.

"Where do you want to walk?" Curtis asked.

"Not in the Quarters; everybody is gawking."

"Where, then?"

"I like it past the fields where there's grass and flowers."

"Okay," agreed Curtis, and they started. He couldn't think of what to talk about, so he blurted, "You've changed since you were a skinny little kid."

"How would you know?"

"I've got eyes."

"I didn't know you ever looked at me."

"At you and others. Know something? You're pretty in that blue dress."

She stroked the very short skirt. "It's new. My ma made it for me last week."

They walked on, saying little. The grass began and the flowers and trees, and they looked at it all, not at each other. Curtis suddenly seemed to be tongue-tied.

"This way," Marie said. "I'll show you something."

He cleared his throat and grunted assent. They turned, going deep into a sort of wilderness, flowers everywhere, especially roses. She stopped, and he did, too. He looked around; he'd been here before, but always on his way someplace and hadn't paid attention.

"Well?" she demanded. "Isn't it super? Look at all the roses!" She ran across the grass to where wild roses, red and pink, were clustered thick, some winding around trees.

"I used to play house here when I was little. I'm going to build a rose house! Want to help?"

Her invitation unlocked the speechless state Curtis was in. "Sure, I'll help," he said. "But I don't see how you can build a house out of roses."

"There's so many little trees it can be done, Curtis! We need to cut some poles with an ax and set them in the ground. Then we'll train the vines to climb the trees and the poles—they grow fast—and we'll have a rose house!"

"What'll you use it for?"

"To sit in and talk. Bring other kids. Have a party."

"You mean it'd be like that Grape House at L'Acadie?"

"Sure! Except we'll do it with climbing roses, roof and all!"

Her enthusiasm got to him. When you're with a girl, he thought, especially one like Marie, you've got to keep her

entertained. This was a snap. They'd have plenty to do,
lots to talk about.

They set right in, carefully moving a long strand of
rose-laden vine, draping it onto the nearest tree, then
onto the next nearest. When that vine ran out, they went
to work on the next strand, a long one, and the next,
chattering about how big to make the house, crying out
when they got stuck by thorns, sucking the blood away,
laughing, their eyes looking merrily on each other.

When it was time to go home, they'd made some
progress. There was the beginning of a wall of roses along
one end. Curtis said he'd bring an ax next Sunday, cut a
few poles. Later, he'd cut some to lay across the top;
they'd cover them with roses to make their roof.

Marie's eyes sparkled. "Can we work on the house other
times, not just Sundays?" she asked.

"Sure. Every day, right after supper, before dark."

"And longer on Sundays?"

"Naturally."

The third time they worked together, Curtis said, "You
know what everybody's saying about us?"

"What?"

"That we're going steady."

"Oh," she whispered.

"Do you care?"

"Not if you don't."

"I don't care. I want us to go steady." He hadn't known
he was going to say it, but now that he had, he didn't
regret it. He was sweating heavily.

"Oh!" This time she gasped the word.

"Will you?" he blundered. "Or is there somebody else?"

"No one else. I want to be your steady, too."

"That's settled, then. We're going steady," he said and
swiped his wet brow. His voice was not quite even, but he
had no control over it. "My pa," he said, "might object.

He doesn't trust me, but I'll not get you into trouble, Marie."

"I trust you," she whispered. "I know you won't. But you're the heir, and I'm only a tenant's daughter. Maybe we can't go steady, you so high, so important."

"I pick my own steady. You're it . . . if you're willing."

"Any girl would be," she said. "You're super. You're strong like your pa, but with the good-looking face of your ma. You get along fine with her. Everybody says it."

Curtis grinned. "I don't get along with Pa that well. We hardly ever agree on the first thing, seems like."

They worked on their house for weeks, and everybody knew they had a project, that they were going steady, and accepted it. The rose house grew slowly. As they worked, they talked, told each other everything, laughed and listened to the little portable radio Curtis brought with him. They became friends, and Curtis liked her too well to get the least bit fresh, and wondered if this was the way you fall into real love.

The day came when the wilderness house was finished. It was three-sided with roof strands of pink roses hanging down on the open side like draperies. They'd made the roof and the walls extra thick with roses. It was, indeed, a house of roses, and it gave off a heavenly scent.

When there wasn't another thing they could do to improve it, they stood hand in hand, gazing at their rose house.

"It's extra super!" Marie breathed. "Oh, Curtis, let's keep it this way, always! We can't let it ever fall to pieces!"

"We won't," he promised. "Know what? We can make this a very special house." His throat was dry.

"How?"

"It can be a wedding house. For us to get married in."

She stared at him, open-mouthed. His heart thundered.

Her ears were singing and her own heart was leaping wildly. She'd so wondered if he'd ever get serious.

"B-but you're still the heir to so much and I'm still—"

"Nuts to that. You're the one I want to marry. I . . . well, damn it, I'm wild about you!"

"And I . . . about you," she whispered.

He kissed her, holding her close, and she was soft in his arms as she kissed him back. He held her so close she felt him, but she kissed, just the same, then pulled gently away.

"How about next Sunday?" he asked. "We'll invite everybody. The wedding will be here instead of church."

"But your family—"

"They like you. Everybody at Rivard likes you. You're the sweetest person at Rivard, except for my Grandma Pearl, and you're just as sweet as she is. You're like her. Why, even Pa says you're a jewel and warns me not to get fresh with you, and he hardly ever thinks my way about anything."

"Won't they think I'm too young?"

He swept a look over her, her maddening figure, her lightly, softly curling hair. "You're eighteen, that's old enough, and we've found out we're wild about each other. They won't say no because we'd marry anyhow."

No one said no. Even Clarence was pleased.

So, on the next Sunday bride and groom and preacher stood inside the bower of pink. Curtis wore his white suit, and Marie was lovely in a soft, full, white voile gown with a little headdress to match. Benjy and Lora were in the front row, their faces lit with smiles, arms around each other.

Birds trilled, butterflies flitted, frogs croaked and answered each other, and squirrels chattered in trees. The mother of the bride wept happily; the father had tears on his cheeks. Babette, mother of the groom, kept wiping away tears.

Clarence beamed. Ben stood with his arm around Pearl, who smiled tenderly throughout. As the young couple made their vows, Ben whispered them to Pearl, and she whispered back, renewing their own vows.

Marie made a daily visit to Babette, her mother-in-law, after she finished gardening each day. Babette grew fond of her son's wife.

"I love having you every day, dear," she said on one occasion. "But you mustn't spend time with me you should spend with your own mother."

"I spend lots of time with Mama," Marie assured her. "I love being with you, and besides, I can learn more about Curtis from you—and from Grandma Pearl—so I can be a better wife."

Babette pressed a kiss on Marie's cheek. She was coming to love this girl and to believe that Marie would, in the future, be a perfect mistress for Rivard.

Marie became pregnant very soon. When the baby, Seth, was born, he resembled Marie in every detail.

Marie was generous with her baby, letting Babette and Pearl and her own mother have him for hours. Even Lora and Benjy had their fair turn and were beside themselves with joy.

"Don't let the kinfolk push you around, them wanting Seth," Curtis warned Marie. "He's your baby, not theirs."

"Our baby, goose! And he is so their baby!" She laughed. "I like their advice; it's good advice. You just watch all of them when they pick Seth up—they feel he's their baby, and I like it that way! As for Lora and Benjy, they play house with Seth, play he's truly the baby they can never have. We can share him, Curtis darling, and in no time at all we'll have another and another and another until Rivard is full of our children!"

Within a year, it seemed as if Curtis and Marie were

already master and mistress of Rivard, so loved were they by all. The tenants called them the young master and mistress, smiling, but in earnest, too.

Their only sadness, as time passed, was that they had no more babies, but they comforted each other that the son they had was perfect. They were content, and though still hopeful for more children, their lives were filled with joy.

Camille Rivard, whose father had been murdered by his twin at the time of her conception, had sung and danced her way to maturity and unexcelled beauty. Her stepfather, John Hall, had married Andrea, her mother, when Camille was a baby. He had lost his heart to the child as thoroughly as he had to the comely Andrea.

"You know," John told Andrea often, cradling the singing little mite, "she's like honey, this baby doll. She's got hair like honey, skin like honey, eyes so hazel, and she wears it all like jewelry. We got to save money, Andrea, save it for her, ev'ry penny."

"Whatever for?" laughed Andrea. She had been happier with this wiry, dark mulatto than she'd ever dreamed she could be after Fred, handsome, passionate Fred, was killed before her eyes.

"It's for when she gets married," John decreed. "She's to have linen tablecloths, linen sheets,—"

"But only folks like the Leblancs have such, John! Unbleached muslin—"

"None of that, not for my baby! The best. Plated silver and a silver coffee service, not even pewter like in Ben's house. And clothes, the prettiest, nicest clothes to be had. And lots of them. And on top of that, the biggest wedding ever given in the Quarters of any plantation on the bayou. That's what I want for my baby, and that's what she's going to have. And any money left over, we keep in the bank for her, case she needs it."

From the start, Andrea knew she had a big job ahead keeping John from spoiling Camille. But Camille, it turned out, wasn't easily spoiled. She accepted what they gave, never asked for more, and shared her bounty with her playmates.

When she was eight, John bought her a secondhand piano. Ben Rivard tuned it, and Andrea and John polished it so the dents hardly showed, and Camille sat at the yellowed keyboard and learned the notes from her Grandpa Ben. Within a year, she was able to play the music as she sang. When they asked what she wanted that Christmas, she wanted only a hymnal, so she could learn to play the church songs.

She was fully grown before she asked her parents for anything they'd failed to provide. She'd just given Andrea and John a concert, singing along when the selection had lyrics, humming when it didn't.

Now she turned the piano stool to face them, smiling as they applauded softly. Then her smile faded, and she looked sad.

"What is it, honey?" John asked. "What's wrong?"

"It's . . . well, Grandpa Ben says he's taught me all the music he knows. He says that I've gone ahead on my own as far as I can without higher training."

"Then we'll get you a teacher in town!" exclaimed John.

"Grandpa says there isn't one who knows more than I do."

John scowled. "Your grandpa have any suggestions?" he asked finally.

"He says there's a fine music school in New Orleans, says I could learn an awful lot there, especially the singing. He thinks my voice is for opera, Papa John."

"How much does this school cost?" Andrea asked. "And where would you live? Who would look after you?"

"Grandpa wrote off for information. The cost is very high." She whispered the figure.

John's mouth dropped open. "That's nearly as much as we've saved for when you get married!"

"And it's only for one year, Papa John, and I'd need to study several years. But at the end of the first year, Grandpa Ben says I could get work singing; then I could pay my tuition and board and clothes out of what I earn. I just need the money for the first year."

"You're so young!" wailed Andrea. "So innocent!"

"I'm well over twenty, Mama, past marrying age! And I'd be living in a dormitory with girls, so I'd be safe. And I'd never go out with a man!"

John, shaken, was trembling visibly. "All our hopes and dreams, the saving... You real sure there ain't just one fine young man on the bayou you'd want to marry, honey?"

Wide-eyed, Camille shook her head. "All I want—ever—is music. If I could learn to be an opera singer, I'd not want anything else!"

"There's wickedness in New Orleans, danger for a girl like you," John said brokenly. "It ain't the money. If you want it for music, that's fine because you sing like an angel and play almost as good. It's the thought of the kind of men you can meet in New Orleans. We want you safe, angel girl, and to us that means a good husband."

"Somebody like your Papa John," Andrea put in, beginning to weep. "And you living right here at Rivard, raising your family. This other way...." She flung her hands apart and the tears flowed.

Camille knelt by her chair, held her and wept, too. "Please Mama...please, Papa. I don't think I've ever asked for anything big before. And this is really big—it'll take all you've saved, but you saved it for me, and this is how I want to use it. Please, oh, please!"

Now John was weeping with his womenfolk, his very

heart ripped out, and they were clasped in each other's arms, the three of them. Thus the parents gave their consent, gave it in sorrow but with love, and Camille felt her heart would shatter to be parted from them, but she was driven to be joined forever to music.

XLIII

Reluctantly René made a request of his grandfather. "Before I settle down to running L'Acadie, sir," he said, "there is a thing I long to do, a favor I can ask only of you."

"All you need do is speak, René."

"It's my music, sir. I'd like to spend a year in New Orleans, play piano professionally. Make some practical use of what I studied in college."

Pierre responded instantly, remembering his year in Saint Louis. "I see no reason you can't have the year," he said.

"It means work for you, Grandpa. Running the plantation an additional year."

Without so much as a glance at René's artificial foot, Pierre spoke reasonably. "If you'd been able to fight longer, I could have run the land. Go, my boy, go with a free conscience."

René embraced his grandfather wordlessly. There was no way to express his appreciation for a year of utter freedom. Everything in him pushed him toward music, and now he could give in to it for a time, and he was ecstatic.

In New Orleans, he took a modest room; he searched for just the right job, going first to the smaller restaurants.

At the second place, he was interviewed by a lardy, oily-skinned man who chewed on a cigar and had an unpleasant body odor. "Play piano, you say?" he demanded, shifting the cigar to the other corner of his mouth.

"Yes, sir. I studied music in college."

"Play rock and roll? The Beatles? I got lively customers."

"I can play that, yes," René said.

Beady eyes darted at his foot. "That fake?"

"Yes, sir."

"How come?"

"Vietnam."

"Don't expect no favors from me, drafted or not. Most of my customers are against that war. Well, set down. Play."

René was angry, but he controlled his voice. "Thank you, but no," he said. "I hardly think I play your beat well enough."

He walked out. He went to other places, but had no better luck. They either rejected him because of his foot, or they wanted him to play only rock, or they simply didn't want live music. He became angry and downcast by the constant rejection.

Finally, René went to Armando's, the newest fine restaurant in the city. Ricardo Armando, a portly man with white hair, auditioned him. René played classical music, ballads, jazz and blues. Armando hired him on the spot.

"Since you're educated in music," Armando said, "maybe you can help me out."

"Gladly, sir. What can I do for you?"

"I want to add a girl singer to the band. One who matches you at the keyboard, one who will be a star attraction. Not a flamboyant type, but a lady."

René was thoughtful. "That," he said, "is going to be quite an undertaking."

"Yes. And naturally, she must be beautiful."

Armando left René with this problem.

Every night René played with the band. Every afternoon he auditioned singers. One singer was pretty, but she had dyed red hair. She began to sing, and he decided to ask her to change her hair, but when she finished her song, she turned on him.

"I won't sing fancy stuff, and you play too much of it," she said. "Count me out." With a swish of her skirt, she turned and left.

When Camille Rivard came in, René didn't recognize her. For one thing, he hadn't seen her in years, and for another, he was taken aback by the outfit she wore.

Frowning, he watched as she moved gracefully across the quiet restaurant toward him. She had delicate features and soft, flowing blond hair. Her coloring made her look as if she'd been dipped in honey, but the clothes ruined it.

She had on a gored, gold-colored miniskirt; her legs were clad in fishnet stockings, the feet in open sandals. Her blouse was also gold, with tiger heads printed all over it, and she wore a matching scarf. The only added touch of color was her bright eyes, which were soft hazel and shone like jewels.

She came to him, smiling.

"I'm Camille Rivard," she said. "I'd like to audition."

"Dressed like that? In a place like this?"

"What's wrong with my clothes?" she retorted. "This is the 'in' thing, just like Armando's!"

"Armando's caters to top society. Mr. Armando would never let a miniskirted singer entertain here."

"I'll bet the girls who wear miniskirts come here, René Leblanc!"

"How did you know my name?"

"I've seen you on the Teche."

"The girls who come here to dine don't wear miniskirts."

"I'll bet they do on the street! This is the sixties we're in—women have lots of new rights!"

"Maybe so. But for you to show up like this for an audition! It'll give Mr. Armando the wrong impression if he sees you."

"I wouldn't wear a miniskirt to perform!" she said, quietly angry. "Surely you have sense enough to know that!"

"I can only go by what I see. And I see too much leg for this establishment."

"Does that mean you won't audition me?"

"Now that you're here, we can run through some numbers."

"Thanks a lot!" she snapped. "Back home on the Teche, we were neighbors. Here—" She flung out her hands.

He took a curious satisfaction that they'd been neighbors. That they came from the same bayou, from plantations whose boundaries had used to touch. It freed him to speak what he thought, to chide her.

He thought of his will. If he should suddenly die, this girl, this leggy beauty, might live at L'Acadie. He didn't dislike the idea, if she'd only dress like a lady.

"You resemble your grandfather a bit in looks," she said. "Once he bought me a sack of lemon drops. He's a kind man, noticing a child from Rivard, buying her candy. He didn't snap, like you!"

She glared at him. Under different circumstances, she'd like what she was seeing—the six-foot height, the dark hair, the strength. Even now she liked his Acadian olive skin.

He glared back at her, and his loins went hot. But he couldn't ignore her immodest dress. Besides, she was Negro and he was supposed by people on the Teche to be white and should conduct himself accordingly. He wondered what she'd do if he made advances. Would she reject him or would she be interested?

"The audition," she said. "Do I get it or not? I've had music training all my life, have sung ever since I could walk, and even before that, my mother says. My grandfather plays a mean piano, and my mother sings in the Rivard choir, lead soprano. I had six months at the music academy in New Orleans. Grandpa Ben urged me to try out here, and I promised."

Wearily, he motioned her to stand in the curve of the grand piano, asked what she wanted to sing.

"Whatever they like here," she said stiffly. "I know everything—jazz, ballads, popular songs. I like the Beatles, sing them a lot. New songs, too, and simple opera. You play, I'll sing."

He played the opening bars of one of his own favorites, and she came in with utter naturalness, sure of herself. She had a clear soprano voice, and her range was wide, layered, and sent small jolts of surprise through him. He played on and on, and she continued to sing, voice and manner enchanting, and the waiters who were setting the tables for dinner listened and sent admiring looks at her. Armando emerged from his office, sat down, listened.

Finally René went to Armando, leaving Camille. "This one, sir," he said. "She's the best I've ever heard. Anywhere."

"I'm impressed by her singing, not her outfit," said Armando. "But that can be changed. It's settled. We'll give this girl a chance."

Camille was overjoyed by the decision. She thanked Armando, agreed to the salary offered, and thoughtfully agreed to let René have control over how she was to dress for performances.

When René coolly invited her to the French Quarter for coffee and to discuss costumes, she agreed, but the warmth which had been in her voice for Armando was not there when she spoke to René. They sat at a sidewalk table and sipped the hot brew as they talked.

She thanked him for helping her get the job. He demurred, said that she'd won it despite his first impression of her.

"You said something about women having more rights now," he said. "What did you mean?"

"Well, everybody's fighting for civil rights, you know that! It's all around! Negroes want the right to register for the vote, women want the right to work at the same job as a man and get equal pay. And women also want the right to choose their own clothes, for goodness' sake!"

Intrigued by her seriousness, René grinned. "Okay, okay! Truce? We're to discuss costumes." He smiled.

Camille smiled back, but angrily. "Agreed. Now. Tell me what costumes to get. I don't want to disgrace you, you're so picky!"

He studied her across the table. "Wear cocktail dresses and evening gowns," he told her. "Simple cut. And gold, always gold. Dress, skin, hair—everything will blend. The gold must always have a tinge of honey—to make you look as if you've been dipped in honey, just one quick dip. No jewelry. Just your eyes."

"I don't have jewelry," she said, and laughed. "The only jewelry at Rivard is wedding rings. Even the mistress, Grandma Pearl, doesn't have one of those because she and Grandpa can't marry." She smiled sadly. "The law, you know. Grandpa being black and her white."

"It's a damn shame," René said. "That law may be changed. If it is, they can get married."

"If they do, it'll be the loveliest wedding you ever saw!" Camille exclaimed. Tears shone in her eyes, and suddenly René found himself almost beginning to like her.

Camille, getting dressed for opening night, knew she was in love. She was in love with her costume, with the music, with her new job, and most of all, if only he'd act decently toward her, she could be in love with René Leblanc!

She had been angry over his attitude, then worried, but now she was neither. What had her upset was that love could try to sneak up on you silently, lying in wait, choosing the moment in which it would overwhelm you. She pushed the thought away and concentrated on dressing.

Her gown was of fine, soft net—gold with a honey tinge. The bodice was fitted, outlining her lovely breasts, its color melting into the skin of her bare arms and modest cleft. The skirt fell in soft folds to the tops of her honey-colored slippers. Her hair swayed on her bare shoulders when she moved, and this added to her grace.

"Perfect! Enchanting!" murmured René when she arrived. "I apologize about the miniskirt! Your taste is flawless!"

She smiled tremulously, her arm seemed to burn his fingers as he guided her backstage to await her first number. He felt strangely drawn to her and even had to crush the urge to take her into his arms and kiss her. Was this attraction, he wondered, or was it sex, or was it both? Lips firmly set, he took his place at the piano.

When she heard her cue, Camille caught her breath. How could she sing when she couldn't breathe? But she moved forward, out into the restaurant, past the band, and took her place in the curve of the piano, feeling naked before the sea of faces.

She glanced fearfully at René. He nodded, and then he winked, and suddenly she could breathe again. Suddenly she wasn't afraid anymore. René was there and he was playing for her, just for her. She began to sing.

The diners set down their forks to listen. Camille held the big, rich room in thrall. The number ended, she inclined her head to the applause, and the diners stood, applauding, and she had to sing two more numbers before they would let her go. This response was repeated at her second show that night, and her third, and every night at every performance. Her beauty and the purity of her voice became the talk of the city.

Armando, delighted, billed her as the Golden Girl and raised her salary. She bought a dozen new golden gowns— satins, silks, lace, sequined. Although she was no longer timid, she would look toward René during performances, and he would signal with a tiny nod, and she would begin to sing, trusting him.

One night he asked to walk her to her room.

"It'd never do," she protested. "You're a white man."

Before she could say more, he had her outside on the banquette and they were walking. "You do know about my will," he said firmly. "Don't you?"

"I . . . yes. I heard about it. And was sworn to secrecy with the others."

"Then you know that Curtis Rogers, your cousin, might inherit L'Acadie?"

"Yes, I know that."

"So you also know I'm not really white. So it's proper that I walk you home."

She looked at him and smiled warmly. This made his heart lift, and he squeezed her arm, and they laughed together.

So began the courtship of René Leblanc and Camille Rivard. They tried to figure out their blood relationship, decided they must be cousins far removed, maybe half-cousins, even further removed, and smiled at its unimportance.

Soon René was urging marriage.

Camille tried to hold him back. "At least people on the Teche think you're white, and you're legally white," she pointed out. "It'd be a scandal for you to marry me."

"I'm ready for all to be known," he declared. "There's

always danger that word of that document of Grandpa's wishes for L'Acadie is going to trickle out—"

"If you're thinking of Uncle Clarence," Camille put in, "forget it. He's strutting proud about that will, threatens to beat up anybody who lets out word about it."

"Why? I heard he was friendly with the Mercers."

"Not any more! He thinks he'll be made master of Rivard and live in the big house if the others go to L'Acadie. He's afraid the Mercers would make trouble for him if they knew. So you can be certain that no one at Rivard will tell, ever. They're proud of it, all of them, but know it'll never come to pass."

"You and I will put an end to that document," René said firmly. "I am going to declare my black blood legally so we can marry. And when we start a family... You see, sweetheart, L'Acadie will never be white, never has been white. There's been the other blood ever since the first Gabriel found that runaway slave girl and fell in love with her."

Still Camille demurred.

He wouldn't listen. "Our marriage will cement the Leblancs and the Rivards," he insisted. "My family?" He shrugged. "They may be doubtful, even hurt, but that's the way it's going to be!"

He drew her to him, and they kissed, and Camille promised to marry him.

They agreed to wait six months, continue their jobs, save money. This would give their families time to adjust to the fact that they were going to be man and wife.

"I'll visit Rivard," René planned, "and take you along. And we'll visit L'Acadie, too, every time we go to the Teche. They'll get used to seeing us together, get used to the idea of a Rivard coming to live at L'Acadie."

"Yes," she breathed in his arms, "oh, yes!"

He held her close, firm in his plan, but knowing that the families might not be so easily won over.

XLIV

René, who had long since persuaded Camille she preferred life with him to the stage, attended to the legal
chore of declaring his black blood and after that, called
first at Rivard with Camille on his arm to get acquainted
with all her people. At first everybody, including René and
Camille, was wary, embarrassed and reserved. Then René
and Curtis discovered they agreed on how to raise sugar
cane, and their conversation flowed, and they felt comfortable with each other.

Ben and Pearl soon joined the conversation, although
the engagement between René and Camille was spoken of
in a tentative manner. One by one the others at Rivard
edged closer and exchanged pleasantries with René.

Pearl, who had watched closely, felt drawn to René. She
knew he was a fine young man or Camille would never
have chosen him to be her husband and given up her
study of music. Pearl smiled and motioned, drawing the
engaged pair into a corner of the dining room.

"If you'll let an old lady—" she began.

"You're not old, Grandma!" exclaimed Camille, and
hugged her.

"Well, if you'll let me speak then. I was in your same
situation, René, when I first came to Rivard. And I'd like
you to know how things went for me at the first, because
you may feel as I did."

"Go ahead, ma'am," René said. "I want to hear."

"I suppose Camille told you how Ben rescued me from

Josie's place, saved me from selling my body, the way my Pa wanted."

"Yes, she did. Your husband was a very fine man to—"

"Not my husband, my true love," Pearl said softly and glanced to where she could just see Ben's shoulder in the crowd. "At first I felt strange and scared being with all Negroes and me so white, the only white. I was even afraid of Ben, and he'd saved me. It's natural that you feel some of what I did—uncomfortable among so many Negroes, getting ready to marry into the family."

"A little strange, maybe," René confessed. "But far easier than it was for you. Because I have Negro blood, remember. That makes a difference."

Pearl nodded. "For me, what made the difference was kindness. All the Rivard people were so kind to me, I couldn't help liking them, and then I got used to them and hardly ever felt different. And now I feel no difference at all. I can't tell you how I felt when Ben moved me into the big house with him, but then I came to love him."

"Well, I already love René, Grandma," Camille smiled. "No obstacles."

"The obstacles will be his family," Pearl said flatly.

"The blood? They've got it themselves—"

"But they've lived white for generations, and with you comes a deeper strain of the black. It's going to take some getting used to for them."

"What should I do if they don't like me, Grandma?"

"Be friendly and kind, but remember that no matter how they may treat you at first, you're blood kin to them and they're good, kind people. Just be sweet; just be Camille. I've been so happy with Ben, still am, I want the same for you and René. Ignore criticism; do what you want to do and marry. Times are changing. You and René no longer have to hide your love the way Ben and I did."

Now Ben himself and John Hall came to them. He put

an arm across René's shoulders, and John Hall, tears in his eyes but a smile on his face, genially brushed Ben's arm aside and replaced it with his own. "Welcome into the family, son," he said to René, and René clasped John's shoulder.

The visit ended in a mood of friendliness amongst all. Camille was so happy she glowed.

But when René took Camille to L'Acadie, things were different. Pierre and Maebelle, though courteous, were cool. Dorcas was cordial. Francie and Josleen scowled, obviously not wanting to be in the same room with Camille.

Irked by the contrast between the two families, René took matters into hand. "You may as well learn to appreciate Camille," he said, his arm around her. "She's going to be mistress of L'Acadie," René went on, "mother of my heir. As for blood—all born Leblancs are on the same footing with all born Rivards. We're equal."

Pierre, seeing that Francie was on the verge of spitting out some venomous words, cut in. "Unfortunately," he said, "René is right. The Leblancs and the Rivards are already intertwined. René and Camille have every right to marry. The day of the wedding, I'll sign L'Acadie over to them."

Pierre's icy tone quieted Francie before she could speak, before she could scream out her belief that William would return from war, that William had a right to the land. But though her tongue remained silent, her vicious mind was desperate—and busy.

When she did speak, she icily proposed a toast and maliciously watched René drink part of his Grape House wine before he set the glass down. But on his wedding night, Francie thought with deadly glee, that would be wine enough.

*   *   *

Word of the upcoming wedding spread fast. The Mercers were amongst the first to hear it. They listened with satisfaction as the bayou folk, shocked to the core, gossiped and gasped and turned to one another in frustration.

Simon's silver tongue murmured to plantation owners, to merchants in St. Martinville, just a word. Slyly it murmured, and then there was no more need. The whole bayou was enraged that René Leblanc—of course he didn't have black blood, certainly not—was going to bring a nigra girl to be mistress of L'Acadie. Seemed she was a throwback, sort of, to her white grandmother. Something should be done to stop it. The law should never allow it, even if René did sign papers that he was black. Leblanc or no Leblanc, René and that wench should not be allowed to get away with what they meant to do. The murmurs went underground, but they continued, and punishment was at the root of them.

As the wedding date approached, the Mercer clan was joyful and busy. The Mercer women laughed and sang. The Mercer men went about their routine, Simon dropping a word here, a word there. For there was, at last, a plan. And their hearts were filled with hatred and glee.

XLV

The first week in June was lovely and sunny with little bursts of rain which washed the greenery and left it glistening. Babette arranged a party to celebrate the fiftieth anniversary of the union of Ben and Pearl. Ben was seventy-two, Pearl sixty-seven; her platinum hair had turned a blazing white. Both were in splendid health, both were handsome. The years together had left only smile lines

and crinkles at their eyes. Their faces in repose were
serene; when they laughed, time was wiped away, and
they seemed as they'd always been.

Even Clarence helped with the preparations, though
mostly getting in the way with his boasting. He'd never
been so happy in his life, not even when he married the
boss's daughter. Only one thing clouded his mood, and
that would never come to pass, he knew it in his bones. —

The whole bayou country was dead set against René
Leblanc taking Camille to live at L'Acadie. Clarence figured that marriage'd never go through. Pierre Leblanc
would stop it; he ruled L'Acadie, not that one-footed piano
thumper. Things just would work out so that Curtis, his
own son, would be master of both Rivard and L'Acadie and
he, Clarence, would be top man at Rivard.

On the night of June 10, 1967, all Rivard gathered in
the parlors of the big house for the anniversary celebration. After a covered dish supper, they smiled and laughed
and talked.

Pearl had been hugged and kissed; Ben's hand had been
shaken, and he'd been kissed by every woman. René, the
only outsider, had congratulated them, had greeted everybody else. At last, he stood quietly with Camille, who
smiled and glowed with pride in her grandparents.

Ben now produced a framed, carefully inscribed document which he read aloud. "This is how I feel," he
announced, "and I want the world to know it." He read, "I,
Ben Rivard, do on this, our fiftieth anniversary, again
pledge myself and all my worldly goods to Pearl. Signed,
Ben Rivard."

He kissed the framed document, held it to Pearl for her
kiss. Nearly everyone wept or had tears in his eyes. A
thrill went down René's spine, and he tightened his arm
around Camille as Ben hung the new document over the
mantel beside the one he'd put there half a century

earlier. Then Ben enfolded Pearl, placed a lingering kiss on her lips, and she returned it. And they tasted each other's lips in complete love.

"Pray God," Ben said then, "that before we die, the lawmakers of this state will make it legal for black and white to marry. When that happens, and it's been talked of, Pearl and I are going to have the biggest wedding ever held on the Teche!"

All applauded. Pearl slipped her very white arm through Ben's very black arm, looked down, and smiled tenderly at the contrast.

After that, the happy pair led the onlookers to the Quarters, where the piano had been set out. René took over the keyboard and two fiddlers backed him up, and he thought he'd never enjoyed playing so much, not even at Armando's.

René and Camille, deeply moved by the anniversary party, decided to keep their wedding simple. Camille explained to the Rivard people that only her mother, Andrea, and John Hall, her husband, Pearl and Ben, Babette and Clarence, and Curtis and Marie Rogers were to be invited. Ben agreed heartily with what she said and passed word that it would be out of place for Rivard and L'Acadie to socialize any more widely.

As the wedding day approached, Bayou Teche boiled with whispers. "That white nigra René—yes, he actually is nigra—signed legal papers that he is—aims to bring a darker one, a Rivard, to L'Acadie as mistress! Granddaughter of Ben Rivard, and Ben's black as coal. It's not to be tolerated. Decent people don't have to take it sitting down. It's time for the Teche to put an end to this, stop it before it gets worse." So ran the talk that was born of the Mercers.

The wedding day arrived. In the big double parlors

gathered those from Rivard, plus the priest, Pierre and Maebelle, Dorcas, Francie, and Josleen. Elizabeth was there, too, and her husband, José Herrera. The tenants of L'Acadie lined the walls.

Francie stood near Pierre and Maebelle, taut but inwardly trembling. She had so little time before she must carry out her plan. William's body had never been flown back like Lee's, therefore, he wasn't dead; Francie wanted him to come home to find his heritage ready and waiting.

The bride and groom entered together and stood before banked white roses. René wore a new white suit and the auburn of his hair glinted under the lights.

Camille looked more beautiful than ever. She wore a glistening white Chantilly lace dress made with a fitted bodice, high neck, and long sleeves which came to points at the wrists. Her lace veil, which framed her honey colored hair, fell just past her shoulders. In her hands she carried a white prayer book; on her trembling lips was a smile, the start of happy tears.

The rooms were hushed. The priest stood before the bridal pair and spoke the words which made them man and wife. René slid the heavy gold band onto Camille's finger, lifted her veil, kissed her tenderly on the lips, and then everybody moved forward to offer loving good wishes.

Francie busied herself at the table which held the wedding cake, decanters of Grape House wine, plates and glasses. Her hand steady, she poured the wine, and Pierre watched approvingly, hoping this was a sign her rigid disapproval would thaw.

Her back to the guests, she added the poison to a glass of wine, lifted the silver tray of filled glasses, went directly to the bride and groom. She handed a glass to Camille and one to René, saying, "It's your wedding. Surely you'll drink it, bitter or not," and René smiled and accepted the glass.

She served the others, even the L'Acadie tenants, her heart jumping. Pierre gave the toast and all drank, including Francie. René drained his glass swiftly, set it down. He looked as if he'd like to make a face.

Trembling, Francie cried, "The cake! It's time to cut the cake!"

XLVI

When the cake was eaten, the tenants left for their cabins. Then dinner was served to the families, now united. René and Camille were so ecstatic that everyone but Francie and Josleen smiled with joy at the happiness of the bridal couple.

Francie nibbled at chicken and salad, watching René for symptoms, but there were none. Afterward, they all drifted back into the parlors where they drank more wine. This time Pierre filled the glasses. Finally the bridal pair, Camille shy and blushing, René openly impatient, said good night and walked toward Honeymoon House.

The Rivards headed for home in their cars. The Leblancs scattered to their various suites, relieved that the wedding was over, hoping the adjustment to come wouldn't be too difficult.

"When you get tired of Honeymoon House," René said as they walked, arms around each other, "we can move into Old House. Or, Grandpa suggested that they all move into Old House and let us have the big one, L'Acadie itself."

"Oh, no!" Camille protested. "Let them stay! Don't upset them! We're young, and I love Honeymoon House and Old House, too! I guess I'm greedy. This way, we'll get to live in all the houses eventually, one after the other!"

He laughed, stopped walking and kissed her, held her, looking forward to the moment they'd be alone in their bedroom. It was then the first sharp pang went through him, and he wondered what he had eaten to cause it, then couldn't remember what they'd been served, he'd been so excited.

They sat in Grape House a few moments and murmured and kissed. René felt a pain in his chest, decided he'd eaten and drunk too much. Suddenly concerned, he thought about asking Camille if she felt all right, then did not. No need to alarm her.

She was laughing, a low, gurgling sound. If he asked her how she felt, she'd sense instantly that he might be sick. And he was well; he just had a touch of indigestion.

They spoke of their future. "I told Grandpa that I'd take over the plantation right away," René said. "Which means no more professional music for us."

She sighed contentedly. "We'll make all the music we need, right at home. Could we move that piano from Old House into Honeymoon House?"

"Of course. It's a fine idea. And I'm going to make a down payment on a new tractor, put more acreage to work."

"And I'll have a dozen babies, and we'll have to move into Old House!" she whispered and held her lips up to his. They kissed lovingly and long, then strolled toward Honeymoon House and their marriage bed.

René turned on soft lights, and the glow reflected in the mahogany furniture. It showed walls of books; in the main bedroom, the four-poster used by so many Leblancs was ready turned down.

They stood in the middle of this room. "I need to undress you, darling," René said. "I want to be the one to

reveal your beauty this first time." An indigestion pain
pierced him; he ignored it, though his impulse was to
double up.

"If I can undress you, it's a deal," she said boldly.

Tenderly he removed the lace wedding gown—the veil
and the white prayer book had been left at L'Acadie—and
slid off the silken bra and panties, revealing the exquisite,
honey-dipped figure. His eyes rested on the sweet thrust
of golden nipples, the sweep of waist, and the matchless
surge of hips that flowed past tender thighs where lay the
blond love nest, down perfect legs to narrow, slippered
feet.

He took the slippers and nylon stockings off her, breath
caught, then loosened her golden hair to fall past her
shoulders. Enthralled by her total beauty, he ignored the
indigestion.

When she began to undress him, he helped, making it
easy for her unaccustomed fingers. His body was ready,
aching for the second when it would claim her. His loins
throbbed with longing.

She knelt, touching the fastening of his artificial foot,
and he lifted her. "I leave it on tonight," he said, swung
her into his arms and started toward the bed.

A sudden, unholy clamor was heard outside. There was
the banging of metal against metal, hoarse shouts, a
gunshot, another. Voices yowled, "Show yerselfs! This is a
shivaree! We want you to entertain us!"

"René," Camille breathed, "people don't do this any
more unless they like the bride and groom very, very
much. Or unless they hate them. And the people around
here hate us—we've outraged the whole bayou!"

"Right!" René agreed, ignoring the pain in his belly.
"Get something on! Fast!"

XLVII

As Camille got into a silk-lined robe, René plunged into undershorts and reached for his own robe. Suddenly three burly figures, robed in white satin, wearing pointed white satin headgear with eyeholes, burst into the room.

"Who are you?" René demanded. "If it's refreshments you want, all we have is Grape House wine."

"We don't care for wine, not tonight," came a silver-tongued reply and René recognized the voice as that of Simon Mercer. "We're here to teach you a lesson!"

They were all Mercers, bound to be, René thought wildly. "Get out of here!" he ordered. "We don't want you!"

One of the figures guffawed, a hoarse, harsh sound, and the others joined him, making an unholy racket in the room. René, holding Camille, put her aside. He took a step toward the one who had spoken.

"I know who you are," he gritted. "Get out or I'll throw you out!"

"René! Don't try!" cried Camille, but he took another step forward. The satin-covered figure stood still, waiting.

The other two sprang, each grabbing one of René's arms, and braced themselves. Camille moved to help René, but three more white-robed figures suddenly appeared, and one swatted her back so hard she staggered and fell against the wall.

She flew back at them. "You let him go!" she shrieked at the men who were holding the twisting, yanking, kicking,

biting René. "Let him go this minute! You have no right to
do this! This isn't a shivaree at all!"

One of them gave René a mighty punch to the jaw, a
punch which yanked his head half around. Camille clawed
to get her hands on the fellow, to rip off his robe, scratch
his face, dig out his eyes. Failing this, she tried to snatch
off one of their hoods, but one man gave her a jolting
punch alongside the head and flung her away. She fell, but
was up in a second, ready to go at it again. Two of the
figures grabbed her, held her in a vise. She tried desperately
to wriggle free, tried to kick, but she was barefoot and her
efforts were useless. The men dug into her arms as she
struggled, and she knew that their thick nails had drawn
blood.

She screamed, and one of them hit her across the
mouth. She knew she bled, for she could taste the salt.
The three who had the violently resisting René were
driving their fists into him brutally—into his face, groin,
kidneys, heart, face again. Camille tried to scream, but
the men who had her, choked her until she was almost
senseless, until she grew so weak they had to hold her up,
but still she fought. René, glimpsing her, bellowed as he
tried to free himself, and the men smashed his lips, which
soon swelled and he could not speak.

The little house was filled with deadly, murderous figures, with guttural, death-dealing noises. The white figures stomped and bellowed in great, rough surges of
sound. They cursed and guffawed loudly and evilly.

Camille never ceased trying to get to René, and he tried
endlessly to free himself. Merciless hands held them
apart; merciless hands stripped off Camille's robe, leaving
her naked.

"What a wench!" roared one figure. "Let's pass her
around first! It'll be a real lesson to Leblanc for bringin'

her here. It'll prove to him he better get rid of her for keeps!"

"No," said the silver-tongued one, "we keep it clean. Rough them up good; teach them a lesson. Then wait for them to sell out, pack up, and leave the Teche!"

"You're the Mercers! Bound to be!" René managed through his split, bleeding lips. "You can't ever scare us off!"

He tried to struggle again, but they held him. Camille tried, but three of them held her, too. She didn't scream again, only moaned René's name over and over. All that mattered was that she get to René, or he to her, that they be in each other's arms. Together, they'd somehow fight off these satin-covered wolves.

Instinctively, she changed her tactics. She stopped pulling away and stood quiet. Voice shaking, she tried to plead with the men, begging them to leave. They roared their glee, bellowed it, drew their guns, and shot out the light fixture. The room went dark.

They dragged Camille and René, now doubled over with that indigestion pain, from room to room, shooting out lamps. Moments later, there was the odor of gasoline, then flames exploded and all Honeymoon House was afire.

The robed throng dragged the naked, struggling Camille and the doubled, helpless René outside to where cars were parked, dropped them onto the ground, piled into their cars, and drove away, bellowing their laughter.

XLVIII

Back at the big house, the Leblancs heard the racket at Honeymoon House. They heard gunfire. They heard Camille scream.

Pierre, fully dressed, rushed to the telephone, called the police. "Trouble at L'Acadie!" he gasped. "Bring all the cars you can!"

Instinctively, he knew it was the Mercers. Word had reached him more than once of how the Mercer clan was spreading venom against the Leblancs. When Pierre turned from the phone, José Herrera was there, also fully clothed.

"Let's go!" shouted José.

They ran, all of them, even the women. Elizabeth and Francie and Dorcas and Josleen and Maebelle all ran as fast as they could.

They got to the blazing Honeymoon House as the carloads of white-robed figures drove away. They heard the evil laughter, saw René, doubled up and writhing on the ground, and Camille, naked, kneeling beside him, calling out his name. "He's sick!" she cried to them. "He's terribly sick! We've got to get him to the hospital!"

"I'll get the car!" Elizabeth cried and left.

"Who was it?" Pierre demanded. "The Mercers?"

"Yes, but it doesn't matter! René's hurt."

Camille cradled René as he came slowly out of a spasm of pain. Dorcas ran forward, also knelt, feeling his brow.

The police cars arrived. Suddenly uniformed officers were in charge.

"So you think it was the Mercers?" the chief asked Pierre. "Which Mercer?"

"Simon, for one," said Camille, who had heard the chief's strong voice. "René knew his voice. They were wearing white robes like the Ku Klux Klan."

"Go after Simon Mercer and Guy and Silas junior," the chief instructed his officers. "Take them in on charges of disturbing the peace and arson."

The police car drove off as Elizabeth drove the Chevy up. They got René, doubled over again, into the back seat. José gave Camille his coat to cover herself, and she, bruised and battered, got into the back seat with René and Dorcas. José drove with Pierre in the front seat and Francie crowded between them.

At the small hospital, René was taken to one cubicle, Camille to another to have her cuts and buises treated. They gave her a long hospital lab coat, which reached to her knees, and she gave José's jacket back to him.

"René?" she asked, though she knew from the look of the others that there was no word. Weak, trembling, she paced the floor where other people with anxious faces also paced.

On they waited, and on. The clock on the wall sent its hour hand around two complete revolutions and started on the third, and still they knew nothing. Camille saw Francie biting her fingernails and wondered, dully, why Francie was doing that. She'd never been overly fond of René; he'd told her that himself. Yet there Francie was, pacing, biting her nails, white as death.

When it had been three hours, a green-coated young doctor came to them and they clustered around him. Pierre spoke for all of them. "What about it, doctor? How is René?"

"We barely saved him. Fifteen minutes later, and we couldn't have pumped out enough poison. Even then we had to work over him afterward."

"The Mercers tried to poison him!" breathed Camille.

Pierre's look went to Francie. He'd noted her strange behavior, too. Now he saw the whole picture.

"The Mercers didn't do it, Camille," he said. "They weren't at the wedding."

"But who—?"

"Which one of you is Camille?" the doctor asked.

"I am—I'm his wife! I want to see him!"

"He's asking for you. Come along to his room."

They left, and Pierre sat down. José and Elizabeth sat

with him. Dorcas curled up in a chair and trembled. Francie paced.

Camille's with René by now, Pierre thought. She's holding her bridgroom close, they're murmuring love words. Francie will have to pay. If I can't prove her treachery, she's got to at least leave L'Acadie. The irony of it all, he thought. The Mercers roughed up René, and thereby saved his life.

He pondered René's near death. That called to mind the will and how it had almost been needed. Relaxing a bit, Pierre took comfort in the thought that whatever happened in future, L'Acadie would be in good hands, would survive and hold its place on Bayou Teche.

ABOUT THE AUTHOR

SALIEE O'BRIEN has been writing for as long as she can
remember, and publishing stories since the age of fourteen.
She was lured away, while in her twenties, by community
theater and radio broadcasting; but they couldn't keep her
from her first love—writing. Stories began appearing in a
wide range of magazines: *Saturday Evening Post, Collier's*
and *Blue Book*. Novels followed, and in abundance. They
include *Farewell the Stranger, Too Swift the Tide, Heiress
to Evil, Bayou, So Wild the Dream, Black Ivory, Cajun,*
and *Cayo*. Ms. O'Brien is married and lives in Florida.

READ THESE GLITTERING BESTSELLERS
BY JUDITH KRANTZ

☐ **MISTRAL'S DAUGHTER** (23800-0 • $3.95 • $4.95 in Canada)

From the '20s Paris of Chanel, Colette, Picasso and Matisse to New York's sizzling new modeling agencies of the '50s to the model wars of the '70s, MISTRAL'S DAUGHTER is a dazzling international tale that captures the explosive glamour of life at the top of the worlds of art and high fashion.

☐ **PRINCESS DAISY** (14200-3 • $3.95 • $4.95 in Canada)

Across an international landscape stretching from the horse-drawn carriages of pre-Revolutionary Russia to the magical whirl of New York's Madison Avenue, Judith Krantz has written a dream of a novel filled with secrets and discoveries, glamour and pain, sadness and joy. And the beating pulse of it all is Princess Daisy—the ultimate heroine.

Buy both of these fabulous novels, on sale now wherever Bantam paperbacks are sold, or use this handy coupon for ordering:

Bantam Books, Inc., Dept. JU3, 414 East Golf Road, Des Plaines, Ill. 60016

Please send me the books I have checked above. I am enclosing $_____ (please add $1.25 to cover postage and handling. Send check or money order—no cash or C.O.D.'s please).

Mr/Ms _____

Address _____

City/State _____ Zip _____

JU3—11/83

Please allow four to six weeks for delivery. This offer expires 5/84. Prices and availability subject to change without notice.

THE LATEST BOOKS IN THE BANTAM BESTSELLING TRADITION

☐	23800	**MISTRAL'S DAUGHTER** Judith Krantz	$4.50
☐	14200	**PRINCESS DAISY** Judith Krantz	$3.95
☐	14628	**WHITE TRASH** George McNeill	$3.50
☐	01487	**MORNING STAR** Kerry Newcomb (A Large Format Book)	$6.95
☐	20823	**DIFFERENT FAMILIES** Alison Scott Skelton	$3.50
☐	23291	**JERICHO** Anthony Costello	$3.95
☐	23105	**NO COMEBACKS** Frederick Forsyth	$3.95
☐	22749	**THREE WOMEN AT THE WATER'S EDGE** Nancy Thayer	$3.50
☐	23028	**WINDBORN** Victor Brooke	$3.50
☐	23026	**CAPRICE** Sara Hylton	$2.95
☐	22924	**PUBLIC SMILES, PRIVATE TEARS** Helen Van Slyke w/J. Edwards	$3.95
☐	23554	**NO LOVE LOST** Helen Van Slyke	$3.95
☐	23071	**A RAGE TO LOVE** Liz Martin	$2.95
☐	22846	**THE DISINHERITED** Clayton Matthews	$3.50
☐	22838	**TRADITIONS** Alan Ebert w/Janice Rotchstein	$3.95
☐	01415	**FLAMES OF GLORY** Patricia Matthews	$6.95
☐	22751	**A PRESENCE IN A EMPTY ROOM** Velda Johnston	$2.50
☐	22577	**EMPIRE** Patricia Matthews w/Clayton Matthews	$3.50
☐	20901	**TRADE WIND** M. M. Kaye	$3.95
☐	20833	**A WOMAN OF TWO CONTINENTS** Pixie Burger	$3.50
☐	20026	**COME POUR THE WINE** Cynthia Freeman	$3.95

<u>Prices and availability subject to change without notice.</u>

Buy them at your local bookstore or use this handy coupon for ordering:

Bantam Books, Inc., Dept. FBS, 414 East Golf Road, Des Plaines, Ill. 60016

Please send me the books I have checked above. I am enclosing $_____
(please add $1.25 to cover postage and handling). Send check or money order
—no cash or C.O.D.'s please.

Mr/Mrs/Miss_____

Address_____

City_____State/Zip_____

FBS—11/83
Please allow four to six weeks for delivery. This offer expires 5/84.